CUTTER'S CLAIM

A BAD BOY BIKER ROMANCE

STEAMY BIKER ROMANCE SERIES

MONIQUE MOREAU

Cover Design by Cover Couture
www.bookcovercouture.com

MEET MONIQUE!

Join Monique's Newsletter (and receive goodies and release information)
https://bit.ly/SteamyReadNewsletter
Join Monique's FB reader's group, she'd love to hear from you
Possessive Alpha Reads
Like her Facebook Page
https://bit.ly/MoniqueMoreaufb
Follow her on TikTok
https://bit.ly/MoniqueTikTok
Follow her on Book Bub
http://bit.ly/MoniqueBookBub
Learn all about Monique's books
MoniqueMoreau.com

1

CUTTER

Beads of sweat slid off the woman's flanks and drenched the bedsheets.

Cutter rolled off her, floating on the high of a good fuck. It had taken the edge off. Tomorrow was the third Saturday of the month. Tommy's day. Lying beside her, he cast a glance sideways and blew out a gust of frustration. It had been a mistake to fuck her twice.

He swung his legs over the side of the bed and planted them on the carpet. Christ, his balls were gonna freeze off. Late March in Poughkeepsie did that to a man.

He glanced over his shoulder at Mandy, her chin propped on her hand, her eyes following his movements with greed. Her red-dyed hair matched the smear of lipstick around her lurid grin. Rolling onto her belly, she jiggled her pink ass at him. He gave her what she wanted, a sharp slap to each butt cheek.

"More, Cutter, more," she pleaded.

Of course, she wants more. His rep preceded him wherever he went in the circuit of motorcycle clubs. He was a magnet for a certain kind of woman with a certain desire. It was common for brothers to deal with women wanting to be their old lady or baby mama, but he got it twice as bad. Women knew about a biker named Cutter, and his knack for satisfying a woman's kink with singular talent. They vied to be one of his "speed-dial bitches."

"The more you beg, the less you get."

The energy roaring through his system crashed like a downed helio. Ever since Prez got sick, sex left him empty. Bracing his arms on the futon, he pushed himself up. Even before Prez, his mind began to wander. He'd switched up his routine, amped up his techniques, but still, he was left worn out. For a man who'd turned thirty a month ago, that was wack.

Buck naked, he disposed of the used condom. He returned from the bathroom, moving around the space and releasing Mandy from the ropes around her wrists. A kiss on the crown of her head and then he gathered his tools. Following a ritual of cleansing, they were returned to their proper places in the drawers. Mandy's lips drew down into a pout. She crawled toward him as he stood by the plastic drawer storage that doubled as a night table and grabbed his hand. Christ, her antics.

Swiping the underside of her breast, he instructed, "Time to go, babe, I got things to do. Be a good girl and drag your panties over that sweet, blistering ass. Make sure the elastic band scrapes up my marks real good." He cupped the back of her neck and gave her a bruising kiss before turning his back to her.

In the bathroom, he twisted the lock. Lifting his head to the cracked mirror above the sink, Cutter took a hard look at himself. He scratched the prickly scruff on his jaw. Been a while since he'd shaved. His deep-set eyes made him look rough enough without adding facial hair. He liked to keep things easy. Chill. Relaxed. Mellow. Those were the words people used to describe him. Except in the bedroom, where he exercised absolute control over women. He was the yang to their yin.

Puck poked his head into Cutter's bedroom and called out, "Yo, Cutter, get out, we got to talk. I'll be downstairs."

After a quick shower, he took the stairs to the main floor of the clubhouse. Puck was sipping a beer, spread-eagled on a leather couch cracked and aged with a scattering of cigarette burns like confetti at a ticker-tape parade. The cloudy midafternoon February light peeked in through a row of back windows and illuminated a pool table. Brothers advanced, retreated, and circled the green felt like hunters on the prowl. A clatter of glasses and dishware being arranged in their proper places behind the bar reverberated in the spacious room. Cutter snatched a water bottle and joined Puck.

Sprawled on the couch, the odor of ammonia twitched his nose, reminding him it was Tuesday, the day prospects mopped down the floors. A splintering sound sent both their gazes toward the pool table. Loki held a broken pool stick in both hands, the jagged edges pulsing in the air. There was a shout from the bar, and he threw them down. He whipped on his leather jacket as he stormed past them.

"He's one moody fucker," offered Cutter.

Puck grunted in agreement before replying, "Loki was never talkative, but ever since Chopper offed himself, he's caught up in a world of shadows."

"At least Kingdom's gotten over it. If our VP's head was still in the toilet, Prez's cancer would have dismantled the Squad. There'd be no surviving that shit."

"Can't compare their situations," debated Puck. "Chopper was Loki's blood brother, not Kingdom's. And Loki's got no woman to pull him through."

"At least the fucker's not blaming Kingdom no more," Cutter noted. Before their truce, there were times the feud got ugly. "Loki pledged his life over to Kingdom. Which was a fucking good thing because a man like Loki doesn't do shit half-assed. Though, thank fuck I ain't like him." Cutter gave out a shudder.

"Would be good if you were like him once in a while," Puck grumbled, unease pricking at his chest.

Cutter straightened. "Christ, tell me how you really feel."

Puck's lips flattened. Puffing out a breath of exasperation, he said, "You're an asset to the Squad, but you're wasting your life. With your skills, you could rise in the ranks. It's a fuckin' shame."

Assessing the empty water bottle, Cutter crushed the plastic in his hands. "Brother, that isn't for me. I'm a chill motherfucker. Stress-free. Responsibilities come with stress, and stress don't agree with me."

Puck flexed his bicep and massaged it. "You're a selfish dumbass is what you are."

Yeah, he was. Sue him if he wanted to make up for his lost childhood.

"I don't see you rankin' up," he pushed back.

Puck began massaging his left tricep, the one that always cramped after a long workout. "I can barely contain my sister. Can't expect me to do more. I'm where I'm supposed to be. You aren't."

"I've been taking care of Tommy my entire life. You don't see me complainin'."

Lifting his chin toward Loki, who was returning from the back offices, Puck observed, "He's the Sergeant of Arms. Kingdom's the VP. Fuck, even Whistle patched in and he's the poster boy for 'Stupid as Fuck.' Sage bails his ass out of jail on the regular. Even so, he's found his place. You wanna stay the same. Never grow up like Peter fuckin' Pan. You"—Puck stuck out his forefinger—"you've dug your heels in like a righteous, stubborn bastard."

"That's cold, bro."

"That's real is what it is."

"I ain't shopping for an old lady and a bunch of kids."

Cutter wasn't one to get riled up, but his gut burned. His skin crackled, choking his body, like a snake before a molt. Forcing a grin, he joked, "Admit it, you're jealous because I get the bitches you ain't never gonna get."

Puck snorted and shook his head. "Those bitches are gassin' you up if they've convinced you tying them up is somethin' special."

"See, that right there proves you don't know half of what women want. Takes a special man to give it to them right and teach them new tricks."

Puck released his upper arm and leaned forward, elbows resting on his knees. Eyes hard, he checked their surroundings before speaking low. "Things are changin' up in here. Your head is stuck in too much pussy to notice."

Cutter's gaze snapped toward Puck, on the alert. "Say what now?"

Puck shifted closer and growled, "I said you're too stupid to realize what's going on."

Cutter's head jerked back. Puck's dander was up. What the fuck? Puck didn't do dander. "The fuck you talkin' about, yo?"

Puck muttered under his breath. Lurching forward, Cutter caught the tail end, something about "another one coming up."

"Hold up. Repeat that," Cutter directed. A slew of curses poured out of Puck's mouth and flew over Cutter's head, making him dip low.

Tipping his head another inch closer, Puck reiterated, "One man's going down and another's gonna rise in his place."

Fucking Puck, with his opaque philosophical shit. Half the time he didn't know fuck-all what Puck was going on about, but apprehension crept up the nape of his neck and raised his hackles.

Cutter grabbed the pack of cigarettes he'd dropped on the low coffee table. He tapped it, and a loose cigarette dropped out. In one swift move, he tossed it between his lips. Bending low with Zippo in hand, he lit it. Sucking in nicotine, he took a moment to regain his balance. Then he surreptitiously scanned the area once more. Puck and he were speaking close, but not close enough to catch anyone's attention.

"Prez is sick."

Cutter let out an irritated puff. "No shit."

"Again. He's sick again and it's uglier than last time."

Smoke poured out of Cutter's partially opened mouth. "Nobody's said anything."

"I'm saying it. Seems I'm the only brother who's got eyes that work. It don't help that the power couple's in denial."

Cutter bit back a smirk. Kingdom and Loki, the power couple. Funny.

"Neither of those bastards can deal with another death, but I know the truth," said Puck.

"And how in the fuck would you know the truth?" Cutter asked dubiously.

"I eavesdropped on Prez."

Cutter's eyebrows shot up to his hairline. "Come again?"

"Get off your damn high horse, you lazy piece of shit."

Where in the fuck was this coming from? Cutter scowled, and snapped, "Don't get pissy with me."

Thumping his chest bone, Puck declared, "Everyone's got their heads up their asses. I'm the only one who bothered to find out. At Prez's last checkup, I drove him. Stood outside the door when he talked to his doctor. I was checking my phone and shit when the door swung halfway open, and I heard the doc's diagnosis." Puck spat out the last word as if it were venom.

A heavy, frigid sensation hit Cutter as if he'd been dunked in freezing water. Scooting to the edge of his seat, he murmured, "Prez did it on purpose. No way you would've heard anything unless he wanted you to."

"Whatever. Doc ordered him to take it easy. From now on. 'Quit your job,' he said, and 'make your health the number one priority. You can't be of use to anyone if you're dead. I've got you an appointment at Sloan Kettering in New York City for chemo and radiation. A colleague of mine owes me a favor. Radiation begins in six weeks.' Can you believe that shit?"

Prez was like a father to him. Didn't matter that his moms hated Prez's guts. He'd been their neighbor when he started the Demon Squad with two other members. Prez had fallen for his moms, and she'd repaid him with revulsion. Good man that he was, he never held it against Cutter. Closest thing to paternal love he'd ever experienced, because he sure as fuck got no maternal love. That had been used up on Tommy.

After he'd patched in with "those hooligans," as she called them, she refused to see him for years. Until she got sick. And then, only for Tommy's sake. He did what she'd asked of him. Shouldered the responsibilities she'd foisted on him. Still, he was kept at bay until her illness took a turn for the worst. One afternoon, he lay down on the hospice bed beside her sleeping form and, caressing her hairless skull, wept like a pussy. His moms. Gone. After the other Squad founders died, Prez was the last one standing.

Cutter hunched over, his gaze cutting to Puck. He cleared his throat, trying to speak, but it took a moment before he got words through the painful swelling of his throat. "Sloan what?"

"Memorial Sloan Kettering, a hospital that has a Cancer Clinic. Place where they take care of people with bad cases of cancer."

"Six weeks till he leaves. For how long?" Cutter asked.

Puck lifted and dropped his shoulders in a helpless shrug. "It doesn't fucking matter. Shit has got to be put in place now. Gotta say, I almost bawled like a fucking kid. Him stepping down will rock the Squad to the core."

After drawing in a deep breath, Puck continued, "It's up to you, Cutter. Besides me, you're the closest thing to a son Prez has. After Chopper's death, you're the closest brother to Kingdom. Loki will flip his shit when he finds out. Kingdom's gonna need you to keep him strong, to push him through the transition. And to keep Loki out of the psych ward. That's gonna be a killjoy, for fuckin' sure. If not done right, it'll be a clusterfuck of massive proportions."

The cigarette dropped from his fingers, burning a new hole into the scruffy rug. Staring down at his open palms, he scrutinized the lines as if he could consult them about the future. The Squad's future. His future. One deep horizontal groove crossed the others, slashing them in half.

Puck gripped his arm and gave it a shake. "You can do it. You'll keep the brothers from blowing up—because they'll be ticking time bombs, for sure. Keep them chill. We'll need a strong hand, not a hard fist. We'll need someone easy."

The cigarette butt died. The rancid odor of burnt rug fibers singed his nostrils. Cutter wiggled his numb fingers to get the blood flowing. Shame and regret double-teamed him. His muscles trembled as if he were lifting weights without a spotter, and a barbell was about to land on his throat. He'd never cast himself as a disloyal brother, but he'd squandered his time on fun and games, on jesting and fucking.

"How much time does he have left?" asked Cutter.

"Dunno, the door shut afterwards. The club is his bitch and his baby. Don't know what's gonna happen to him without it." Puck strained to rise, leaving Cutter to replay the times he'd messed around, this week alone.

Thump.

Two shots materialized on the coffee table. Lifting a shot glass, Puck saluted, "To the best of us."

Blindly picking up his shot, he raised it to match Puck's gesture, and downed it. The liquid blistered his throat, coating his tongue with a bitter aftertaste. He wasn't one of the best. The day he walked away from his mother and Tommy, at age eighteen, he put himself first. Made him a selfish bastard, but it was the only way to make up for a childhood shackled with taking care of his uncle twenty-four seven. Puck included him in the toast, but it was a damn lie. Prez, Kingdom, Loki. Even Puck himself. But not him. Cutter scrubbed his face roughly. He had a debt of honor to pay off; he'd work himself to the bone and earn a place on the throne, alongside the heroes of the Demon Squad.

2

GRETA

Greta pulled out her clipboard with the completed forms she'd gathered earlier.

She twirled a pen around her fingers. Fussing with her long skirt, she steadied her legs, leaned back, and smiled at the woman sitting beside her. She had recently gotten her paralegal certificate and already Sage, her "boss," entrusted her with a new type of client her firm represented. Pretty big deal. If she could manage to keep her shit together.

The woman's gaze flitted nervously around Sage's office. Before finally settling on Greta, her eyes screamed caution despite her tentative smile.

"Good to see you again, Christine. I've read over your paperwork, but I'd like to hear, in your own words, what's happened." Greta held up her clipboard and pen. "I may take notes, but anything I write is strictly for myself and Sage. Do you remember what I told you before?"

"Everything I tell you is confidential. You will share it with Ms. Cameron and no one else unless I give you permission."

Okaaay, that was a word-for-word recitation.

"I'm glad to know that you've been paying attention, but remember, you may call her Sage."

Christine whooshed out a breath, although she had not entirely surrendered her intense grip on the worn purse on her lap. "When it comes to this, I'm always gonna pay attention."

Greta gave her a soft smile. "I wouldn't expect anything less of you."

Twitching her skirt into place once more, she crossed her ankles, the tip of her pen poised against the clipped sheet of paper. "Just pretend I don't know the details of your case and start."

"Sage helped my brother, Jackie that is, stay out of the pen after he smashed up my asshole of a husband's face." Christine flinched. "Against a brick wall. Messed him up pretty good. I screamed for him to get off and tried pulling him away. I didn't want the brother I love to get into trouble for my stupid mistake. You see, what my husband did to me, my father did to our mom, and Jackie couldn't stop himself. I tried hiding it from him, I did."

Fury thrummed through Greta's blood. The part about Christine's father gutted her. In a previous interview, Jackie told Sage straight-out that if Christine wasn't taken care of, he'd be back with another assault charge or worse. Without helping his sister, there was no helping Jackie. It led Sage to help Christine, and others like her, free of charge.

At first, Greta hedged. She wasn't a trained social worker, but a paralegal, and she didn't want to get vicariously fucked up by working with a survivor. Like now. Greta paced her breathing to keep her pulse steady.

Wringing her hands, words tumbled out of Christine. "My husband won't leave me alone, and if he doesn't, someone's going to end up dead. For once, I'm afraid for his safety, because Jackie will kill him. I was stupid enough to fall for a loser, and I'm paying the price. Jackie shouldn't have to. You know how my brother is." Tears leaked from the corners of her eyes, and she swiped at them with the back of her hand. A sob slipped out.

Greta seized her hand. "Christine." She squeezed hard enough to cause her a twinge of pain. "Take a deep breath."

Instead, Christine released a storm of sobs, and her purse toppled off her lap. Greta deftly picked it up and placed it on the table before caressing her back. Tears pricked at the back of Greta's eyes. After a few minutes, she didn't know how much more she could take, so she firmly shook Christine's shoulders.

"It's not your fault. Wipe that thought from your mind. Abusers are experts at manipulation and putting the blame on their victims. If you want to save yourself and your brother, it's going to be a tough fight. But, trust me, it's winnable."

Her professional demeanor almost broke, but she clamped her lips shut to keep from confiding that she'd once been in the same position. Perhaps she hadn't taken the physical blows, but she'd lived in a world of violence. Hers was a story of escape and survival. Of starting over and building her life from scratch. Of success in creating a new life. Despite her resurrection, fear was imbedded in the marrow of her bones.

Shaking off her nervousness, she said, "Breathe with me."

Nodding weakly, Christine breathed alongside her.

"Again," Greta directed. They took the second breath in unison. "Let's do a one-minute breathing exercise."

Greta closed her eyes and concentrated on the center of her forehead. Their inhalations and exhalations overtook the room. Sixty seconds seemed excruciatingly long, but they got through them together. Her heart rate was unsteady, but at least when she opened her eyes, her focus was back.

"Are you ready?" She didn't bother to ask Christine if she felt better. That was a ridiculous question. Her long fingernail tapped the papers balanced on her knees.

"Why don't we start with going through the legal forms allowing our law firm to represent you? Then, we'll return to this. Please take out any documents you were told to bring and put them on the table, and I'll go through them one by one. I understand that you're out of the house and staying with a co-worker. Great first step. And you've changed your cell phone number. If we're lucky, you won't see him again until the court date."

"I don't think that's going to happen. He's sworn up and down that he'll never let me go and he's already stopped by my workplace once. Made a hell of a scene. It's only a matter of time before he strikes again."

"Let's get through this paperwork, and then we'll work on other ideas," Christine said, blowing out a huge breath.

"Yeah, okay."

"We've established contacts with organizations who have committed to working with us. I'm going to give you the contact info of a great social worker. Her name is Abby, and she already knows about you. You should call her and set up a meeting within the next few days to create a safety plan for you. You'll have access to a support group and a therapist. But, Christine? No matter how much support you have, you're going to want to go back to him a hundred times over."

Christine's eyes widened and her eyebrows touched her hairline "How could you tell?"

"Trust me, I know."

The statistics were dreary. It took survivors several times, sometimes many times, to ride the merry-go-round of hell before they got off for good.

Boundaries. The stories walking through the door were

going to get worse. How would she handle seeing a kid with a busted lip or broken bones? She had to stick to her part of the script, the legal part. That's the only way she could make a difference.

"Right then, let's get to it," she said.

Once they were done with their consultation, Greta walked into the reception area and nodded to Sage, who gave her a worried look. Her heart hammered against her breastbone and sweat plastered her shirt to her skin.

Man, did she need a breather. Good time to get lunch. Knowing Sage, they'd both be starving by the time Christine left.

GRETA JOGGLED a large paper bag of takeout on her knee as she shimmied the front door closed. Whew, no clients. After depositing the bag on her desk in the reception room, she locked the door in case of a wayward client. Implementing a policy to close the office for half an hour for lunch had been a struggle, but otherwise Sage would never take a break to eat. It had the added perk of getting Kingdom out of her hair, because he'd made it a habit to randomly check in on Sage to make sure she took care of herself.

Greta was setting out the various containers when Sage emerged from her office. Dragging a visitor's chair across the carpeted floor, she sat down with an *oomph*. A whiff from an open container drifted up. Shooting Greta a brilliant smile, she said, "Yummy, I'm starving." Armed with chopsticks in one hand and a spoon in the other, Sage scooped up a spoonful of broth, and blew on it.

"How'd it go? For you, I mean," asked Sage.

Through a mouthful of rice, Greta garbled out, "Alright, I guess."

Sage wrangled a serving of *pho* noodles with her chopsticks and spoon. Between slurps, she asked, "Want to debrief?"

"I like the way you use rice noodles as a perfect foil to poke around my head without being blatantly intrusive."

Sage clutched her string of fake pearls and gave her a look of horror. "How dare you suggest that I use food for anything but nourishment? Getting my favorite dish from my favorite Vietnamese restaurant is a form of obstruction and a low blow. Even for you."

"Okay, okay, lawyer lady, I'll stipulate to that count. Listening to the details was rough. So many details," her voice ended in a low whisper. Her head and shoulders drooped. Spine curling inward as if she could coil into a tight ball, the adrenaline in her system crashed, leaving her a little woozy. "I went over her documents and gathered more evidence. Then we covered how to keep her safe. Well, as safe as she's willing to be."

A furrow broke the smooth skin between Sage's brows.

Greta assured her, "She's going to yo-yo. Get back together with him, then leave, come back, leave again. The typical cycle."

"It's true, the process is long and arduous, but at least we're part of the solution." Leaning over, she grasped Greta's hand. "Anytime you need a break, I'll cover for you. Time we recruit volunteers and train them, because we'll need help. And to give you space if you need to step away for a while."

Sage was amazing. Sophisticated, sharp as a tack, with intuition and empathy in spades.

"Why don't you take a break this afternoon," suggested Sage. "There's not much going on."

Greta stifled a huff. "Yeah, right, you're overloaded as it is."

"You with your savior complex. Take the afternoon off and let me feed my inner monster with work. Anyway, Kingdom's coming over later to pick me up."

"Why didn't you say so in the first place? It relieves me of playing babysitter."

Sage gave Greta a saucy wink and gestured with her chopsticks in the air. "You act as if he has magical powers."

Greta snorted out, "He's a biker, so yeah, I'd say he does. Especially when it comes to you."

Sage snatched a carton before Greta could put it away and said, "Just go before I get angry at your assumption that he can rein me in."

Greta came around and gave Sage a quick hug. With a peck on her head, she grabbed her purse from under her desk. Shrugging on her biker jacket, she unlocked the front door and said, "Alright, I'm off."

"Go to a library or a used bookstore. I'm sure you'll find a treasure trove to add to your colossal collection at home."

Her plan was to go browse alright, but not for books. Window-shopping at the Harley Davidson dealership was on the menu. Some people went to church, some went to yoga. She went to look at bikes to re-charge.

3

CUTTER

Cutter was late meeting Kingdom.

He'd stayed longer than he intended, sparring with Puck at a boxing gym they were checking out as an investment for the club. His thigh muscles screamed from overworking them. A week had passed since his conversation with Puck about Prez's condition, and he'd been working out harder than usual to burn off the irritation churning in his gut.

Normally, he wasn't one to hurry, but he lengthened his strides on his way to his bike. Passing by the Poughkeepsie Coffeehouse and Bar, he did a double take and screeched to a halt. From the other side of the windowpane, a pair of brilliant green eyes stared out at him on the busy avenue and quickly snapped away. Too late. The instant their eyes connected, a deep burn seized his muscles as if he'd caught a fever. He *had* to meet her.

Fuck me.

She was fucking beautiful. Those lively eyes of hers popped out of a heart-shaped face. Straight black hair cascaded down to her rib cage, pink ends brushing a leather bustier. Better yet, the bustier showed off the tops of plump tits. Which he appreciated since the rest of her was encased in a bulky sweater. Damn, he'd suck and bite those tits of hers for days.

Her almond-shaped eyes swept his way again, pinning him in place. Cutter broke into a wide grin. This one looked like she was about to spit fire. After a moment's hesitation, her lips tilted upward slightly, and that small smile of hers cinched his balls like a harness.

The pretty girl pivoted to speak to the person by her side, and his scalp pricked at her dismissal. At the edge of his vision, her friend waved in his direction, attempting to get his attention.

Sage. With an excited smile, she urged him to join them. Hell yeah, perfect timing. This was his chance to press Sage into service before Prez left for radiation. He grabbed his cell and sent off a text to postpone his meeting with Kingdom by an hour. Didn't hurt that he'd get a closer look at the green-eyed woman with tits that made a man quick to sin. And he was a sinner down to his core.

Once inside, he bent down to smack a kiss on Sage's upturned cheek. Pulling back, he inspected her.

"Whattup? You look mighty fine today," Cutter complimented smoothly.

"You're such a flirt," Sage chided. "We just finished up in court and ate lunch before heading back to the office."

Sage's eyes gleamed with purpose, as if she was giving him the go-ahead with her friend. Interesting. Not that Sage's approval mattered, because he was on the bitch's scent, and he sure as fuck wasn't going to be put off by anyone.

"I don't think you've met Greta. Although, I'm sure you've heard of her," Sage guessed accurately.

Greta. Sage's personal warrior bitch.

His jaws clanked like a steel trap. This was the same woman who'd hidden Sage away in some bumfuck state near Canada when she skipped town on Kingdom.

Greta eyed him, her plump red lips on the brink of a snarl, daring him to step to her. She stood up to Kingdom, toe to toe, after he'd fucked up with Sage. During their confrontation, Kingdom had come down hard on Greta. Not only did she refuse to give up Sage's location, but she told him to fuck off along with choice words about his behavior. Truth was, she'd done her job too well, because Cutter's efforts to find Kingdom's woman had also failed, and he was a tracker, dammit. Pissed him off that he'd rescued soldiers held hostage in Iraq but couldn't track down one bitch in his own damn country.

This, then, was the infamous Greta.

Cutter jiggled the long keychain attached to the wallet in his back pocket. Like a dog whistle, the jingling put this woman on full alert. Her chest rose and fell like bellows. Coincidence? Not if his life depended on it. His fingers twitched with the desire to redden her ass. He could sniff out a subbie in Times Square on a rowdy New Year's Eve at the stroke of midnight.

She'd caught his knowing smirk and scowled like a pit bull ready to maul him. Little did she know pit bulls were his favorite breed. He had a talent for making them straight-up docile in his hands.

He braced one hand on the back of her chair and the other on the table, caging her. Fenced in, her gaze fell on the prominent veins snaking around his forearm, lined with tattoos. Feisty Greta liked what she was seeing. Bending low, until there was but a mere inch separating them, he murmured, "So. You're Greta."

He drew in a breath and her scent hit him like a tsunami. Caramel notes of burnt sugar, mixed with cinnamon and spice. She averted her bright eyes and nonchalantly picked at imaginary lint on her skirt. Biting down on his lower lip, he nudged her. "Aren't you a pretty little girl?"

Her body went as taut as a leather restraint. "I'm no one's '*girl*.'"

A challenge? He hadn't had a test in a long-ass time. Game. Fuckin'. On.

"Do you mind? You're being rude," Sage interjected, as she patted the seat beside her.

"Sure thing, babe." Cutter dragged the chair Sage motioned to and placed it right up against Greta. He eased back in it and draped his arm around the back of hers. "I'd do anything for you. After all, you're the Squad's number one old lady."

"Why bikers insist on calling their girlfriends and wives 'old ladies,' I will never understand. Either way, we are not having this conversation again."

"Sweetheart, make our lives easier and just accept the fact that you're our savior."

"Nothing has changed," she huffed.

"See, you're wrong there. The writing is on the fuckin' wall. It's happening."

Switching her gaze from one to the other, Greta queried, "What's going on?"

Sage bowed her head, intently focused on her empty cappuccino cup, and fiddled with the spoon. "Cutter is leading a campaign to convince Kingdom to become president."

Greta's eyebrows shot up. "Seriously? Why haven't you mentioned this before? That's a huge step, you know. It will affect every aspect of your life, including the time you have for your cases." She held her breath before adding, "And our other project."

Sage looked up at her beseechingly. "Exactly. Kingdom

hasn't said much on the subject, so this is a Cutter pipe dream." Muttering low, she finished, "Hopefully." Squinting up at Cutter, Sage complained, "Since when do you get riled up about club politics, anyway? That is simply not your MO."

Cutter gave her a shit-eating grin. "I saw a need, and I got involved. Time to suck it up, babe."

Sage's mouth fell open. "Who are you? And bring back the Cutter I know."

"Times are a changin'. You'll end up doing it my way." He added a wink to his smug smile.

Greta thrust the butt of her palms against Cutter's chest. His heat clung to her fingers, and she clenched her jaws to keep from curling them over his pecs. "It's not good for her to get embroiled in the Squad more than necessary. Old lady to the VP is one thing but being the senior female of an entire MC is a completely different scenario."

Cutter deadpanned, "This is club business."

"Whatever. Sage isn't getting caught up with criminals. Not on my watch."

His eyes bored into hers, and he chastised, "Manners, little girl. Watch them or I'll take you over my knee. That what you want? Because that's what you're in for if you don't watch the attitude."

Clenching her fists, she banged them on the table, her voice unsteady. "You'll do better to kill me than lift a finger to any part of me."

HOLY HELL.

The biker staring her down from the street moments ago was looming over her like a grizzly bear. She was so close to blowing up. The only thing holding her back was the disapproval vibrating off him. Nervous tension pulsated in her gut. Sage reached out to place her hand over Greta's shaking fists.

"Oh, Greta, I'm so—"

"Don't touch her," Cutter commanded in a cold tone.

Sage's hand hovered in midair before returning to her lap. Stiffly, Greta focused on a spot in a far corner of the bustling shop. What the hell was happening to her? She hated bikers. Wanted nothing to do with them, but, here she was, trembling. *This is dangerous. This I have to fight.* A hand seized the back of her neck and pulled her sideways until she smashed against a massive chest. She jerked slightly and rubbed her cheek against the leather of his vest, better known as a cut, in a subtle movement.

He held her still until she got ahold of herself and indicated that she wanted to sit up. He slid his hand down her spine before releasing her. Mortified, she was about to leap up and run screaming from the coffee shop, but another—stronger—part of her kept her glued to her seat. A shiver went through her. The struggle between her body and mind was beginning to overwhelm her when he slipped his hand beneath her hair and massaged her nape. His calloused fingers left a trail of electricity crackling on her skin.

"Apologize." Cutter's baritone shuddered down Greta's spine, and she cringed inwardly. She'd butted in and snapped at Sage.

Without thinking, she obeyed. "I'm sorry. I shouldn't have snapped at you."

"Good girl," he praised. She flushed at his compliment, and pleasure surged inside her. Sage's eyes bugged out in shock. Oh, fuck. She'd outed herself. *Not that Sage doesn't know, but still.*

Shoving her chair backward with a screech, Greta stood

up with her spine straight as a javelin. Cutter held her wrist for a moment before deciding to let her go. *Smart move, buddy.*

"Excuse me," she muttered mulishly, spun on her heels, and stalked away.

At the counter, she requested a glass of ice water and emptied it in one go. She was desperate for something stronger than water, preferably a shot of vodka. Her head spun, but she'd be damned before she ran away. Stomping back to the table, she heard Sage giving him a piece of her mind.

"You can't just grab people! Especially women. Grab, grab, grabby. You're like a caveman."

Greta placed a hand on Sage's shoulder. "Relax, it's no big deal."

Ignoring Sage's reprimand, Cutter kicked Greta's chair out to make space for her. He slanted his eyes toward her and then over to her seat. When she hesitated, he raised one eyebrow. Growling under her breath, she threw her shoulders back and swept into her chair.

Cutter's open arm settled on the back of her seat. Again. Blood rushed to her head at the weight of his stare. His blue eyes were at half-mast, praise for heeding him. A frisson ran down the length of her spine, because, asshole or not, he was devastating. A satisfied grin curved his full lips, his upper lip plumper than his lower. Like a pretty boy, only nothing else about him was pretty. Certainly not his square jaw, sporting a scruff of hair so blond it was almost imperceptible, but she noticed every detail about him. Like the curls on his fair head that she wanted to weave between her fingers and tug on as it moved between her legs.

What the fuck? Ugh, he's a biker, and not the weekend type either. Pure, unadulterated alpha biker.

She schooled her features and settled for a scathing look

that ordinarily froze men as if they'd looked into the eyes of Medusa. Unfortunately, he wasn't cowed in the least. Was "subbie" emblazoned on her forehead? Changing tactics, Greta graced him with a fake, bright smile. Although he'd won this round, she'd be ready for him next time.

And there would be a next time, because she planned to fight him for Sage's soul. At all costs.

4

CUTTER

lick-clack, click-clack, click-clack.

The cover of Cutter's Zippo snapped up and down, the percussion of metal on metal sounding through the twilight air. Cutter leaned against the brick wall of the back of the clubhouse, lighting the cigarette he'd pulled from his pack. Taking a long drag, the burning tobacco created a perfect circle of red light.

Kingdom waved his arm and the motion-sensitive porch lights flashed. Placing his coffee mug on the ground beside him, Kingdom coughed and hit his chest with his fist, complaining, "Are you going to quit that lung cancer shit?"

Ignoring the complaint, Cutter turned toward Kingdom, his shoulder scrapping the brick wall.

"Prez can't keep up anymore. Since the second round, he hasn't been the same. If you want what's best for him, talk to him about stepping down. You've been skirting the issue for over a year."

Kingdom scowled and noted, "Don't you lecture me. I'll start talking to Prez."

Cutter shot his brother a look of shock. "All those behind-the-door sessions and dinners at his house, and neither one of you spoke about it? Not once? Is that what you're telling me?"

Dead silence hung between them. Kingdom wasn't a pain in the ass on purpose. Although both their moms died of cancer, Cutter had never had a brother die on him. Chopper may have technically been Kingdom's surrogate brother, but when he self-destructed, Kingdom had fallen apart. Luckily, he'd found Sage. The brothers groused about Sage not being from their world, but Cutter had recognized her potential from day one. His instinct had been right; she was one strong bitch and she'd pulled Kingdom out of the rubble.

"Yeah, that's what I'm telling you. It ain't your fucking business how we conduct ourselves."

"Christ, you're both in denial."

If Kingdom hadn't spoken to Prez about it, then it was worse than he thought. Didn't faze him, though. Nothing stopped him from a mission. He took care of his moms. *Check.* Took care of Tommy. *Check.* Finished his tour in Iraq. *Check.* Finished his associate's degree, like his moms insisted. *Check.* Never mind that he didn't do fuck-all with it. The one thing he'd done against her will was join the Squad. She'd rejected him for it until she needed him to take care of Tommy.

"What's up with Sage's guard dog, Greta? She had the gall to dictate club business to me." Fuck, he sounded like a pussy.

Kingdom gave Cutter a sidelong glance. "What in the fuck are you babbling about?"

"She tried to shut me down when I talked to Sage about you bein' the new president."

Kingdom's fingers paused in the middle of poking at his cell. "You talkin' club business? More importantly, you bothering my woman?"

"I'm not bothering her. I was discussing her new role."

"What role would that be, exactly?" Kingdom asked in a careful tone.

"Why are you actin' thickheaded? Old lady of the president."

"Not sure I want that for her."

"Why the fuck not? Sage is more than up for the job."

Kingdom's gaze skittered around the backyard. "If it's not good for my woman, then I will not become president."

The floor underneath him bottomed out. "Are you saying we're not good enough for Sage? Because the Sage I know would disagree. She loves the club."

"It's not about what she wants, it's about what's best for her. My woman comes first. Period. The end."

"Both can happen at the same time."

"Maybe, maybe not. The verdict's still out. She's a criminal attorney and we're not exactly clean. Sage's legal career is important to her, and I'm not going to place it in jeopardy."

"We're cleaning ourselves up. Besides the bar, Puck and I checked out another boxing club. This one's promising. We're getting a proposal ready. After that's up and running, we'll be in the clear."

"Cutter, we've got a few big jobs left, during an internal shift of power. We need the money more than ever with Prez's medical bills. That's a whole lot to chew off in one bite."

"You can do anything you put your mind to, Kingdom," he argued.

"It would put her in a vulnerable position, and I can't have that."

"We'll protect her."

"I'm not putting a target on the backs of my woman and kid," Kingdom ground out.

Shock reverberated through him, leaving his blood drumming in his temples. He was at Kingdom's side, clapping him on the back, but Kingdom put a hand up to stop him.

"She miscarried," he said in a weary tone.

His hand fell away. "Fuck."

"I'm working on putting another one in her belly. Went to the OBGYN, and the doctor explained that shit happens. She's healthy. I'm healthy. No blank bullets on my part. No problem on hers. But I'm not about to put my old lady and a kid in a potentially explosive situation. Ever."

Cutter backed away. "Let's say, for argument's sake, that I can guarantee her safety. Sage would do it in a heartbeat."

"Even if I said yes, Greta's gonna fuck up that plan of yours."

His jaw locked, but Kingdom continued, "Sage won't do it if Greta says it's a bad idea. She trusts Greta, and Greta's not a fan, to say the least. Bad enough she hates bikers, but she hates bikers who do illegal shit more. In the beginning, she tried scaring Sage off me with tales of violence. Or, best case scenario, that I'll be locked away for years."

"I'll take care of Greta," he snapped.

Kingdom pocketed his cell phone and bent down to pick up his mug of coffee. He gulped down a mouthful and muttered, "You don't know her if you think that's easy."

"I know something you don't know about that little submissive," he retorted.

Kingdom spewed coffee down his own shirt. Choking and plucking at his wet T-shirt, he huffed out, "I don't want to fuckin' know that shit."

"Whatever, you fucking prude," Cutter said with a wave. "Talk with Prez. See where his head is."

"Assuming shit goes down the way you want, there's one more issue." He paused. "Loki."

Yeah, that was a definite issue. Between gritted his teeth, he declared, "And I'll take care of Loki."

Kingdom's eyes shot wide. Barking out a terse laugh, he said, "Since when do you want to take care of anything. Un-fucking-believable. The boy's all grown up."

"Yeah, don't get used to it," he griped.

The thought of confronting Loki was about as fun as getting punched in the face by a dude with fists of granite.

Shit was about to get real.

5

GRETA

Greta bent over to tuck some papers away in one of the filing cabinets lining the wall behind her desk. Sage's hip was perched on her desk. Swinging a leg in the air, she commented casually, "I have a few minutes before my next appointment."

Rising, she saw Sage's eyes twinkling with mirth. "Whistle's appointment. Yum."

"I take it you like the pretty boy."

"Oh yeah! A pretty boy dressed up in biker gear is the best eye candy ever."

"Yet you've sworn off bikers," Sage hedged.

"That doesn't mean I can't drool." Greta flicked through the files one by one. Whistle and she had established a routine of harmless flirting. "It's not a secret. You've met my mom. I'm sure you got the general picture of my life before I went to college."

"True, although she only gave me the bare bones. The rest was deduction on my part."

The door swung open and Whistle sauntered in, sporting a panty-dropping grin. Although he'd settled down a bit since patching into the Demon Squad as a full member, he was always a magnet for trouble. Once Sage finished with one legal tangle, he'd be back with another, without fail.

Following close behind him came Cutter. Greta almost swallowed her tongue and crouched low to the ground. What was he doing here? He'd never accompanied Whistle before. In the week since she'd met him, Cutter had preoccupied her thoughts more than she'd admit to another soul, but if Whistle was eye candy, then Cutter was hard candy. The kind of candy that a person sucked to the roof of their mouth. The addictive kind that left a row of cavities and thousands in dental fees. Cavities, and the bittersweet taste of heartache. She caught her lower lip between her teeth and bit down hard. His aura sucked all sober thoughts out of her, but no way would she let him hijack her control like last time.

"Hey, Whistle. Hey, Cutter," Sage greeted them. Smacking her cheek, she gasped, "Oops, I just forgot about a call I have to make. Give me about five minutes."

"No problem, Ms. Sage."

Sage snorted loudly at Whistle's all-to-proper address. Cutter explained, "After he missed his last appointment, Kingdom gave him another lesson about respect. Ain't that right, newbie?"

Damn his voice. It was sexy smooth as bourbon.

Whistle muttered, "I ain't no newbie or prospect anymore."

"You might've been voted in by the brothers, but you're a newbie to me until you prove otherwise."

Sage waved her hand to cut off their bickering. "Relax, it's all in the past. We've turned over a new leaf, and I'm certain you won't have to ensure that Whistle comes to his appointments on time."

"Doubt it," Cutter grunted.

"Since when are you Whistle's babysitter?" Sage inquired. He gave Greta a lazy once-over, and drawled, "Since now. Take your time, sweetheart, I've got things under control out here."

Greta clenched her fingers before she succumbed to the urge to slap that cocky expression off his face.

Sage's office door closed, and Cutter took the seat closest to Greta's desk. He stared her down with those marine-blue eyes of his. She was *not* going to let him rattle her this time. Swatting away a pink-tipped lock of hair that had escaped her chignon, she plunked down on her seat and stabbed away at her keyboard. Whistle propped his butt on her desk, and said, "Hey, babe, ain't seen you for a while. You're lookin' prettier than last time."

A growl rumbled from behind them before a harsh voice boomed, "Get the hell over here, boy."

Whistle jumped to attention and beat a hasty retreat. The command in his voice left her heart pounding, but she stamped down the flurry of butterflies in her belly. Butterflies were so overrated. Stealing a quick look, her pulse tripped as he drilled into her with those grim, deep-set eyes. A vein throbbed on his temple. Even better. Hell yeah! He was trying to ruin Sage's life, and he was too arrogant by half.

"You're being an asshole. To think, you have a reputation for being chill?"

His features turned hard. His eyes clashed with hers, penetrating her with perceptive eyes. One by one, he cracked his knuckles. "This here prospect," he nudged Whistle's boots with his own, "has to start acting like he deserves to be in the Squad. We can't afford any weak links."

Whistle visibly paled.

That was a low blow and he only delivered it because Whistle had dared flirt with her. She clamped her hand over her mouth before she wailed into him. Drawing in even, slow breaths, she hunkered down behind her screen. Wiggling her fingers over the keyboard until she'd released the tension, Greta then scrolled through her list of favorites and clicked open the Harley Davidson website.

Better the bike than the biker.

It was fun riling Greta up a bit. Her hair was slicked back to hide the pink in a tight bun by her nape. If she thought she had toned down her sex-kitten vibe, she was clueless as shit. The black velvet jacket that hugged her figure flapped open and revealed a bondage-like belt, with two large D rings on each side. Rings used to tie a woman down where you wanted her kept. Hot. As. Fuck. He crossed his ankle over his knee to give his swelling cock a bit of space in his tented jeans.

Glowering at the monitor Greta was hiding behind, Cutter murmured, "Damn, you're a fine bitch."

Greta's head swiped left, her eyes zeroing in on him. Her mouth twisted sardonically. "You'll never get to her. Not on my watch."

Cutter leaned his elbows on his knees. His fingers contracted as he imagined tweaking her nipples while she squirmed, her pussy clenching on his cock. "Little girl, stop wasting your breath. Put that pretty mouth of yours to better use."

Splashes of red colored her high cheekbones, and her eyes spit out fury. "You wish," she replied, "but, all joking aside, I'm watching out for Sage. It's one thing being associated with an MC, but she's an attorney. She can't be linked, on the highest level, with an organization involved in questionable activities. Back off. Otherwise, I'll take care of it myself."

Christ, she was making it sound like they were career

criminals. It wasn't his job to set her straight about the level of involvement she was so worried about. Either way, if the pulse point at the base of her throat was any indication, she was enjoying their tit for tat as much as he was. And, she couldn't keep her eyes off him for more than a few minutes at a time. He threw his head back and laughed out loud. "You've got sass in you, for sure."

"You're too stupid to live if you think I'll let you get away with anything."

Damn, she was begging him to dirty up her mouth. Whistle sent him an astonished look. The fucker had better turn away before he got the beating of his life. He opened his mouth to cut into Whistle when Sage stepped out of her office and sing-songed, "I'm ready now. Come on in."

The tension in the air stopped her in her tracks, gaze swinging from Greta to the men, and back. Cutter subtly adjusted his erection, but when he stood up, he caught Sage's smothered laugh. Irritated, he slapped the back of Whistle's head. The kid yelped and muttered, "What the fuck?" As Cutter passed by Greta's desk, she returned his hard stare with one of her own. Oh, he was gonna make her pay for trying to mess with him. And for being a cocktease.

6

CUTTER

Cutter pointed to Whistle and then to the office door. "You. Outside. I've got business with Sage. I'll get you for your appointment when I'm done."

"Brother, it's freezing out there. Why can't I wait here?"

"'Cause I said so." He narrowed his eyes. "And don't call me brother until I give you permission."

Sliding over to a seat farther from Greta's desk, Whistle promised, "I won't talk to her."

"Did I fucking stutter? I don't give two fucks what you say. Out!"

Without another word, Whistle flew out of the waiting room. Walking to Sage's office, Cutter opened the door and swept his arm out for her to enter before him. Over his shoulder, he caught Greta's bared teeth before she masked it quickly with a saccharine smile. He winked at her before clicking the door closed behind him.

Sage settled in behind her desk and folded her hands together in a gesture he'd seen many times. "What's going on, Cutter? Did something come up with Whistle that I should know about?"

"Not here about Whistle. You'll take good care of him, as you always do." She beamed at his compliment. "I'd like to talk about Kingdom and the Squad."

Her face fell. In a neutral tone, she asked, "Is that not club business?"

"Officially, yes. Unofficially, it has everything to do with you."

"Me?" she gasped.

"Kingdom refuses to become president without your approval," Cutter explained patiently. He understood her position. She still considered herself an outsider and didn't want to overstep and get involved in club business. Unfortunately, that ship had already passed. She was now Kingdom's second half, and on top of that, he respected her opinion.

"Of course I approve. I love the Squad. You know that."

"Let me rephrase. It requires your persuasion," clarified Cutter. "*You* must persuade him. He thinks your safety will be compromised and he's worried that a deeper association with the club will blemish your reputation."

"Would I be in danger?" she asked, her head cocked to the side.

"Not going to lie to you, as the old lady of the president, you'll have more exposure."

Fiddling with a pen, she remained silent. Eventually, she lifted her gaze to him and said, "I don't think my reputation will be at risk. I've represented the club enough times in court that any blowback would have already occurred. If people should find out, and that's a big *if*, I don't believe it will make a difference. To outsiders, even criminal attorneys and prosecutors, there isn't a great distinction between being in a relationship with the Squad's vice president or its president."

"Good." He blew out a sigh. "There's the primary issue of your safety, but I will figure out a way to take care of you. I will *personally* make sure you're always under protection. Especially since you'll be having a kid soon."

Instantly, her gaze snapped to his. In a cautious tone, she said, "What makes you say that?"

Shrugging nonchalantly, he noted, "You and Kingdom have been solid for a while, and he's not getting any younger. You've got time, but the longer you wait..." he trailed off.

"Not getting any younger, huh?" She smiled sardonically. "Well, thanks for your input."

"Don't you want a family?"

"Of course I do! In fact, Kingdom and I have talked about it quite a lot recently."

They were more than talking about it, but he wasn't going there with her. "Starting a family makes a man nervous. Kingdom is already more possessive than the average man. Or the average biker, for that matter."

"As you well know, some of the brothers and the women in the club have not always been welcoming of me."

"That was in the past," he insisted with finality. "You've proven yourself repeatedly. God knows you've saved their asses too many times to count. The thing is, you've got to convince Kingdom it's in your best interest, and that of your kids. When your mom and brother died, you learned what it's like to have no one. Kingdom hasn't experienced that, but you can give your kids the kind of family that neither of us had. They'll be protected and surrounded by people who would lay down their lives for them. Not to mention, everyone will want a part of them and spoil them rotten."

Sage chuckled. "I don't know that I want them spoiled rotten."

"Hey, that's a luxury."

"Very true. But, wouldn't that happen whether Kingdom was president or vice president?"

"Your kids will be royalty," Cutter clarified. "It's a whole other level, babe."

Sage opened a small drawer in her desk and took out a folded American flag. Between her fingers, she caressed the stitches on the border. "I know what it's like to have no one at all." Inhaling, she smoothed out a wrinkle and returned it to the drawer. A small smile graced her lips. "My brother."

Her brother had been in the military. Middle Eastern metalwork and ceramics were scattered around her office. A small, intricate bronze bowl filled with Iraqi coins stood by her penholder.

Tossing one of the coins in his hand, Cutter confessed, "The Squad is my life. It's my only family. Where will we be if it's dismantled?"

"Kingdom wouldn't allow that to happen."

"Anything can happen. Without a firm hand, all hell could break loose. We need a leader who's trusted, respected, and feared. Imagine what will happen to a boy like Whistle? Fuck, he's barely manageable as it is. Without the Squad?" Cutter shook his head. "I don't ever want to go there. He's not the only one. Hoodie was found on the side of the highway, beaten half to death."

Sage inhaled sharply.

"Both young men and women found a haven in the Squad. As Kingdom's partner, you'd have the power to direct the club in any direction you wanted. Be more involved in protecting survivors like the ones you're already helping. Your impact will be huge."

Sage's eyes glowed. "I never thought of it that way."

Cutter cracked a smile. "Babe, that's why you have me. Not just any old lady will do. The Squad deserves better than that, and you'll make it greater than it already is. Charity rallies,

Toys for Tots...whatever you decide. Dozens of people will chip in to help you."

Sage's chair creaked as she fell against the back. "I'm flattered you think so highly of me, but it's a bit overwhelming."

"You can do this, Sage. For Kingdom. For your future family. For all of us."

Shadows cloaked her bright eyes. "Greta won't like it. She's adamant that I don't get involved deeper into the club."

He ground down on his molars. "Greta doesn't know jack shit about the Squad. From what I've heard, the club she came from was screwed up. She's biased. As for Kingdom, he plucked the decision right out of your hands and made it for you. Don't you think it's time you made up your own mind? Without Kingdom's influence or Greta's bullying. How does that make you feel, strong woman that you are?"

The muscles of her jaws twitched. "Not good at all. He's so bossy!"

"That he is, but don't let him boss you around. If you don't put your foot down, he's going to run right over you. You've gotta train him now. Teach him that he can't make unilateral decisions." It was a low blow, but Cutter wasn't above going there. "And if you're not going to take it from Kingdom, then why should you take it from Greta? She's your girl, and I hear that, but it's your decision. I would honor it, even if I didn't like it. Are they showing you the same respect?"

Narrowing her eyes, she scrutinized him. "You're very persuasive when you put your mind to it. All these years, you've been keeping this superpower under wraps. I believe you've just outed yourself."

Cutter shook with laughter. "Yeah, alright. You get Kingdom to take over, and I'll step up to the plate."

Slapping the palms of her hands on her desk, she replied, "Deal!"

Reaching the door, he turned the knob and pivoted around. Leaning back against the door, he crossed his arm and said, "Since we're partners, I've got one last favor to ask you."

"What's that?"

"Greta. I'm going for her, and I'd like you to back me up."

"Your chances with her are slim to none. Forget about it."

"Doesn't she deserve to have what you have with Kingdom?"

"Is that what you're planning? Honestly, Cutter, your middle name is promiscuous. I'm not going to stand by and watch her get hurt."

"I would never hurt her, but a woman like her is begging to be set free. I'm good at what I do, and I would never fuck around on her. Do you believe in me?"

"I'm beginning to, yes," she admitted.

"Then trust me, she'll be safe in my care."

"If you can catch her," Sage scoffed.

"She's as good as mine."

"You will crash and burn, but, fine, I won't get in your way. If you bring her out of her shell, then I will support you. God knows, I've been trying to set her up with men for ages."

At the thought of another man touching her, his fingers dug into his biceps. "I'm what she needs. Trust me on this."

Sage pursed her lips while she considered him. "She is attracted to you, but she's afraid." Focusing on her nails, she whispered, "You've got to promise that you won't hurt her. She's been through enough."

"I won't hurt her. Ever," he assured her.

Sage pressed her lips inward as she flicked at the top of the planner on her desk with her finger. Nodding, she acquiesced, "I give you my blessing. Good luck. You'll need that, and more."

7

CUTTER

Cutter leaned back on the sofa in Kingdom's office, waiting for him to wrap up his call. Christ, he was catchin' feels, and they pinged around in his chest like pinballs. Two days ago, Greta was sassier and sexier than the day at the coffee shop. Time to get that shit under control. He couldn't remember the last time he got as heated as he had the moment when Whistle had flirted with her. After the appointment, he taught that wet-behind-the-ears boy to never talk to her again. As of today, she was off-fuckin'-limits.

"What do you want?" Kingdom grumbled as he typed away on his laptop.

"Greta," he replied solemnly.

"You've got zero chance with her. Forget about it."

Almost the same exact thing Sage had said.

Cutter scowled at him and bit out, "You wanna bet, asshole?"

Confusion lined Kingdom's forehead. Not exactly the right way to talk to your soon-to-be president, but he didn't give a fuck.

Kingdom snorted. "I'm not betting on you. It'd be like taking candy from a baby."

"You doubtin' my skills?" he snapped.

"Bro, you got no skills to doubt," Kingdom retorted. "My advice is this. Don't get wrapped up in her, 'cause she doesn't go for bikers."

"See, that's where you're wrong. She's dying for biker dick," he said confidently. She might act like she didn't want him, but he saw through her ruse. That bitch wanted him, hands down.

Kingdom angled his head, watching him keenly. "I'm not sayin' she doesn't want it, I'm sayin' she won't take the bait. She's got history." Kingdom fake shuddered. "Fuck, she'd rage on a brother if he stepped to her. You see the way she dresses."

Yup, he sure as fuck did. Greta's wardrobe hid too many of her sexy curves, like she was confused or some shit. The touch of bondage was real, though.

"Didn't notice her clothes," he mumbled.

"Bullshit, you tallied up a list of every detail. There's only one reason a biker bitch like her leaves her club and becomes a hard-core feminist. She's been burned. She's not your regular bitch. Since she was too young to be an old lady, I'm guessing she's someone's daughter."

Say what? Hard-core feminist? He hadn't seen that one coming. Cutter popped a cigarette into his mouth.

"Sounds about right," he concurred as the unlit cigarette bobbed between his lips.

"You remember what happened when Sage dropped out of sight. She might as well have gone into the witness protection program. Greta hid her out in the mountains with her mom. A woman doesn't drop everything to hide a person she doesn't know for two weeks unless she's been in a fucked-up situation herself at some point."

Kingdom's expression took on a grim, possessive look. "Sage told me about Greta's mom and her man. They're members of a club in Vermont, but they work as part of a covert network for women escaping abuse. Not just any kind of domestic violence...the killing kind."

No good came from letting Kingdom dwell on the ugly. Shaking his hand as if burned, Cutter said, "Wherever she came from, Greta cleaned up real good. She's sizzlin' hot, yo."

"Did you not fuckin' hear what I just fuckin' told you?" he grumbled.

"Oh, I heard you. It just doesn't change my plans."

Kingdom shook his head. "Forget it, man. Greta's a tough nut to crack. Too tough for you. She was in college on a scholarship when she became Sage's receptionist. After, she went on to get a degree in paralegal studies. Sage treats her like a partner. When I fucked up, Greta set up Sage's escape plan and got her out of town within *hours*. She ran that office on her own until Sage came back. She doesn't joke, yo."

A grin spread on his face as Kingdom queried, "You're sniffin' around her like a bloodhound. She ignoring you or what?"

"Fuckin' woman flirted with Whistle," he groused.

Kingdom's mocking laugh twisted Cutter's guts like a knife.

"Never thought I'd see the day when you were jealous. Damn, you're a goner. Listen bro, she's not interested in boys. She's looking for a man who doesn't fuck around and you're the furthest thing from that. Then there's the fact that bikers are strictly off-limits for her. When Sage and I hooked up, Greta warned her that bikers ain't worth nothing. Stressed Sage out about our less-than-legit business organization. We don't have the worst, for sure, but we're not squeaky clean either. She told Sage that if I didn't get murdered, I'd end up in jail. Needless to say, it took a while for Sage to come around."

Sobering, he finished, "Greta's not the kind of woman you want to fuck with, and I don't say that lightly. Fact is, she matters to Sage. She isn't an easy woman to deal with, and if she gets hurt, Sage will hurt along with her."

Cutter blew out a breath, and then complained, "Women."

"Pretty little thing like her ain't gonna stay single for long," Kingdom mused, rubbing the scruff on his chin.

Cutter's eyes tapered into slits, his stomach roiling. In a flash, he was around Kingdom's desk, hand clamped on his friend's shoulder. Brother or not, he was about to take the motherfucker down.

"You ain't fuckin' interested in her," he declared in a deadly, cold tone.

Kingdom shrugged out of his hold and skewered him with a vicious look. "You gotta be fuckin' crazy. Get out from behind my desk. Fuck man, it's not like you haven't drooled over my woman or come over uninvited to cockblock me and mooch food off my woman."

Cutter wiped his hand over his face. What the hell had gotten into him?

Flashing an impish grin, he cracked, "What can I say, I can't fight the temptation to mess with you and fill up my belly at the same time."

"I know you," Kingdom warned. "You've checked out Greta's tits and fell in love with them. Get it through your head, dumbass. She is not for you, period. The bitches you go for show off skin like strippers. She wears hippie skirts and crystal necklaces."

Cutter blithely added, "And leather bondage heels and biker jackets."

"She's not a blonde," he shot back.

"That's what bleach is for."

"You are one fucked-up brother," he said with a laugh.

"That I am, brother, that I am."

Kingdom's laughter tapered off and threatened, "Either way, I'm not giving you the go-ahead. Leave her alone."

The hairs on the back of Cutter's neck prickled.

Like hell he would.

8

GRETA

Greta passed rows of bikes blocking half the street, the light repeatedly glinting off all that beautiful, polished chrome in the setting sun. After driving around the block a few times, she finally found a parking space one street over. Based on the sound level as she strode up the clubhouse, Sage's birthday party wasn't popping yet.

Gulping, she stared up at the awning emblazoned with the logo of the Demon Squad, three demons on Harleys, likely representing the original members who founded the MC. A man approached her as she passed through the fence. A recruit, by the looks of him. He wore a leather cut with a single bottom rocker patch.

He surveyed her from head to boots. She had on tight jeans and her motorcycle jacket because she wanted to blend in, for Sage's sake. She couldn't deny that the weight of it fell comfortably on her shoulders. Her clothing must have passed the biker-bitch code because he ultimately waved her through. Bikers could be as snobby as a fashionista during New York Fashion Week.

"Where's Sage?" she asked.

"Out back. Go straight that way," he gestured.

Nodding her thanks, she wrapped her jacket around her chest and passed another set of gates to the backyard. A bonfire was flaming in the center, and several picnic tables were set up with food and drinks.

Greta took a bracing breath. It was just your run-of-the-mill party. God knows, she'd been going to them since she was in her mother's womb. Stopping next to a tub filled with drinks, she was reaching in for a beer when her wrist was seized from behind. She froze as thick fingers wrapped around the bones of her wrist, demanding her attention.

Cutter pulled the bottle out of her grasp, popped the lid open with a flash of white teeth, and ordered, "Tip your head back."

Towering over her, his shoulders blocked out the last rays of the sun setting behind the row houses. In the growing dusk, his command shimmered with unrepentant sensual dominance. Instinctively, she tilted her chin upward and her lips drifted open. Deftly, he brought the cool glass bottle to her lips. She took her time wrapping her mouth around the rim. Inch by inch, he leveraged the bottle until liquid slid over her tongue and down her throat.

After she swallowed, he brought it to his mouth and finished half of it. "That's real good, baby girl."

Greta crossed her arms and then uncrossed them. She cleared her throat and forced out, "You better not bother Sage tonight with your nonsense."

"Come on, it's her birthday. I'm not a *monster*."

"Actually, I'm pretty sure you are," she quipped.

Cutter gave her a slow once-over and paused at her harness. She'd chosen a silk top that displayed every crease along the leather straps caging her chest and looping around her neck. More straps joined the wires in the bodice pushing her breasts up to display them to their best advantage. The tip of his incisor clipped his bottom lip. *Damn*. The evening was frigid, but heat flooded between her thighs.

"Truce tonight," he rumbled.

"Oh, you're so magnanimous," she countered.

"I'm showing my patient side, but don't underestimate me, Greta. I'll get what I want in the end. I always do," he promised, his tone dripping with arrogance.

"You're such a pompous ass." She turned to leave, but he dragged her against him until her nipples chafed against his chest. The irises of his easy blue eyes had changed into a dangerous gunmetal grey.

"If you want to drink, you come to me. I'll be the one to quench your thirst," he warned.

His natural cedarwood scent surrounded her, short-circuiting her brain. She was thirsty alright. Thirsty to fall to her knees and swallow his cock to the back of her throat. She wiped the sweat beading along her hairline.

A knowing smirk spread over his face, and he gave a crisp swat to her ass, catching her in a sensitive spot between her butt cheek and upper thigh. In place of a curse, a whimper slipped out, and she had to consciously stop herself from rubbing the spot on her bottom.

That swat snapped her back into reality.

"I'll choke on my tongue before I ask you for anything," she gritted out.

He laid his palm on her hip and prodded her forward.

"Go find Sage before your smart mouth gets you into trouble," he cautioned.

Regarding him over her shoulder, her tongue darted to the

corner of her mouth. He followed the movement before his gaze dipped to her harness.

In a throaty timbre, he warned, "Watch yourself, little one."

Tugging the ends of her jacket together, she lifted her chin. The bastard had thrown her off her game *again*.

Cutter crossed his arms over his wide chest at her defiance and let out a low growl. An actual growl. Unfortunately, her body was primed, her nipples painfully tight. Giving him the middle finger, she mouthed "fuck you" and hurried toward a group of women standing by the fire pit. Her heart pounded against her rib cage like a jack-in-the-box gone rabid.

Greta turned her back on the stacks of liquor bottles to the side of the buffet table. She was damn thirsty, but no way in hell was she going to drink a drop if it meant asking Cutter for anything. What he'd done to her was too good by half. Her peace of mind was shattered because, at his signal, she'd have dropped between his legs and unbuttoned his Levi's. Have him give it to her dirty and crude, the way she craved it. Jesus, she must be broken inside to be fantasizing about him like this.

Sage sidled up to her and slipped her arm into the crook of Greta's arm. She flinched, but Sage's smile calmed her pulse. Dusk had already fallen when Cutter had pulled his little stunt, so Sage hadn't seen any of it Greta planned to keep it that way. Sage inquired, "How are you?"

"Good," she muttered.

"I hope you're telling me the truth. I know it isn't easy for you to be here. Any time you feel uncomfortable, I'll leave with you," her bestie promised.

Greta rolled her eyes. Like she'd take Sage away from the party. She was a type A, overachieving, overworked attorney. And that was with Kingdom setting hard limits on her. There was no way Greta would drag her friend out of her own birthday party.

"I know this isn't super comfortable for you, but I'm so glad you're here," Sage murmured.

"Girl, I wouldn't miss your birthday party for the world. And it's not so bad. When I visit with my mom, I hang out with her man and his brothers."

"You *stay* with your mom. You don't set foot inside their clubhouse," Sage remarked.

"Eh, it's not a big deal."

Sage squeezed her closer. "Come on, let's get you a drink and mingle."

At the mention of alcohol her gaze skittered around the space and screeched to a halt on Cutter.

Nearby lights illuminated him, lounging back on a picnic table, his arm wrapped around a woman's shoulders. Across a yard full of people, she could hear his distinct laughter.

Sensing her attention, his eyes met hers. His smile fell away, replaced by a hard-set jaw and immobile features. She expelled a little sigh and saluted him with her closed water bottle.

Absently, Greta said, "I'm good with this."

"Seriously? No alcohol?"

"I'll catch up, don't worry," she lied.

Sage frowned but shrugged. They'd reached a group of women, and Sage belted out, "Hey everyone, this is Greta! Some of you already know her, but let's welcome her to the way we party!"

Before Kingdom, she'd never seen Sage giddy like this. Greta snagged Sage and hugged her tightly. The smokiness coming off the firepit brought back memories of playing tag around bonfires. She smiled at the women as she was introduced to them. Like the prospect outside, they looked her over meticulously. One of the older women nodded to her, and the others relaxed collectively, pulling on their beers, or taking sips from their Solo cups, and resuming their conversations.

9

CUTTER

utter watched Greta release Sage from a hug and stride into the clubhouse. Where the fuck was she going? *Better not be going inside to dance and rub up your sexy body on some other bastard.* Getting up to follow her, Cutter found her plastered against a wall facing the large dance area, dark and pulsing with the heavy bass of hip-hop.

A woman in daisy dukes and a tube top waved her hands above her head, then dropped them to the bar in a sultry move before all eyes were drawn to her twerking ass. The air was humid and hot from the wall-to-wall crowd of people dancing and drinking. He caught sight of his brother Puck dragging his younger sister, Sammi, away from a man she was grinding on.

Cutter wove between swaying couples toward Greta as she edged around the side wall. He tracked her as she skirted the crowds, checking each hallway of the main floor before going down a corridor. He sprinted to keep up and almost caught up with her when she slipped into a bathroom at the last moment.

Waiting, he leaned back against the wall facing the bathroom. The door swung open. Greta stumbled out, screeched, and smacked into his rib cage. His hands cupped her elbows to steady her, and he felt her little nails dig into his biceps.

Thunder brewed in those dark green irises, overtaking their natural grass color. She looked like one pissed-off biker princess. She looked glorious.

He skillfully moved her until her spine hit the wall and then slapped a hand beside her head. The sound echoed between the narrow walls of the empty corridor.

"Time to go home, Cinderella," he intoned.

She huffed out a laugh. "Cinderella. Funny." Then, she grimaced. "I don't like being called a Disney character. One thing I know for sure is that I'm not a damsel in distress. Been there, done that so you don't need to save me. I can take care of myself, asshole."

He arched an eyebrow. "Oh, yeah? Think what you want, but when you're in my club, I call the shots and I say that you're leaving and I'll be the one seein' you home safe."

Greta curled her upper lip. "I don't need a bodyguard. I'm more than safe on my own."

"I'm not giving you a choice," he declared.

"What the hell are you talking about?"

He breached the remaining space between them until they shared the same air. His knuckles stroked the top of her chest and followed the curve of her breast to the center of the leather harness.

He yanked her closer until she could feel the outline of his hard dick. An obscene moan slipped from her lips and washed over him, zip-lining a surge of power and hunger straight to his cock.

"I decide what's best for you. Bad enough you're wearin' a harness, advertising your nature to every dominant male within a ten-mile radius. I bet there's a matching collar somewhere, but, lucky for you, you were smart enough to leave it at home. As it is, you wouldn't last the night without some asshole getting up in your face, bossing you around."

She snorted softly, the sweet scent of her dancing across his cheek. "You're talking in riddles because that's exactly who you are. Funny, you're the only man who's been getting in my face and bossing me around."

"Yeah, but I'm the asshole you want so I determine when it's time for you to leave. I decide if you're gonna ride on the back of my bike. I decide everything. Feel me?"

"Hold up, you did not just say I'd ride bitch on the back of your bike." Shaking off his hold, she waved her hand and said, "Whatever, that's beside the point. Let me clear something up for you right this instant."

With a finger poking the center of his chest, she stared at him with a fierce look and ground out, "You. Don't decide. Anything for me."

He pressed her back against the cement blocks of the wall, crushing her pointed finger between them. She might be on the slimmer side, but in no way was she petite. With three-inch boots she towered over most men, yet she'd have to go onto her tiptoes to lick the line of his jaw.

"Not gonna lie. Been waiting for a woman like you, Greta. Bitchy on the outside, but docile on the inside. You don't know it yet, but you've been waiting for me."

"Okay, you're babbling nonsense. Are you drunk?" she asked.

"I'm gonna do you a favor," he replied, ignoring her question.

She rolled her eyes. "Can't wait to hear this one."

He chuckled before finishing, "I'm not gonna turn you against the wall. I'm not gonna rip your jeans off or take my hand to your ass until it's bright red and you're screaming yourself hoarse. "

Squirming under his bulk, she tried to shove him away, but ended up grinding against his erection. He slid his thigh between hers and increased the pressure. His balls drew up as he imagined her pulling out his swollen cock into her waiting hands.

He captured her wrists and raised them above her with a smack against the wall.

"Ouch!"

"You hurtin'? Seems to me you're not a good listener, but I have ways of getting bad girls like you to start actin' right. To listen and follow whatever I say."

"Fuck you and your club," she snarled.

"The word 'fuck' is the first real one you've said all night. Fuck, as in fucking your mouth or fucking your pussy? Or do you like takin' it in the ass?"

He tilted his head, his gaze running down her side to her butt. "I'm partial to your ass."

Oh, she was feeling him now. Right between the legs, because the heat coming from her pussy was singeing him like a Taser. He adjusted his grip, taking her wrists in one hand and cupping her butt with the other. Her ass cheek filled his hand, soft and bouncy. He kneaded it, and she barely stifled a yelp while the inner muscles of her pussy clenched and released against his thigh, in tandem with his massage. Spine arching, her torso jutted forward to give his large hand more space to grip.

"You like that. No wonder you have an attitude, baby girl. You haven't been fucked right." Her breath stalled, but she made sure to toss him one of her signature salty expressions. "Don't play with me. I've barely touched you, but your fuck-me eyes are begging me for a nice, sharp slap as an appetizer."

She shifted her attention away from him, but he snapped his fingers in her face and dragged her focus back to him.

Eyes narrowed, she spat out, "You know nothing about me."

"You've got spunk, that much I know. I also know that I like it," he responded in an amused tone.

His fingers returned to her buttocks, diving deeper into her supple flesh. A snicker came from behind him and the sound broke the intensity of the moment.

Checking over his shoulder, irritation bubbled in his chest.

"A new woman. How you find them…"

Fucking Puck.

Thinking he was distracted, Greta squirmed to get away, but before she could escape, he cupped her mons. She stilled her struggles.

"Clear out and don't let anyone back here," he ordered Puck.

"Come on. You never minded an audience before," Puck replied soothingly.

"Fuck off, Puck. Do what I say."

Puck raised his hands in surrender and backed away. "Alright, alright."

Once Cutter was comfortable with Puck's distance, he flicked the buttons of her jeans open and snaked his hand down the front.

"What the fuck? I barely know you," she hissed. Her words were harsh, but she bit back a groan the instant his fingers slid between her wet, fleshy lips.

"Princess, you're gonna let me do this," he pronounced.

Her gaze roved over his hard torso, from the cords of his thick neck to V-shaped grooves of his abdomen, outlined beneath his thin Henley. Trapped between the wall and his body, his mouth claimed hers. Devouring her orally, his thumb and forefinger latched on to her clit.

"What I'd do to lick your pussy right now. Not the time and place for that, but lucky for you, I'm in the mood to play."

Small gasps puffed out of her as he thrust inside and ground the heel of his palm against her pussy. Groping, she found the ridge of his stiff cock and stroked hard. He tore her hand away and shoved it against the wall again. Clinging onto his shoulder with her free hand, she clamped her leg over his thigh and rode his fingers.

A base growl that he barely recognized rumbled through him. His hand gripped her breast, holding her in place, as her orgasm tore through her like an oncoming train. Shivers crashed through her in waves. Her nails came out and raked the side of his face as her hips gyrated until she was left panting. He pressed in again, but she was so sensitive that she jerked and shook her head for him to stop.

Satisfied, he slid his hand out, her juices coating his fingers. Eyes on her, he sniffed them and then slipped them into his mouth. Her scent brought forth a sultry summer afternoon, rich and heavy. Fertile, like a soil meant to receive his seed.

Pulling them out with a popping sound, he touched her chin with his sticky fingers. "You're gonna go home, take a shower, and rub yourself down with lotion. No touching that swollen little clit of yours. Not until I allow it."

Her chest heaved, air sawing in and out of her lungs.

"You're not the boss of me," she protested.

"Baby girl, my cock is hard as steel. Don't tempt me 'cause you don't want me to show you who's boss right here. It won't be pretty or gentle." He eyed her up and down. "I see you, woman. But you don't want pretty and soft, do you? No, you want it *dirty*."

Batting his hand off her, she disengaged herself and fled down the hall, hurling out a *fuck you* over her shoulder for good measure. Puck stepped aside for her.

Once she'd slipped around the corner, he said, "You outdid yourself. I timed it."

He waved his cell phone. "Three minutes and twenty-seven seconds. I'm keeping score with the brothers who can get a bitch off the fastest."

"Where's your sister, huh? I'd check on her if I were you," he rejoined.

With the taste of Greta on his lips, he stalked into the bath-room, slammed the door shut, pulled out his cock, and stroked.

That bitch is mine.

10

CUTTER

I t was too fucking early to get out of bed when there was a warm body beside him, but Cutter's chances of cornering Loki without eavesdroppers were limited.

Like clockwork, the brother woke up at five or six, some fucked-up hour in the morning, like a damn monk. Rubbing the grit from his eyes, Cutter dragged himself out of bed and stumbled down the darkened stairs. Roaming the first floor of the club, Cutter flipped on the lights, grumbling about how he was gonna kick Loki's ass.

Turning into the kitchen, Cutter found him bent over a collection of knives set out on the island counter. The bastard was sharpening them. Loki kept himself to himself and didn't want to know anything more than necessary. The brother was like an IED ready to explode.

That said, he was a good brother. One of the best, if you didn't count the time he tried to take Kingdom out over Chopper's suicide. Loki was an officer with a sophisticated set of skills that acted on command. End of story.

The only question that remained was whether he'd stay after Prez stepped down. Civilians thought bikers were renegades, but nothing was further from the truth. They did not follow normal rules, but it made their commitment to their club more powerful. Bikers lived and died by the oath they pledged to their colors.

Best way to solidify Kingdom's reign was to corral Loki into supporting him. Who knew, it might pull his ass out of his monastic knife obsession.

"Want to know why I take out my collection to clean at the ass crack of dawn?"

Fucking hell, he had no choice but to take the bait. Leaning over the island, he dropped his chin on the heel of his hand. "Why?"

"I come down, in the early morning, to be in peace and tend to my knives. You're fucking with my meditation time. Best be quick about it or I'll jab a blade in your junk."

"Guess a man can learn something new every day," he snorted. "Cleaning utensils: a form of meditation."

"Your ignorant ass doesn't know shit. These aren't kitchen knives. Samurai care for their weapons like real men care for their women."

Here we go. Picking up a long sword, Loki began, "The *katana* was their primary weapon. A *katana* is an extension of a warrior's arm. It is a spiritual object, and like anything on a shrine, I must keep it pure. We're dirty motherfuckers, and it's a warrior's responsibility to return the object to its original, pure form after he touches it. Respect the knife and you will be worthy of handling it."

If a man gets poetic about his knives, it's time to jump ship. Unfortunately, Cutter didn't have a choice but to listen and pray he didn't get stabbed for his troubles.

"Men abuse their weapons with their ignorance and lack of respect. A Japanese steel *katana* is a work of art. It's as demanding as a woman beggin' to come. One of the most important ways to respect your blade is to clean it when it encounters impurity."

Loki cut a look Cutter's way, wordlessly telling him that he was as impure as they came. Cutter rolled his eyes.

"Blood," Loki emphasized. Aww, shit. Loki was going down a dark path. Fuck, this was painful to listen to. "Blood taints a clean blade. The best way to maintain the blade is to not touch it or use it. But life doesn't work that way, does it now? Situations arise that require the use of a weapon." He raised his hands, palms outward. "The tips of my fingers are dirty—no matter how much I scrub them. Imagine what that does to a blade."

Loki closed his eyes and inhaled a full breath, held it, and released it slowly. "It's carbon steel. Since you're an idiot, you have no fucking clue what that is. I'll tell you what it's not. It's not stainless steel like the swords dumb-fucks like you buy on the internet."

"You're scaring me, dude."

"That's because you're a pussy."

"Am I gonna get to talk, or are you going to chew my ear out much longer?"

Loki gave him a doleful look. Raising his eyes to the ceiling, Cutter muttered, "Go on, but wrap it up quick. I've got a bitch in my bed."

Loki held up two pieces of cloth, one clean and one soaked with oil. "There are native materials, like rice paper, that Samurai used instead of cloth. Many items can be substituted, but"—Loki cradled a silk ball in the palm of his hand—"an *unchiko* ball can't."

"A what now?"

"In traditional sword care, the *unchiko* ball is used to prevent rust." He held it in front of him with outstretched hands. "It's filled with the fine powder of a special Japanese stone."

Concentration furrowed his brow as he tapped the silken ball on the stainless-steel countertop. Cutter touched the soft powder, like ash, flowing from the silk. For some damn reason, Loki's lesson was beginning to interest him. Loki wiped the blade from hilt to tip in one precise motion.

"I'm removing the excess oil from the carbon steel. I would normally polish it, but I won't since you're here."

Holding the *katana* in midair, he slashed downward. Cutter stood close enough to feel the whip of air against his cheek. Loki canted his head to the side, inspected the gleaming metal and his facial expression relaxed. He took a clean, light cloth and applied a new coat of oil. Bringing the sword closer, he mused aloud, "It needs sharpening." With a cutting look and a smirk, he continued, "To optimize, ya know, to slice up flesh."

"Christ, you're sick. The way I am with women is the way you are with slicing flesh? No thank you, yo."

"Like I said before, you're a pussy. Pussies only know one thing, how to control other pussy."

Cutter was at the point where he was about to rip the hair out of his scalp. That's what talking to Loki did to a man.

Carefully placing the sword down, his gaze pierced into Cutter. "Respect. Life has no meaning without respect. I show respect to my blade. I demonstrate respect to the maker of the blade. To the hundreds of years it took for a culture to create the blade. I work to deserve the *katana* in my hand. Like my club. What do you revere? I sure as fuck don't see you treating anything with respect, except the pussy in your bed. And once they step out of your room, they're back to being nothing."

Cutter threw his hands up in the air. "Get off your high horse for once in your fuckin' life. You don't touch women. It's not natural. Only shit you play with is knives and guns. You hide behind them."

"And you hide behind twisted pussy," Loki countered.

"Fantastic," he responded derisively. "We're even, so let's squash this bullshit. You talk big about respect for the club. It's time to show it because the Squad is going under. Are you ready to take one for the club if it brings your ego down a notch, you condescending motherfucker? I'm not big on pride, but you pride yourself on everything, including shittin' on the pot, like a damn king. Only one king here."

"What in the fuck are you talking about?"

"Are you wantin' to know something from me? Damn, guess there's a first time for everything. I thought you were the all-knowing guru." Cutter motioned with his hand, taking in Loki's sword and materials. "Then you don't know that Prez is on his way out."

Loki's large frame tensed; his eyes flat, dead.

"Yeah, that's right. The position of leader. You're sure as fuck not steppin' into it. A few of the brothers may want the job, but they don't have what it takes. That leaves one person and you know who that is."

"Fuck!" Loki bellowed. He took the handle of the purified *katana* and whipped it through the air.

"Is that the way you *respect* your toy?" Cutter commented drolly. "I've got a woman upstairs tied to my fucking bed, waitin' on me, but I came down here to speak to you. You put me through my paces with your knife cleaning, ritualistic bullshit. It's time you fuckin' man up." Stabbing his forefinger at Loki, Cutter growled, "Shit's goin' down, and you're gonna give your oath to Kingdom. He's our future and you better fall on the right side of it."

Swiping his hand down, he backed away and held the

swinging door open. Before exiting, he instructed, "You go back and play with your toys. I'm done."

Behind him, Loki grumbled, "Never thought you had it in you, Peacemaker."

Whatever. Up till this point, he'd tried his best to avoid drama. Taking the stairs three at a time, Cutter paused on the landing. The sounds of snoring coming from open doorways reverberated in the hallway.

He tiptoed into his darkened room and pulled out some workout gear. After slipping on a pair of boxing shorts and tying up his running shoes, he quietly slipped back out the door, the image of a certain raven-haired beauty with haughty eyes plaguing him.

GRETA

Sage had planned a girls' night out after work, since Kingdom was out of town. Greta stepped out of the office bathroom, freshly dressed, as Sage's cell rang. Kingdom had come home early. Sage arranged to meet him at a bar downtown, and then pleaded, "Come along."

"No way," she answered. "I'm not cockblocking Kingdom, and I'm not about to be a third wheel with you lovebirds. Your public displays of affection are downright embarrassing."

Lying back on one of the office couches, Sage flung off her high heels and wiggled her stocking-clad toes.

Trying to be sly, she side-eyed Greta as she remarked, "Cutter will be there as well. It's been a week since my party, and don't think I didn't notice how you guys checked each other out. His baby blues didn't leave you once."

Greta laughed. "I'm pretty sure they did. He had some bitch hanging all over him."

"Pfft," she replied with a dismissive wave of her hand. "He's a biker. The PDA code is totally different. It didn't mean a thing."

Goosebumps swept down her arms to the tips of her

fingernails. *Seriously? I never knew nails could tingle.* Thank God Sage wasn't privy to her body's automatic reaction to his name.

"Hell, no" hovered on her lips when Sage cut her off. "Biker or not, if you're going to experiment, you should do it with him. I trust him to take care of you."

Greta's lower jaw detached, and her mouth gaped. They'd danced around the topic of her bent predilection but had never spoken about it outright.

Conspicuously avoiding Greta's gaze, Sage hurried on, "At the end of the night, you decide who drops you off at home. The ball is in your court."

Unbelievable.

Sage was pimping for him.

Clearing her throat, Greta replied, "You've certainly thought this through, but him being my type is irrelevant. I don't want him manipulating you, Sage. You have no idea what you'd be signing up for."

"I respect your opinion, but this is between me and King-dom," she replied pertly. "Not you. Not Cutter either."

"And what does Kingdom say?" she queried.

Sage's lips flattened. "I don't appreciate the way you and Kingdom are acting about this."

Huh. That meant that he wasn't on board with being president. Good to know. Even so, her accusation rankled because it was Cutter's doing.

"We want what's best for you," she pleaded.

"Kingdom is being irrational. Since my miscarriage, it's like I'm made of spun glass and, quite honestly, I'm getting sick of it. My birthday party proved that the brothers and bitches appreciate me."

"It was a party," Greta implored. "Bikers are at their best when they're drinking and whoring."

Sage raised her nose and sniffed. "I understand that you

have issues, Greta, but you have to admit that you're a bit jaded."

"And you're too damn naïve to see the truth," she fired back.

Sage breathed in sharply and Greta squeezed her eyes shut. *Shit, I'm being harsh again.*

"I'm not an idiot," she said in a small voice.

The hurt in her tone made Greta want to slap herself. This was her issue, not Sage's. Yes, she was worried. Yes, she was right to be concerned. But, she didn't have the right to spew her issues all over her friend.

Wrapping her arms around Sage, Greta insisted, "Of course not! They do love you. Who wouldn't? The problem is that it takes so much to head an MC."

"It'd be Kingdom, not me," she sniffed.

"It's all-consuming," Greta forged on, "and I don't want you shackled to a club filled to the brim with idiots. I mean, you've seen Whistle and the other prospects. Am I right?"

Sage cackled, "Yes, well...they *are* idiots."

"That they are," Greta confirmed with a resolute nod of her head.

Sobering, Sage pulled away gently, and implored, "But they need Kingdom. Cutter's right about that and I'm not going to jeopardize the club's future. Kingdom should take the position. It's the right thing to do. It's the best thing to do for the club and the club saved Kingdom. It's his life."

Damn that Cutter.

"Please, tell me what Cutter said so that I can set you right," she insisted.

Greta cringed at the face Sage made. *Oh, no*, she'd pricked Sage's savage avenging streak. If there was someone out there to save, Sage would swoop in to do it.

"Please don't make any hasty decisions," she pleaded. "This is a super-serious, life-changing decision."

"Since the miscarriage, I've thought long and hard on how to raise my children. They should grow up as part of a community, with people I trust. I've never had that, Greta. For you, it was dysfunctional, but the Squad is not the Dark Horsemen."

Understatement of the fucking year, but still...

"All MCs are dysfunctional," Greta muttered.

"That's not true," Sage argued stiffly.

Greta was going to murder that son-of-a-bitch biker.

"What did he say to you?" she ground out.

Guilt flickered over Sage's face. "Cutter has been feeding you bullshit. What did he say, exactly?"

"It's not something he said—" Breaking off, she approached Greta with quick strides, and hugged her fiercely. "I know you only want to protect me, but I'm asking you to stop it. Focus on yourself, not me. I'm sick with worry about you. You're beautiful. You're an incredible person and you deserve to enjoy life a little. Even if you're not interested in Cutter, you have a chance to discover whether this...this lifestyle works for you."

A wave of embarrassment swept over Greta.

Squeezing tighter, Sage persisted, "I may not understand everything you like or what you're going through, but you've told me enough, and I'm honored that you have. When it comes to sex, judgment and intolerance is woven into the fabric of our culture, especially for women. But if I could attain happiness in the brief span of time we have on this godforsaken earth, then I'll do anything to find it for you, too."

Greta's nose burned, pressure building behind her eyes. Sage had pried open a gaping hole she struggled every day to shut down and bury away. She hadn't been touched in forever.

Tone stiff, she lied to her best friend, "I'm not interested in Cutter."

"Yes, you are," Sage refuted. "At least enough to hook up with him. He'd never hurt you and he's experienced. For Pete's sake, we aren't talking about a relationship here, we're talking about taking advantage of an opportunity. That's all it is. An opportunity, and I'm insisting that you take it, Greta."

Sage clung onto her as Greta rolled her head, landing it on Sage's shoulder, and groaned, "He drives me crazy, and not in a good way."

"Oh, please, that's only because he pushes you out of your comfort zone. Come out tonight. It will only be the four of us and he knows how precious you are to us. If there's one thing I can say about Cutter is that he doesn't force women to like what he likes. If they do, then they hook up. If they don't, he leaves them alone."

"We haven't exactly seen eye to eye," Greta insisted.

"So what?" Sage scoffed. "He's ready to eat you alive." She gave Greta a sly look. "And you're interested, I see it in your eyes. You can pick up arguing with him another day. Just take a break for tonight and see where it goes."

I guess I could kill two birds with one stone. Experiment with him and maneuver him into giving up his ridiculous quest. But was she seriously considering being intimate with a guy she resented? The image of Cutter at the party, his pretty-boy lips licking her juices off his fingers, poked at her. The yummy sounds he made as he sucked off his fingers brought on a shiver racing down her spine. The desire to return the favor, to taste him, had preoccupied her ever since.

"Does Kingdom know?" she asked, looking at Sage suspiciously. She didn't want any of the brothers knowing her business. Those men were worse than a pair of grannies sitting on a park bench.

"Don't worry about him," vowed Sage. "I'll keep him distracted and he won't notice a thing."

Greta doubted that, but she'd let the white lie pass.

With a teasing lilt, she noted, "My, you've thought of everything."

Sage stroked her hair. "It's wrong to waste time, baby. You're so special to me, and I will make sure you have nothing to fear." She shrugged. "Anyway, it's not as if anything serious would come of it."

Her last sentence hit Greta like a slap to the face.

Mistaking her expression, Sage hurried to add, "I mean because he's a biker and all."

Greta swallowed through the elastic band constricting her throat. Of course, she was right. He was a biker. Lust must be melting her brain, because, for one insane moment, the thought of more than a hookup slipped through her defenses and it hadn't mattered who he was who. But he was who he was, and she was who she was. No compromise could change the facts.

Right, she had nothing to lose.

"Fine, I'll do it," she breathed out.

12

CUTTER

Kingdom came back early from Virginia, smuggling in contraband smokes, and contacted Cutter to meet up with him at a warehouse. Several hours of waiting for the pickup while his brother paced, poking away at his phone, nearly drove him insane. Finally, their counterpart showed up, they loaded up the merchandise, and they were free to ride away. Kingdom crossed through various neighborhoods, toggling his cell between his shoulder and jaw, talking to Sage.

Smoke blew out of Cutter's nostrils and he twisted his head toward the open window, biding his time until he was free to prowl for fresh meat.

After disconnecting, Kingdom threw his cell on the console and faced him. "Sage is bringing Greta. Her way of torturing me for being away. You're comin' along to distract her."

"What happened to your lecture about her being off-limits?" he asked, eyebrow arched.

"Fuck that, I can't have her using Greta as a shield. We had a disagreement about the club." Eyeing him carefully, he added, "Don't bother denying that you're behind it. You owe me, so you better take care of Greta for me."

His momma didn't bring up no fool. Hell, he wasn't one to contradict a direct order.

They rode down to the Brewery District to some dipshit yuppie bar, where they ordered a round of whiskey. Being among yuppies didn't stop a slew of women from blatantly checking them out, though. As the woody flavor with hints of vanilla rolled on his palate, Cutter settled onto the barstool with a satisfied sigh. Tasted like Greta's cream on his tongue. His teeth clicked as if he was latching on to her clit.

Swiping his hand down his face, he rubbed the bristles on his chin. Fuck, he wanted that woman.

Cutter spun the dark liquid in the glass in looping coils when the nervous tapping of Kingdom's fingers on the bar halted. He looked up. Sure enough, the women were standing by the hostess.

Greta threw her head back, laughing in response to something Sage was saying. From his vantage point, those brilliant green eyes of hers called to him like beacons. And her hair. Fine, silky locks of black ink lay over her breasts, tipped in pink, begging to be wrapped around his fist.

Moving toward him like a sleek goddess, she wore the most revealing outfit he'd seen on her yet. The smooth, tanned skin of her bare arms gleamed under the dim light of the bar. But what cinched it for him was her choker. Three layers of pearls. Classy, and tightly wound around the tendons of her neck.

It was like a cattle prod to his balls.

"Babe, you've got no idea what you've unleashed," Cutter whispered under his breath.

"Huh?" Kingdom asked.

"That bitch is fine," he said aloud.

Her choker was a green-fucking-light and, he was well-versed in the stoplight colors. In his world, the stoplight was the basic method of communication between sexual partners. Green meant his partner was ready. Yellow meant that he was pushing her limits. Red meant "back the fuck off." That choker was as green as the color of her eyes.

As she glided toward him with the grace of a dancer, his muscles locked up. Desire, mixed with nerves, rolled off her and poured molten lust into his bloodstream. Drawing near, she cocked a hip, and her hand straddled the curve. His dick got hard so fast it practically punched out of his button-fly to get to her.

The first words out of that sassy mouth of hers were, "Stop staring. It's rude."

After a day wrangling with Kingdom's moody ass, his patience was running thin. He caught her wrist and hauled her up to him.

Bringing his mouth to her ear, he said, "You keep this up and you'll find your plump backside red. And don't think being in public will hold me back. It won't."

Christ, his voice almost cracked.

A flush started on her high cheekbones and spread down to her collar bone. He bet it ran down over her tits and darkened the nipples puckering beneath her shirt.

"I'm going to leave if you get bossy," she warned.

Fuck that.

He was about to tell her what he'd do to her mouthy attitude, but Sage glared at him and ordered, "Play nice."

Cutter grunted and gestured Greta to the stool next to him, away from Sage and Kingdom.

A look passed between her and Sage. Sage gave a slight nod and Greta seated herself on his other side.

He drew close, caging her in his arms, and backed her up

against the bar. Her high tits jutted forward, taunting him to suck them through the stretch cotton of her shirt. Craning her neck to maintain eye contact, her pupils discharged flashes like flare guns. He ran a calming hand down her silken tresses, as smooth as satin ropes. He lifted a fistful and brought it to his nostrils.

Her scent was rich and earthy, with a dollop of honey. It wrapped around his cock like a tourniquet.

He whispered seductively, "What do you want to drink?"

Greta closed her hand over her hair and tugged it out of his grasp. His jaws locked at her demonstration of control, but he let go to play nice. Soon enough, he'd get her alone and unleash his dominance over her without anyone to stop him.

She glanced down at his drink. "Whiskey."

"Chaser?" he asked.

"Nope. Straight."

There it was again. Her maintaining control.

His arms locked as he glared down at her. "I'll allow it. For now."

She glared back at him. "You allow nothing. If I want a whiskey straight, I'll drink a whiskey straight."

Fuck, she's going to pay for that.

13

GRETA

Cutter thought she couldn't hold her liquor.

Pu-lease.

High tolerance was in her blood. She discreetly rubbed her sweaty palms against her skirt. Holy sweet Mother of God, he was the hottest thing ever. Messy blond hair and blue eyes, with the body of a god. A shower of tingles rained down on her.

He handed her the glass and she tossed the drink back like a pro.

Swiping her tongue over her lips, she handed him the empty glass. "Another."

He gave her a vicious scowl and she struggled to suppress a laugh. So easy to rile up. He called to the bartender and joined her in another. Clanking their glasses together, they took their shots at the same time.

His fingers tensed around the glass, lips flat in a tight line. "Bartender!"

Within a second the poor man slid another round toward them. Stopping her as she reached for her shot, he lifted it and brought it to his mouth. The cords of his throat shifted as he worked the liquid down, and she bit down on her lip so hard that she almost drew blood. He'd hijacked her drink, but, boy, was it worth it.

Cutter's hand covered hers. "Slow down. I have plans for you later and I wanna make sure you feel everything I do to you."

She almost groaned aloud, but kept her expression unimpressed. "You're being a bit presumptuous. You have yet to prove that you're worth my time."

"Prove?" he sputtered out. "Baby girl, you do not want to test me right now."

"Oh, but I do," she crooned, batting her eyelashes at him. "I'm not going anywhere with you until you show me that it's worth my while."

A wicked smile curved his lips. "Alright. Let's bet on it."

Adrenaline raced through her veins like a speedball of heroin and cocaine, and the first words out of her mouth were, "Make me come and I'll go home with you."

"I'll make you come. Then I'll feed you. After that, you'll go home with me," he declared arrogantly.

The whiskey must be hitting her hard because, for some reason, her mind tripped over the feeding part. "What?"

"Confused, sweetheart? I said, I'll make you come. Then, I'll feed you dinner. Afterwards, I'll tie you to my bed and fuck you senseless. Clear enough?"

"You can't possibly get me off in the middle of a bar," she gasped.

Grabbing her hand, he called out to Kingdom, "Get us a table. We'll be back in ten."

Shaking her head, she gasped out a laugh. "As in ten minutes? You're friend timed us last time, remember? It took less than four minutes, if I recall correctly." She tutted. "You're losing your touch."

Over his shoulder, Cutter threw her a smirk. "Not likely. I tagged on extra time in case there's a line."

She huffed out a laugh.

He was insane.

TAKING A KNEE BEHIND GRETA, he pressed her over the sink in the tiny, white-tiled bathroom.

"Brace yourself," he commanded.

She hadn't finished curling her fingers over the edge, when her skirt was up and tucked into her waistline. Cutter cupped the globes of her ass. In one deft move, her panties were off and thrown into the corner. His lips suckled her flank and then, he wedged his head between her thighs. She yelped, and he snaked a hand around her front and slapped her pussy.

"Spread them. I'm hungry," he growled. Impatience came off him in waves.

Greta splayed her feet, and taking advantage of the space, Cutter licked her slit from end to end.

A strangled moan slipped out of her.

"Cutter, *ohmygod*," she panted.

His scruff rasped against her pussy and her knees almost gave out, but she bent over until the sink was taking most of her weight. The moment his velvety smooth tongue plunged deep inside, she heard angels. Every stab prompted waves of wetness to gush out. Her spine arched to give him as much access as she could.

He used his lips and tongue to flick, nip, and suck on her tender flesh until her lower back seized. Her cheek was plastered to the mirror as she ground down on his mouth. Cutter rubbed his bristled face through her folds and thrust her over the edge. Raw screeches hurled from her throat.

A fist pounded on the door and cut her off mid climax. Another shriek came out, this time in fear, but Cutter slapped his palm over her mouth and engulfed it.

Without a hint of embarrassment, Cutter spoke loudly, "I slipped and almost cracked my head open. You're fuckin' lucky I don't sue this place."

Braced against the sink, she huffed and puffed through her nostrils. Behind her, Cutter was on his feet, his quick fingers moving like a piston inside her.

Leaning over her back, he licked the arch of her neck, and ordered, "Ride my fingers, princess. We're not leaving till you're done."

At his command, she came so hard her pussy convulsed. Legs unsteady, she caught herself before she tumbled to the floor. Back on his knees, his tongue continued to worship her until she came down and released one final shudder. Standing up, Cutter ground his jean-covered cock against her, the rough fabric scraping her bare ass. Swiping at his cell phone, he waited for facial recognition and then poked it.

"You're not taking a pic!" she yelped.

"Fuck no," he growled. "Under eight minutes. Damn, I'm good."

A cocky smile in place, he admitted, "I timed myself."

"What the hell? I'm not a contest," she spat out.

"Nope, but I promised ten minutes, and I achieved my goal," he replied proudly.

Grabbing paper towels from the dispenser, he nudged her to the side, and swept them under the stream of water. Gently, he brushed her thighs clean of the juices and saliva tightening her skin. Leaving a pert kiss on her raw pussy, he yanked her skirt down and prodded her toward the door. She swooped under him in search of her panties. An arm wound around her waist as he dangled them in front of her.

"Got those, too. Come on, time to feed you."

14

GRETA

True to his word, Cutter fed her. As in, literally, fork-to-mouth feeding. After saying their goodbyes to Sage and Kingdom, he led her outside to his bike. Straddling it, he unstrapped his helmet and handed it to her.

Pushing it away, Greta shook her head. "I'll get an Uber and meet you at the clubhouse."

His brows gathered in a frown as he shoved the helmet into her hands. "Get on the bike, Greta," he ordered, oozing dominance.

But she wasn't about to back down. She had to set a precedent where she retained control, especially if she was going to relinquish it in his bed, so she battled him with a glare of her own.

Biting back a grin, he declared, "I don't fucking repeat myself."

Slamming it in his gut, she stepped away, but he caught her elbow. "There's no way in hell I'm letting you ride with a stranger. Kill that thought 'cause I sure as fuck ain't having you in an Uber."

"I don't ride," she said between gritted teeth.

He rolled his eyes. "You're a biker bitch, of course you ride."

What part of her sentence did he not understand? *But of course, he's a biker so he doesn't take no for an answer.*

"I didn't say that I don't know how. I said, I don't ride," she reiterated.

Crowding her, he grabbed her wrist, rotated her arm behind her back, and bent her over his forearm. Cutter paused to let her feel the ache. Not hard, but enough to get his message across. He was such a pushy asshole.

"I don't give a fuck what you say, feel me. I give you an order and you snap to it. Either you get on by yourself or," he bent down and pulled a red paddle out of his side bag, "I drag you behind the restaurant and discipline you. The end result will still be you, perched on my bike."

She glared at him over her shoulder and seethed, "You wouldn't dare."

Eyes drilling into her, he affirmed, "Fucking try me. Let's get one thing clear, straight away. Your pussy is mine. Your mouth and ass are mine. You argue with me any longer and I won't let you come for the rest of the night." He tapped the paddle against his thigh. "Midnight is two hours from now. You wanna test me? You want me eating your sweet cunt for two hours and not let you come?" His lips curved up in a mischievous grin. "The choice is yours."

She wriggled out of his hold, grabbed the helmet, and slammed it on her head. The Kevlar padding muffled everything but the sound of her heavy breathing, which condensed and fogged up the windshield. Sweeping herself behind him, she scooted over and wrapped her arms around his waist. "You better make me come."

CUTTER TOSSED her onto his bed. Her ass bounced and she almost toppled over, but he caught her and settled her safely in the middle. Swiping long strands of hair off her face, Greta threw him a pissed-off glare. "I'm not a rag doll."

"Your words, not mine," he quipped. Goddamn, he was antsy, wanting to take her *right now*. Grab the top of her dress, rip it down the middle and claw it off her body. Slip his finger beneath her precious pearl choker and feast on her full tits. But the initial step of breaking in any woman was a moment to be relished. His balls tightened and drew up against his groin.

In a startled tone, Greta asked, "Wh-what are you going to do?"

Hugging herself, she took in his room. It was basic. A California king-sized bed with stackable storage drawers on one side and a lamp. Above the bed was a mirror to watch while he fucked. Was she expecting a torture chamber with whips on the walls and a swing hanging from the ceiling? Not a bad idea, but he'd have to get his own place first. Which was happening if he took her on full-time.

"Isn't it obvious? I'm going to fuck *with* you. If you're a good girl, then I might reward you and fuck you for real."

Her pulse thumped against her delicate throat like a manic rabbit. The wind was going hard, and the tips of the branches scratched against the windowpane above the nightstand. He grabbed the back of his T-shirt and tugged it over his head. Greedy eyes traveled over his bare chest. Good, he liked her eyes fixed on him.

"Take off your panties," he commanded.

Rising to her knees, she jutted her chin out and tensed for battle. "Fuck. Off."

He grinned openly. She wanted to fight him. Oh, this was good. Too fucking good.

"Princess," he replied, "you're wantin' this the hard way, but you've got no idea how hard I can play."

Greta spun around, hurtled off the bed, and streaked past him. He lunged for her, lifted her off the floor, and unceremoniously dumped her back on the bed. Straddling her, he clamped down on her wrists and stretched her arms out. This alpha female *would* submit to him. Kicking and flailing her legs, she bucked to throw him off, but he bore down on her chest.

Her breath puffing in his ear further hardened his already stiff cock. "You fucking asshole! Get the hell off me!"

"You set the tone, Greta, I'm just following your lead. I was gonna go easy on you, this being your first time and all, but your defiance has to be dealt with."

"Defiance! This isn't defiance. This is me wanting to beat the hell out of you," she screeched.

"Mm-hmm. Time to give you the rules and regulations," he mused.

Straining her neck, she snapped her teeth at him. A faint red mark bloomed on his bicep. He released one of her hands and reached for the strap attached to his headboard. She thrashed to dislodge him, but he expertly tied her up. Sitting back on his haunches, he admired his handiwork while she writhed beneath him, mussing the sheets beneath her.

Cutter crawled over her, letting the tip of his hard cock drag over her tummy, until they were eye level. "We haven't even begun to play, and your first move is to take your teeth to me? That's a motherfucking game changer, girl."

A strain of desperation bled through her voice. "It wasn't a real bite. I'm sorry, okay, Cutter? Okay? I'm sorry."

She was mouthing the right words, but there was no remorse in the emerald flames of her eyes.

No, she wasn't sorry. Not one bit.

"Apologizing already?" he taunted. "Didn't expect that until your ass was a nice shade of red."

She threw out a string of curses as she twisted every which way, searching for a weakness in the knots of her restraints. Cutter spread her thighs, enjoying the feel of her straining against her bindings. *So fucking pretty.* Her skirt rode to the top of her thighs, exhibiting the wet spot in the gusset of her panties.

Fingering the hot, wet silk, his teeth scraped his lower lip. She was as authentic as they came. He'd expected a fight, and she hadn't let him down. Not one bit.

"We could've done this half a dozen ways, but an attack requires containment," he lectured.

"The brothers are going to break down the door when they hear me scream," she threatened. "They're going to beat your crazy ass."

His shoulders shook with laughter. "The brothers won't do shit. Once a bitch enters my room, it's sealed tight. They've heard worse than you."

"I'm not a bitch, asshole." Her throat worked as she swallowed.

Finally, she was starting to get it. He languidly drew his index finger down the side of her neck and the delicate bumps of her collarbone. Placing his palm on the area above her breasts, he massaged until her breathing relaxed. Rapt, he noted every signal of her body.

Once her pulse slowed down and her eyes dilated, he proceeded. "I mean a biker bitch, and you damn well know the difference."

She licked her dry lips and bit down on the plump bottom one. He bit back a groan on that last move. With an encouraging smile, he raised the hem of her shirt, inch by slow inch, and dragged it off, leaving it twisted above her head.

Unclasping her bra from the front, he pulled it above her to join her tangled shirt. Dark nipples puckered on plump breasts that swayed from side to side along with her rapid breaths.

Greta, bare, was a gorgeous sight.

He attacked her lips. She tried to rip herself away, but he captured her jaw and coaxed it open to lunge into her moist, hot mouth. He expected her to bite him, but, to his surprise, she raised her head and met him with an assault of her own. Angling her head, she sucked his tongue up into the roof of her mouth. The pressure was exquisite.

Damn, he risked losing his sanity with this woman.

He yanked the cuffs off her ankles, threw her legs up on his shoulders and began to finger-fuck her. Greta immediately wrapped her legs around the base of his spine, and warmth suffused his chest.

Priceless.

"You get a little reward," Cutter asserted as he molded the curve of her breast. His mouth dipped and his tongue drew lazy circles around her pert nipple. With each subsequent loop, he swirled closer. Her rib cage stilled as she watched him, mouth gaping open. He flashed her a wicked grin and then sucked her nipple into his mouth. A strangled sound gurgled from her throat. Tugging her throbbing nipple between his teeth, he shook his head like a puppy with a new toy.

He then unhooked her legs and poised himself above her until their noses almost touched.

"Before I reward you, you gotta learn your manners."

"I'm not a child for you to reprimand. You couldn't hurt me if you tried, you worn-out biker trash," she lashed out between gritted teeth.

Cutter chuckled with glee, causing her to growl with indignation. Her attitude was popping up. Ignoring her, he coolly adjusted her bindings so he could shift her onto her belly. Stripping off her skirt and panties left him with a perfect view of her plump, jiggling ass. The sight drained whatever blood was left in his body into his already engorged cock.

Greta tested her restraints, but after adjusting herself, she went lax beneath him.

Poor girlie, she had no idea of what was going to happen to her next.

A sharp crack pierced the air.

Her head whipped over her shoulder; her eyes were two wide green orbes. The burn from his slap sizzled his hand, and he took a moment to savor the sensation.

Her mouth worked open and shut, but before she could scream, he popped her ass again. Her breathing stuttered and her lithe body began to tremble. He smacked her lightly a couple times, on each side.

His balls were drawn up tight, and his cock was begging to explode, but he squeezed his shaft through his pants until the pain pulled him back from the edge. Cutter caressed her from her shoulders down to her ankles, and back up again, until her shudders passed.

Time to go at that fine ass of hers, for real.

His palm clapped down in a series of three. The only sounds in the room were the flat of his hand connecting with her ass and the delicious rasps of her breathing. Her nose nuzzled his hand that lay flat on the mattress beside her, distracting him from the beautiful pink shade of her buttocks.

Her incisors caught a knuckle. She'd nipped him again. His hand was too calloused for her love bite to hurt, but it required a response.

"You made the wrong move, sweetheart," he said as his hand curved over her mouth. Beneath the muzzle, came snorts and grunts. "Wipe that look off your face. If you misbe-have, then you need to learn to take it like a grown woman."

Greta thrashed her head rebelliously, conjuring up all the ways she wanted to kill him. Too bad, so sad. She had no fucking idea what it took to be a man like him. A man with respect for the power he wielded over a woman. He held her while she battled it out with him, but eventually, she let out a huff and averted her eyes.

Bingo.

"I'm going to lift my hand. Be quiet till I'm done talking. To make sure you behave, one hand will be in your hair and the other one will be..." His hand cupped the mound of her pussy, "Right here."

The temperature hit him first, but holy shit, her juices.

She. Was. Drenched.

He swallowed hard. Moisture even stained her inner thighs. A few taps, and he positioned two fingers on either side of her clit.

Greta squirmed, and his cock practically tore out of his Levi's. Thank fuck he had the presence of mind to keep them on.

"Don't move," he gritted out.

Greta pressed her lips together like she was about to argue but then nodded in agreement. Thank Christ 'cause he was close to whipping out his cock and mounting her from behind.

"You," he smoothed a hand over her warm buttocks, "will defy me to test how strong I am. Babe, I guarantee you that I'm strong enough to take anything you throw my way." He gave her ass cheek a little love tap. "But I'm counting on you to be a fast learner."

She harrumphed, yet her eyes didn't stray from his.

"See now, it wasn't so hard to follow my direction," he

praised, "I told you not to speak and you communicated without breaking my command."

Chortling softly, he predicted, "You're gonna make me real proud. You fucked up on purpose to see what you could get away with." He shrugged. "It's in your nature. That's fine because it's in *my* nature to teach you who's boss around here."

Greta snapped at him again with her teeth, but this time she didn't touch him.

Her inner animal was like scrappy like a raccoon, but she was learning the limits.

"Go on. Talk," he ordered.

"You can't possibly know what I need," she sputtered the moment he lifted his hand. "We barely know each other. And you're a biker."

"Babe, I've been doing this for a long time. There are many reasons people want a bit of kink with their fucking. You carry the weight of the world on your shoulders. Sometimes you wanna do you. No fighting. No thinking. Just chillin'. Me being a biker doesn't make a difference either way." Raising an eyebrow, he reminded her, "You could have used the stoplight method when I started in on your ass. Or you could have tapped my arm or given me another signal, but not once did you shut this down. Why? Because you like what I give you."

15

GRETA

He had her there, the bastard.

She hadn't said "red." It would have halted him irrevocably, but it hadn't even occurred to her. Cutter turned her over and tucked a pillow underneath her head. Overheated by his powerful presence, she had a beeline view of his cock, pressing against his denim.

Her belly flip-flopped and her nerves lit up like the Fourth of July night sky. It was maddening not to be able to move around, but one thing was immediately clear. She was seriously, grippingly aroused.

Somberly, she pronounced, "I shouldn't be enjoying this."

Cutter coiled her hair in a tight twist. Scalp stinging, she screamed, "What the hell?!"

She cringed at the look of fury on Cutter's face.

"You haven't done anything wrong. You sure as fuck weren't ashamed when you bit me. You like getting slapped on your ass. So fuckin' what? Christ, get over yourself, Greta."

She blinked her eyes briskly. Eyelashes batted away the tears pooling at the corners of her eyes. Shame was the reason she hadn't hooked up in years. Simply because she couldn't get off unless she got manhandled a little. And that's saying a lot for a twenty-five-year-old millennial. She was a strong woman, and dammit, she'd earned that moniker, which meant that she did not bow down to anyone. Certainly not in bed. To her great dismay, that wasn't the way her body worked.

"What you're feeling is normal. Male subs struggle with this more than you," he explained.

Greta stopped squirming beneath him. He was right that she was gung-ho on shaming herself, but she'd had no problem going after him. The first time she bit him, her intent had been to rip off a permanent piece of him.

"Okay, you make a valid point. Which is surprising from a man who I wouldn't label the sharpest knife in the drawer," she said.

Cutter guffawed at her insult. "Well?" he asked, clearly waiting for an apology.

She opened her mouth, but it clanked shut.

Giving her hair another tug, he cajoled, "Come on, you can do it."

His sweet tone stabbed at her chest, so she tried, but no apology came out.

"I see," he drawled. "You want me to do it for you."

He shook his head in disappointment, and she almost cried. It wasn't fair. He was asking too much, too soon. Flags of heat burned her cheeks.

Fine. Having failed to follow his command, she'd provoke him instead. Her fingers tightened against the ropes and she hissed, "Go find yourself a weak bitch, you sadistic bastard."

"I'm the first to admit that I'm a selfish prick, but you're not going anywhere," he replied casually. "You're perfect and I'm keeping you. I've worked hard lately, and I deserve a reward."

Greta rolled her eyes. "How do you figure that? Working hard to ruin Sage's life so she can save your precious MC? As for perfect, believe me, it's not reciprocated, you conceited asshole."

"Babe, have no doubt. I'm exactly what you need."

"In what way? You mean sexually? Please, I've lived without good sex—"

"Mind-blowing sex," he interrupted.

"Okay, however you want to phrase it. I've done fine without it, thank you very much," she groused.

"A woman like you without sex is a fucking waste. Hell will freeze over before I allow that to happen," he swore.

The sudden sensation of soft lips on her abdomen startled her. Turning her over again, he placed soft kisses on the welts of her bottom. Her hips jerked when a finger slipped between the folds of her slippery sex, penetrating her with ease.

"Been waiting on someone like you for years. I've seen a fuckload in my life, but no woman as responsive and pliable as you are. You're perfect. Fucking perfect," he murmured.

Her thoughts grew hazy and slinked out of her grasp as his fingers stroked between her slack thighs, weaving their magic on her pussy. He settled in behind her and took hold of her hair again. He seemed to have a thing with her hair, and she was already in love with the demanding tone of the act.

She bowed her spine backward to push against his easy thrusts while he slathered wetness over her reddened ass. He landed a sharp swat, and she gasped loudly. The wetness accentuated the blister of his blow.

Fingers back in her cunt, he humored her, building her up, hard and fast. Short moans escaped as he assaulted her clit, and her stomach muscles tightened. "Oh God, I can feel it. I can feel it coming. I'm close, I'm so close."

Pinpricks of delicious heat licked across her flesh like flames, leaving sparks in their wake.

"This will take you over the edge," he promised.

Pulling her butt cheeks apart, a thick digit entered a place no one had ever touched before. He circled his finger around the rim with precise movements, pressing in deeper with each rotation.

"What are you doing?" she panted.

"Stretching your ass," Cutter informed her blithely. With that, he pushed past the barrier of tight muscles. A sharp wave of pleasure-pain zipped to her pussy, and Greta bucked as she rode the palm on her clit and the finger in her ass. If she pushed forward, her clit pressed against his hand. If she tilted back to relieve the pressure, his finger pushed in deeper. There was no way to find relief but to take hold of her climax and ride it like a marauding bull. Her eyes sought his for contact, but he was completely focused on the movement of his finger.

"You're the most beautiful thing."

She let out a scream, but he swallowed it with a lash of his tongue. Breaking off, he demanded, "Stay in position, princess."

Her thighs smacked shut, but he forced them apart and took a long lick of her, from clit to ass. *Like, who does that?* After the last aftershocks of her climax, she spread out like a melted puddle of ice cream, spent. He loosened the ties binding her wrists and massaged the feeling back into her hands. "You've never come like this, have you?"

Wheezing, Greta's head wobbled from side to side.

"Thought so," he said smugly.

His fingers slipped away, and he strolled into an adjoining bathroom. Water ran from the sink, and then he was back, prowling over her like a sleek jaguar. Naked. With his cock jutting out from his massive thighs.

She gulped.

Swear to the great goddess above, Cutter was a true sex

gladiator, and what he was packing was big. As in *big*, big. Although certainly not a virgin, she'd gone without sex for a quite a while.

His shoulder muscles bunched up and biceps bulged when he grasped his cock. The ridges of his six-pack clamped in unison as he stroked his shaft. Grabbing a rubber from the nightstand, he held the tip as he dragged it over his penis.

Her lower lip jutted out.

"Don't get pouty on me. I'll take you bare when you prove yourself."

Her chest tightened. How had he guessed her fantasy about being taken bareback? Rummaging through the drawer again, he pulled out lubrication.

Rolling her eyes, she implored, "Please, Cutter, I'm wetter than I've ever been in my life."

The tube slipped from his hand and dropped on her hip, the cool plastic causing her to flinch. She followed his gaze. It was locked on the tat branded on her upper thigh.

Her ink.

Everything inside her screeched to a halt. Her blood turned to ice. Shuttering her eyes, she whipped away from him, dragging the sheet to cover herself. As if it was so easy, as if it was possible to unsee what he'd seen.

"Eyes on me," he grunted.

Huddling into a tight ball, she rasped, "No."

He took her by the waist and pressed her onto her back. Lifting off the sheet, he traced the ink with a touch so light it made her thigh tremble. "The Dark Horsemen."

"Yes," she whispered, imagining the disgust on his face. Cutter had a tat of the Squad spanning his back from shoulder to shoulder, yet their ink couldn't be more different. She wore the brand of her first owner, the Dark Horsemen, and like a brand, it marked her as their property. Her greatest dishonor.

"Untie me. I'll leave. You won't have to set eyes on me again." Incredibly, she had been so taken over by lust that she'd forgotten she was with a biker who could decode it. *Get it over with and get out of here.* Before he threw her out himself. Unclenching her eyelids, she stole a glance at him.

Concern churned in his darkened eyes. Not disgust. Not pity. Somehow, that only served to gut her more.

"No wonder you hate bikers," he spoke in a rough voice. He cupped her hip, hiding the tat from her view under his large hand, and lifted her chin until their gazes found each other. "You're safe now."

Maintaining direct eye contact, he pressed her legs together and settled them against his left shoulder, her right thigh exposed.

All it took was one thrust. One thrust and he tore through her soul, bottoming out in her pussy. Greta tilted to adjust to his girth, but she had only a second before he slammed back inside.

"Damn woman, I knew you'd be snug. You haven't been fucked right, but that's gonna change tonight," he swore.

With a grip over her tat that guaranteed to leave a bruise, he rooted himself inside her.

She rocked into him, pleading, "Slow down, you're huge."

She wiggled to accommodate his length, and mercifully, he paused long enough for her to catch her breath. Leading her finger to his mouth, he sucked down lightly until her hips flicked to meet his pummeling. Her fingernails scored down his flank as he continued to slam into her.

"Can't get enough, can you?" he said with a smirk.

God, the arrogance of the guy.

"Uh, uh, uh," she grunted with each impact at his raw pace, his heavy balls slapping against her.

She clamped down on his steel cock, fighting for every

inch. Every thrust had her clutching his shaft harder. Cutter steadied himself with a hold on her breast as he lunged and withdrew like a consummate fencer. Eventually, his pace slackened somewhat, and glided his thumb over her swollen nub. Brushing and plucking her clit prodded her into a gallop. Greta arched her neck, burying her head into the pillow as she volleyed toward another climax.

Cutter pulled out of her, plucked off the condom, and gripped his cock.

Panting, she stared at him wide-eyed. Rivulets of sweat dripped down the sides of his face as he fucked himself with vicious strokes.

He came with a roar, his warrior body shuddering as ropes of come painted her belly.

Planting a hand beside her head, he speared three fingers into her sopping pussy. Her hips twerked against his fingers, and he had the audacity to remove them.

A deep-throated command penetrated the postcoital fog in her brain. "You're not coming."

Her mind sputtered. She was sprawled out on the mattress. Her vagina clenched on the ghost of his fingers, and her body screamed in desperation.

"Don't punish me because of the tat," she cried out.

He knifed off the bed, blond strands flying in various directions, and swore, "You're not theirs anymore, you're mine. I do with you what *I* want."

"You want to torture me, is that it?" she screamed.

She crumbled into herself and broke into sobs.

Undoing her restraints, he cradled her, rocking her until her weeping tapered off.

"I'm not above torture, but the point of this exercise is for you to internalize the fact that you're mine. Your body won't easily forget being left on the edge, primed to come. It's a better teacher than any verbal reassurance I can give you. The wait will be harder after the climax I did allow but wait you will. Until I *choose* to let you come. Why? Because I am the master of your body," he finished.

Stretching out, he curled her into his chest, and ordered, "Now, get some rest."

Burrowing into his neck, she inhaled to imprint his essence on her soul.

Sheesh, she must be as twisted as he was, because his reasoning actually made sense to her. Despite the painful ache between her legs, it was a caring gesture on his part. She would take as much kindness as he was willing to give. After all, this couldn't last. A biker from an MC like the Squad would never want a cast-off daughter from another clan.

16

CUTTER

Cutter slumped down on the ratty sofa in Kingdom's new office. His thigh muscles burned from his workout, his right leg pulsing with a dull throb. He stretched his hands out and made a fist, inspecting his torn knuckles.

Been a while since he used the punching bag till his hands rashed up, but there was no other way of shaking off the dread tugging at him since he spotted Greta's tattoo a week ago. The shadow of fear in her eyes had gutted him.

For the past week, they'd been rutting whenever they got a chance. In the morning, after fucking her into oblivion, he walked her through the clubhouse with his arm over her shoulders. A wake of open stares and slack jaws followed them, but he didn't give a fuck. He was branding her as his property, any way he knew how.

A powerful MC like the Dark Horsemen didn't slink away with its tail between its hind legs. Especially over a princess like her. And he had no doubt that she was coveted. No female could replace Greta. Not. Remotely. Possible.

He sank lower into the couch.

Feet propped up on his desk, Kingdom pivoted back and forth on a rolling swivel chair. Each scrape of the casters on the hardwood floors was like nails on a chalkboard to his ears. Cell phone in hand, Kingdom ignored him as he scrolled through god-knows-fucking-what. Every so often the fucker chuckled, grating on his nerves.

Eventually, Kingdom slanted him a sly look, and inquired, "What is it?"

"Nothing," he grumbled.

One hand gripping the side of his head, Cutter cracked his neck. The stiffness eased somewhat, but he covered his head and tugged at the strings of his hoodie.

Kingdom scanned him up and down. "Why did you come into my office if you were going to mope like a fucking bitch."

Cutter threw him a fuck-off-asshole look.

Kingdom slapped a palm to his chest, an injured expression on his face. "Ouch." He smirked. "Did I hurt your pretty little feelings?"

Cutter's head dropped back, scraping against the rough wall texture. "Tell me, Kingdom, what in the fuck-all am I doing?"

"You're busted up is what you are," his friend quipped without missing a beat. "Keep yourself out of the ring for more than one day and she *might*—and that's a big might—want to see your ugly mug again. Your bitches might like kinky, but no bitch likes ugly."

Kingdom squinted at Cutter, considering, "It's a long shot but, if you take a break, you might look human again."

Scrutinizing the cracks in the ceiling plaster, Cutter declared, "I don't know what I'm doing."

"You're sulking like a bitch is what you're doin'. Mind you, I'm not judging. The brothers out there," he jutted his thumb toward the door, "they're judgin'. But not me. You witnessed my near-death experience when Sage left me and disappeared." His last sentence almost ended in a shout.

Cutter smirked. "Touched a nerve, much?"

Kingdom leaned back with his hands looped behind his head. Tilted backward on the legs of his chair, he joined Cutter in staring up at the ceiling. "Those cracks look like a rabbit."

Cutter considered them. "Yep. It's a fucking bunny rabbit, alright."

"I ain't high. You high?"

"Nah, *brah*, it's a fucking rabbit."

"Fuck me." Kingdom swung his legs off the desktop and his boots landed with a thump. Slapping his hands on his knees, he said, "Thanks for stopping by. It's been real. A grown man telling me there's a rabbit on my ceiling. Good times."

"Whatwashelike?" Cutter asked.

"Speak up, bro. Hell, a two-year-old uses words better than you."

"What. Was. She. Like?" he enunciated. "I know she's a Dark Horseman."

Kingdom's gaze snapped to his.

In a cautious tone, he acknowledged, "I didn't mention it before because it was none of your business. Didn't think you'd bag her. S'pose it's time to tell you the truth, though."

Cutter's stomach collapsed on itself. "I'm not fuckin' around with her, Kingdom. She's mine."

"I can see that. Sturgis was the first time I set eyes on her. She was about sixteen, I'd say. The spitting image of the crazy-ass president of the Dark Horsemen. Goes by Scorpion. No one passes Scorpion without taking a long look to make sure they don't get jumped as they pass, know what I mean? Anyways, no one could miss a beauty like her."

Cutter popped up off his seat and flew to the edge of the couch, fists clenched.

"Calm the fuck down," Kingdom snapped. "She was jailbait and her father's fucking Frankenstein. I'm not into Greta. Never have been. Never will be. But that doesn't mean I don't have eyeballs in my head."

Cutter pressed hard on his brow. "Continue."

"We ended up in the same bar as him and his crew, so I got to see her up close. She didn't act like a princess. Among the hardened bikers, every one of them big and mean, she was quiet. Too young to be a biker chick or an old lady. Honest to God, she looked like she was shy. A nerd. She didn't belong. Hell, I bet you the mega millions lottery she was a virgin.

"And she was watchful, like a prisoner. Everything about her was young and innocent, except for those eyes of hers. Those eyes had seen things. Knew things. She surveyed her surroundings like a pro. And she hid."

He imagined Greta as she was back then. Still a baby, with smaller tits and slimmer hips. Sweet, like the way she was with him. Okay, maybe not with him *yet*, but soon.

Cutter clenched his fists, holding himself back from smashing the wall like he wanted to do to Scorpion's face. Her father had fucked her up, there was no doubt in his mind. He'd seen her reaction when he recognized her Horseman tat. She expected him to toss her out like she was trash. That hit him in the solar plexis, and he swore, then and there, that he'd do anything to protect her. She was his.

His head felt like it was about to explode at the thought of her suffering, young and alone. No wonder Greta was encased in an armor cast. Only time the real her came out was when she was in his arms.

"She hid behind a young kid. Older than her, but still a kid. If a biker checked her out a little too long, he'd block their view. Especially if Frankenstein turned his attention on her. They were never far from each other. He was her designated bodyguard, but the boy took his responsibility too seriously, if ya know what I mean."

Another man was in her life before him? He didn't like that one bit.

Legs braced in a fighting position, abdomen tight, he raised his fists and roared, "Why the fuck didn't you tell me before?"

"Sit your caveman ass down. It was a damn decade ago and her situation is complicated. The boy grew up with her. He protected her. They were close. Were they more? Who the fuck knows. But whatever it was, it's over with."

Prowling around the room, Cutter dragged his injured leg behind him.

"He stayed. She left," Kingdom continued, trying to appease him. "If that's not your answer, then I don't know what is. She lived a lifetime away from him and her club. For a bitch, she found the one place they'd never look, a damn 'Gender Studies' department in a college. Focus on today, Cutter, and take care of her now. She's long gone from who she used to be. I mean, who the hell plays with crystals and chains, dresses like a bondage hippie, and talks like a feminist professor?"

"Greta, that's who. Someone's going to pay, yo," he swore.

Bondage was more than a fashion statement. Her choice of clothing was an advertisement of her deep needs. Any dominant could see that.

"Let's not forget the nerd in her," Kingdom joked. "She was a princess thrust from hell into the normal world. She survived. Although," Kingdom rubbed the stubble of his chin, "seein' as she has more books than Sage, I'd think twice about keepin' her."

Kingdom's attempt at a joke rolled off him. In fact, the corners of Cutter's mouth bracketed; his forehead furrowed with dense lines. "How do you know how many books she has in her house?"

"Because I've been to her house, dumbass."

Cutter asked tersely, "Why in the fuck are you at my woman's house?"

"She's your woman now?"

"Don't change the damn subject."

Kingdom leaned over his desk, growling, "Who do you think fixed her leaky faucet or amped up her security? The tooth fairy? No, asshole, it was me."

"Me!" Cutter pounded on his chest. "I should be doing that shit. Not you. No one but me."

There was a knock on the door. Kingdom called out loudly, "Get the hell away from my door."

The knocks stopped, and they waited until the pounding of boots faded away.

"She's fuckin' *mine*," Cutter pronounced, gripping the fabric of his shirt.

"Brother, I didn't tell you so you could act crazier than when you first walked in," Kingdom snapped back.

"I'm losin' my mind over this woman," Cutter confessed. "It's been two weeks and I want her for permanent, though I'll be damned if her pussy isn't as sweet as the day she got her cherry popped."

Kingdom put up his hand. "Stop right there. I can't listen to your personal shit no more."

"I want to be her past, her present, and her future. It makes no damn sense, but there it is. That's the truth," he confessed.

"You're a biker, of course you wanna guard what's yours, but you gotta accept her past and recognize that it's done with. You can't let her past eat away at you, Cutter," he counseled.

"See, that's where you're wrong," Cutter replied. "It's not over. It's in her, and it's going to be a wedge between us. She's not free. Scorpion will come for her at some point, and she'll be helpless. Yeah, yeah, you and Sage will watch out for her, but it ain't the same. If she's not my property, she'll be screwed, and I don't see her ever becoming any biker's property. Not officially."

Kingdom stiffened. "Tell me what you've seen."

"Nothing yet, but I've got an ugly feelin' in my gut, and my gut don't lie."

Kingdom drummed his fingers on the desk. *Tap, tap, tap.* "You stay on her like a fly on shit. Anything you see, you report to me. No way will that motherfucker get close to something that's mine."

Cutter's eyebrows shot up. "Yours?"

Exasperated, Kingdom slammed his fist down on the wooden desk. "You know what I mean."

He did. Official or not, Greta was under the protection of the Squad. "She's not gonna like it."

"Whose gonna tell her? Not you or me. Raised in an MC, she's aware of her surroundings, so make sure she stays distracted. That should be easy for you. It's your specialty, after all."

Cutter rubbed his hands on his knees. His biggest leverage was his dick and he had zero issues using it to his advantage. The pressure in his chest eased a fraction and he took a deep, bracing breath.

Yeah, he had this. He had no other choice.

17

CUTTER

I t was no hardship distracting Greta.

Cutter took her to the dive bar the Squad was in the process of negotiating to purchase. Kingdom hadn't committed to becoming president, but his determination to push the Squad into going legal was a good sign. The brothers stopped by on the regular to check the place out. Different days, different hours, to see whether it was a business worth investing in.

The bar was packed on Saturday night. Music was pumping through speakers that had seen better days, as they made their way through the entrance with another surge of people. Tucked into his side, he pushed Greta through and joined the brothers at the far corner of the bar. He elbowed one asshole out of the way, who'd toppled off a barstool and almost bumped into Greta.

Hoisting her onto a stool, he caged her in between his legs. He liked manhandling her and then getting into her space like an overbearing fuck. Scanning a hipster to his left, Cutter caught him checking out his bitch's tits. He couldn't blame the fucker, but still.

Leaning over, he growled in his ear, "Do you want to fuckin' die, man? Stop looking at my woman and move the fuck over."

The guy eyed the patches on his cut, and then the brothers by his side. Fucking finally the fucker slid off the stool. Scooting it close to Greta's, he sat down and grabbed the bartender's hand as she dropped two shot glasses in front of the brothers. "Get me a tequila shot and a Coors."

She beamed him a big smile and leaned over the bar with a saucy wink, "Why don't you take a body shot off me?"

He pulled back. "Nah, I'm good."

She gave him a practiced moue and flittered away, down the bar to get their drinks.

"I want a shot," Greta grumbled. "And what the hell. She just propositioned you in front of me."

"Jealous? You're getting a beer. After last time, you don't get to order for yourself. I'm irresistible, but you damn well know better than to think I'd touch that hoe."

"Don't call women hoes. It's disrespectful," she said loudly over the ruckus of the bar.

"She just hit on me in your face," he said incredulously.

"Yes, and if she does it again, I'm going to mutilate her, but you can't call her that."

"Babe, I like your savageness but there's no difference between hoe and bitch," he said.

Greta's features took on a pinched expression. "We'll have this discussion in greater depth at another time, but don't fight me on this one, Cutter. Please."

The word *please* was what saved her. Clamping down on her hip, he slid his hand down to her ass and said, "Yeah, alright. I'm gonna fuck you in my bed instead. Happy now?"

"Much," she replied dryly.

Puck sidled up to them, his platinum blond fauxhawk gleaming under the lights.

Squeezing in between them, he asked, "Who do we have here? What's your name, beautiful?"

He damn well knew her name, but he was pretending so he could find out as much as he could, nosy bastard. Cutter wanted to shove his brother into the crowd and pray that he got caught in a stampede.

Greta squinted up at him.

"Aren't you the guy who…" she trailed off.

"Timed you when Cutter got you off." Puffing out his chest, he grabbed the sides of his cut proudly. "Yep, that's me."

"I know it's too much to ask but, fuck man, can you leave us the hell alone?" Cutter groaned.

"No can do, brother. A chance like this comes once in a lifetime and I ain't passing it up."

Glancing at his cut, she squinted up at him with a wrinkled nose. "Your road name is Puck?"

Slapping one hand over his chest, he bowed slightly. "At your service, my lady."

Puck's gaze dipped to Greta's bodice. Normally, Cutter was all about showing off her assets, but this was starting to piss him off. "Eyes off her tits, Puck."

Greta threw Puck a scowl that could hobble a brother. Unfortunately, the bastard had more lives than a fucking cat on steroids.

"What can I say, I'm a dog," he confided with an outrageous pout. "Woof."

He grinned at her as he took hold of one of Greta's tresses. "Can I touch?" he inquired politely with a gleam of mischief in his eyes.

Cutter snatched it out of his fingers and replied, "Fuck no, you can't. Don't you have somewhere to be or someone else to fuck with?"

"Nothing is better than fucking with you," Puck countered with a wink.

Greta's eyes were swinging from Cutter to Puck and back.

Scowling at Puck, Cutter snapped, "If you don't fuck off, we're going to leave."

Puck's gaze dropped to his crotch. "In a hurry? You wanna take Greta to the bathroom again?" He whipped out his cell phone with a grin that stretched from ear to ear. "I'm on duty when it comes to timing. Anytime, anyplace. Just gimme the signal."

Greta turned toward Cutter, and said, "I don't think I like him much."

"No one does but me," he grumbled, "and that's not gonna last much longer."

"Move over," Puck said. Greta puffed out a breath of surprise. "Yeah, get on his lap. I gotta sit down."

Cutter swept Greta onto his lap. Her ass squirmed, making his cock stiff as a steel pipe. Looping her arms around his neck, she nestled into him. Turns out Puck was his bestie after all. He ran his hand up and down her arm, and she continued to rub her delectable ass on him.

The little vixen knew what she was doing. Puck was asking Greta about herself, but Cutter couldn't pay attention with her side plastered to his front. She flung her head back, laughing at something his brother said, which had the added benefit of pressing her tits against his chest. Perfect fucking bird's-eye view of them, too, down to her dusky nipples. Which were as hard as diamonds. *That's it. Gotta get her underneath me.*

He set her on her feet and interrupted their convo. "Babe, we gotta go."

Giving Puck a fist bump, he guided her through the horde

of writhing bodies and out the door. Cutter planned to take a long ride to cool off in the bracing wind, but when they got on the bike and Greta wrapped herself around his back, his cock was back in a choke hold. His plan had been seduction, not subjugation, but fuck it.

Good intentions firmly tossed away, he swerved his bike in the middle of the road and turned in the direction of her house.

In front of her house, he paused long enough for her to hop off and then parked while she opened her door. By the time he waltzed in, her jacket was gone, and she was pulling bracelets off her slim wrists. One by one, they plonked in a bowl sitting on a low bookcase by the entrance. She loosened one earring. It hit the glass of the bowl. *Ding.* The other followed. *Ding.*

Cutter moved past her and settled into the couch, watching avidly as she made her way toward him, hips swaying from side to side. He was certifiably panting by the time she was within arm's distance.

Yanking her against him, he'd knocked a breath out of her, and her honeyed scent brushed over him.

His mouth was on hers. Tongue pushing in, he explored her heat. The combination of her scent and taste made him feral.

His hands gripped and grasped every part he could reach. Her tits, her hips, her ass. One hand on her nape to hold her still, he ran his other hand over her mound, palming it roughly. He plunged his hand into her panties and growled when he felt her wet heat. Greta's mouth moved from his mouth and paused to nuzzle the rough prickle under his jawline. Angling to get a better view of her expression, he frowned. A haunted look snaked around the edges of her eyes.

He tugged her off him and asked, "What is it?"

"Nothing," she said, her breath rattling out.

"Tell me," he commanded, his tone dropping low and hard.

"You know, you don't have the right to every thought that passes through my head," she snapped.

"Yeah, right," he taunted. "I'm a determined man so you might as well give up and tell me now."

"Not all women tolerate being bullied. You want a fight, then let's do this," she ordered.

Cutter seized a thick handful of hair and breathed into the curve of her ear. "In the end, your submission will be enforced. Better retract your nails, my pussycat, before it's too late."

She glared at him sideways and snarled, "You're the one being coy. Playing serious isn't a good look on you, Cutter."

There she went again. Challenging him. The drive to dominate cinched him by the balls.

He twisted her hair around his fist. "Feel that sting?"

"Yes," she muttered tightly, although her eyes rebelled boldly.

"You don't know the half of what I'm capable of."

She stretched up and took a slow lick up the side of his neck, ending in a nip of his earlobe. "I'm not one of your gazy-eyed bitches panting to get in your bed, and you don't have enough of the bully to scare me. Believe me, I've dealt with worse than you."

She didn't know jack shit about him. Loosening her hair, his spine hit the back of the couch and he spread his arms out wide.

Donning one of his iconic panty-dropping smiles, he promised her, "Don't change the facts. I won't stop until I've got my cock pounding you."

She jumped off him and exploded, "Grrr, you're impossible."

She thrust her face in his, trying to loom over him as if she had the right. Unacceptable. This meant a punishment needed to be doled out.

Lacing his tone with gravel, he commanded, "On your knees."

"Hell. No," she sneered.

"Fuck. Yes," he countered.

Snatching her hair, he effortlessly brought her to the floor in a crouched position. She clawed to get away, but he maneuvered her until she was braced between his thighs. She reared back and twisted this way and that to escape. Much stronger than her, he held on until she wore herself out.

A defiant growl rattled between her clenched teeth when she finally settled down.

"You threw down the challenge, little girl," he warned her.

The endearment he'd casually used did not go down well. Her bronzed skin didn't go bright red like with pale girls, but a telltale flush of fury brightened her skin.

"I'm a grown woman and I've been doing a damn good job of taking care of myself," she choked out. "I put myself through college. I could've gotten help from Scorpion, but I refused to turn to that rat bastard for anything."

"Babe, you're a fierce bitch and a witch rolled up into one," he concurred.

She shoved him in the chest and then pointed to the door. "I didn't get away from Scorpion and rebuild my life from scratch to hand it over to a man. Get the hell out of here."

A rumble started deep in his chest and a growl rolled off his tongue. He released her suddenly, and her butt slammed down on the floor. Hands fisted by her sides, she glowered at him. He returned it with a steady stare of his own.

Flinging her arm out, she motioned to the door again. "Out!"

Cutter's jaw slammed together. He wanted to pound out his aggravations about the club, Puck's taunts, and her issues into her sweet pink pussy. He couldn't though.

Although his job was to protect her, he couldn't if she fought him every minute of every day. Time for a tactical retreat.

She wanted his cock, that much was evident. All she needed was a little shove in the right direction. How did he know she'd make the right decision? He didn't exactly, but he trusted the little subbie dwelling inside her. That part of her was dying to curl up on him. Rub her pussy over him and roll over on her back. She'd been starved, and no way was the subbie going to let feminist Greta get the drop on her.

For that to happen, though, he had to bounce.

Throwing his jacket over a shoulder, Cutter strolled to the entrance.

Still on her knees, she sputtered out in a hurt tone, "You're leaving me?"

Catching the doorknob, he flaunted another signature smirk. "Highness, I enjoy swatting that tight ass of yours as much as the next man, but you gotta come clean with yourself. Give me a holler when you're ready to act like a grown woman."

Greta gasped. She scrambled up and followed him out onto the steps. A hand gripping the doorframe, she hurled out insults as he straddled his Harley.

He counted them off...twenty, twenty-one, twenty-two.

His little subbie was spitting mad, but he planned to make her pay for every insult with the switch of a crop to her ass.

18

GRETA

Greta was in a foul mood.

Not that she didn't deserved to have Cutter walk out on her. She had turned into a volatile shrew. *Gah!* Grouchy and teary-eyed, she dragged herself out of bed, stumbled through her morning routine, and somehow managed to get to the office on time. Which was a near miracle since she drove like a tweaking meth addict. After refilling her coffee twice, her brain chose to cooperate, and she made it through the workday somewhat productively.

At home, she beached herself on the couch where they'd argued and grabbed the closest book. *Gender Disparity in the Workplace. That'll work.* Until it didn't.

Twitching her lips, she flipped the pages of the hardcover book, then flung it away. She cringed at the crunching sound when it dented the wall. Digging around in the couch, she pulled out a Zippo lighter. A dark figure on a rearing horse was engraved on the metal.

God knows why she kept it after so much time. A scowl pulled the corners of her lips taut. The day she'd found it was ingrained in her mind. It had been after a raging party at the Horsemen's clubhouse. Trash and used condoms littered the couches and floor like flotsam as she waltzed through the clubhouse in the early morning light. She found the lighter abandoned on the kitchen counter. Her thumb stroked the lighter like a meditation stone. It wasn't long after Shadow had enlisted as a prospect that she'd found his favorite possession. Her hand grasped the smooth surface and she froze, listening.

No one was around.

Slipping it in the front pocket of her jeans, she hurried through the clubhouse and out the backdoor. Zipping across the dirt yard, she jumped a low picket fence and hoisted herself up to her bedroom window. She shimmied over the windowsill and tumbled onto the mattress.

Escaping her room was a piece of cake, but she wasn't tall enough to get back in without crashing to the floor, so she always shoved her bed against the window to catch her fall. Next year she'd be a sophomore, old enough to scramble in without rearranging furniture before she slipped out. Old enough to get close to Shadow. Soon, the difference between a fifteen- and twenty-year-old wouldn't matter anymore.

Plunking down on a rickety, thrift-store chair, she caressed Shadow's lighter. He'd be livid, searching for it everywhere. Another biker or a hanger-on would get the blame for her theft, but hey, life was a bitch. It was hers now. Like he would be... someday.

Shuddering, Greta shrugged off the past. Her first love might have been a farce, but there was a huge contrast between Shadow and Cutter, and she couldn't keep holding herself back because of her history.

Springing to her feet, Greta stomped over to her trash can

and pressed down on the pedal. The top popped open and she chucked the Zippo inside.

Greta lifted her cell phone up to initiate facial recognition. Her fingers hovered over the keyboard. She swallowed a lump, namely her wounded ego, and took the plunge.

GRETA: HEY

It was the best she could do. No way would she grovel. Jiggling her foot, she glared at the screen as she braced herself for his response. *Ping.*

CUTTER: WHERE ARE YOU?

She almost swooned on her feet, imagining his husky baritone.

GRETA: HOME

CUTTER: BE THERE IN TWENTY

She stumbled to the couch and crumbled against the arm. Pent-up stress whooshed out of her and she pulled a deep breath of relief into her lungs.

CUTTER STRODE through her door with arms wide open. With a whimper, Greta cannon-balled into him. Scooping her up, he rained kisses down on her. She wrapped her legs around his waist and slanted her mouth over his, a greedy moan vibrating around his tongue. Fuck, that felt good. Winding his hair between her fingers, she yanked hard.

Nuh-uh. He wasn't going straight to fucking.

This time around, he'd play his cards differently.

The fact that he could send her from spitting mad to lolling against him gave true meaning to his life.

Prying her fingers from his hair, he unceremoniously dropped her on her feet, but caught her before she tumbled to the ground. His fingers flexed around her delectable ass and lifted her until her toes skimmed the floorboards. "Easy, babe."

Mutiny glinted in her eyes, but she stepped away.

Last time, he hadn't paid attention to a thing in her house and he meant to do it differently this time. Standing in the middle of her living room, he pivoted around on his heels, taking in every single detail.

It was typical Greta. The place fit her like a glove. Wandering over to the couch, he laid a hand on the American Indian blanket draped over the back. Beside it stood a dark-blue velvet armchair, the velvet of the arms was mostly rubbed off, showing how well-loved it was. Between them was a low rectangular coffee table with chipped veneer. That was the extent of the actual furniture, but there were throw pillows everywhere, as if she spent much of her time reading on the floor, propped up on an elbow.

Her place was a small, compact rambler, the living room doubling as her office. Her tidy desk was topped with books propped against the wall. Spanning the wall were three posters. One was a popular poster of a woman in a red head-scarf, wearing a jean shirt and showing off her bicep with the words "We Can Do It!" It reminded him of old, inspirational posters like the "Uncle Sam Wants You" army poster. Another poster was an illustration of a book with the words "Women Who Read Are Dangerous" printed over it. The final poster was "The Future Is Female" in hot pink over a vintage photo of a crowd of women.

And that brought him to the books. Kingdom hadn't been joking about the books this girl had in her house.

Rows and columns of books stood like good, little soldiers on makeshift bookshelves fashioned with bricks and planks of wood, on the coffee table, and along the fireplace mantel.

He frowned. Candles rose precariously on top of high

columns of books. Not safe, he wanted to tell her. It wasn't like she didn't already have half a dozen glass prayer candles lying around, sealed in images of saints. Although, come to think of it, if one toppled and crashed to the floor, it'd light the place up like a beach bonfire. Her books were as good as kindling.

He liked wax play as much as the next guy, but he was getting rid of them within the next twenty-four hours. For a smart woman, he couldn't believe she'd survived this long on her own.

He peeked through the arches leading to the kitchen, where a square-shaped table stood, covered with a worn green tablecloth printed with yellow flowers. A large, tarnished silver platter stood in the middle holding plates and cutlery. Unlike Sage's house, there was not a plant in sight, not even a cactus. While Greta's hippie, boho clothing had an edge to it, here, there were no edges.

Posters aside, everything was flowery and feminine.

A fierce, demanding desire to protect the innocence in her floral, book-bound, fire-hazard sanctuary hit him in the chest. This woman deserved everything her heart desired. It was as if her home had torn a piece of his soul off and tucked it away in one of the tidy nooks in her house of books.

He turned to face her, about to gobble her up, when he paused to take in her pajamas. His girl was wearing pj's with bright yellow ducks on them. Quirking his lips, he quelled a chuckle.

Covering her chest with her arms, she snipped, "I like ducks, okay. I don't care what I wear to bed. Bed is for sleeping, and sleeping is utilitarian, not sexy."

"Not anymore it ain't. Bed is for fucking, and you get the mandatory fuck before I give you permission to go to sleep. Grab you're shit for the night. We're leaving."

"Bossy," she muttered, before piping up, "where are we going?"

"You'll see. I'm not waiting for you to change so wrap up in something that'll keep you warm."

19

GRETA

They rode through an unfamiliar part of the city.

Darkness had fallen by the time they rode past a scruffy neighborhood, bare trees lining the road. Halfway down a sloping street, Cutter stopped along the edge of the sidewalk and gestured for her to hop off.

She shook as the wind whipped around the thin flannel of her ducky pajama pants. Rolling onto the sidewalk, he expertly guided his bike past a set of crenellated iron gates. Once the motor was off, he strode up the stoop where she waited, unlocked the house, and ushered her in.

Greta gulped warm air into her shivering body and her shoulders dropped in relief. Cutter came in behind her and hugged her close. Then he turned her around and gently tugged off her riding gloves. Riding in upstate New York, in pajamas no less, was not for the faint of heart. He divested her of her coat and put it away in a nearby closet. Coming behind her again, he wrapped her into his radiator of a torso until her teeth stopped chattering.

Eyes swerving around the living room, she remarked, "I thought you lived at the clubhouse."

Some brothers liked community-living at the clubhouse. They didn't pay rent, and there was always a party.

"I did."

"What happened?" she questioned curiously.

"I moved," he replied succinctly.

Okey dokey, not very informative. Standing in the foyer, it was obvious that he hadn't moved in long ago. A couch, coffee table, and flat-screen TV, all black, held court in the middle of the room. There were a few paintings on the walls. Interesting. She hadn't taken him for the artsy type. Tilting her head to the side, she noted the bold brushwork of the oil paintings.

Before she could get closer to inspect them, Cutter's broad shoulders obscured the view and his fingers nimbly unbuttoned her pajama top. "No more talking. I have more pressing things to do with you."

Dragging her to his bedroom, he tossed her onto the bed, as was his wont.

Folding his heavily tatted arms across his chest, he said, "Take it off. All of it."

She rushed to tear off her ducky pajama bottoms and plunged under the sheets. He smacked a string of rubbers down on the surface of a brand-new nightstand. She lifted onto her forearms, dropping the sheet, and baring her breasts. The cool air swept over her peaked nipples.

Cutter's heated gaze swept over them, and she rushed to cover up. He displayed his own torso, and her fingers itched to rub the crinkly blond hair on his chest and trail down the ridges of his musculature to his low-slung jeans.

While she couldn't hold still, he took his sweet time removing his motorcycle boots and unbuckling his belt. Slipping it from the loops of his jeans, he folded it in half, and smacked it against the flat of his hand. The sound resonated in her eardrums and she clamped her legs together to hide her arousal.

Finally, finally, *finally*, he dragged his jeans down, revealing thighs carved of marble, his hard shaft bobbing between them. She loved knowing that he went commando. Ready to fuck, anyplace, anytime.

He turned to place his clothes on a nearby chair, giving her a view of his fine, taut ass. What she would do to take a bite out of one cheek and chew it down like the flesh of a crisp, crunchy apple.

Then, he rose above her, cock swinging. Greta was dying to track that thick vein snaking along the underside of his shaft with her tongue. Lap underneath the jut of his crown and swallow him to the back of her throat.

"Greta," he called out, but she didn't hear him. Her attention was riveted on his magnificent erection in her line of sight. A flick of his wrist and the sheet was whipped off her, snapping her out of her stupor.

Instinctively, she scurried back against the headboard.

Brows knitted together, Cutter noted, "You're acting like you're ashamed of your body again. I thought we covered this."

Discreetly, her hand inched down her thigh to hide her tattoo.

Catching her hand in his own, he dragged it to his lips and kissed her wrist. "I want every part of you, babe. You're beautiful, including your tat. It's a badge of honor. Tells me you're a survivor."

Cutter eased her to her side and nuzzled her tattoo, tracing its long length with this tongue.

She flinched, wheezing out, "Please don't."

His palms wrapped around her knees and squeezed once, telling her to keep them in place. With a grip starting at the base of his cock, his hand pawed the length of it. She watched with bated breath as beads of come slipped over the top of his knuckles and disappeared between his blunt fingers.

"Hold yourself open for me. I want a good look at your tasty cunt," he demanded.

Her eyes practically rolled to the back of her head. Exposed to his gaze, blistering heat in her core zapped out in every direction.

"You like to rebel and you love dirty talk," he murmured. "Said it before, you're my perfect bitch."

He dragged his cockhead between the lips framing her slit and pressed against her clit. She took a quick lick of her dry lips as the throbbing in her clit reverberated through her trembling thighs and fluttering belly.

"You love being fucked dirty, too. Don't keep me waiting, girlie. Go on, open wide."

She hooked her forefingers between her lower lips and stretched them out. A shiver racked her as he teased her with his cock, breaching her opening and then pulling away. Her chest rose and fell rapidly.

Batting her eyelashes, she begged, "May I touch your cock, sir? Please."

He sat back on his haunches but didn't give her permission. Fuck, the drive to touch him was clawing at her, inside out.

Curling her fingers, she scraped her nails down his flanks, and whined, "You're not playing nice."

She cringed at the desperation in her voice.

"Watch your tone," he commanded. "Put your hands back on your pussy."

Her hands shook as she did as she was told. He began pumping his fist from the root to the crown of his shaft, and enthralled, she held out her hand like a supplicant, quick to catch his seed.

"Move your fuckin' hand away."

He swatted her roughly, but, compelled to disobey him, she fisted his cock roughly. A spurt of come splashed over her slim fingers. Greta rushed to suck his cock into her mouth. His salty, beguiling taste exploded on her tongue. He pulled out of her mouth with a curse, so she taunted him by licking the remnants of come off her open palm.

Eyes drilling into hers, Cutter jacked his cock in a series of fast, brutal movements. He came with a roar and a rush of scathing pain spewed over her.

Abruptly, he rolled her onto her stomach, yanked the nightstand drawer open, and pulled out a red paddle.

Palming the back of her neck, he gave her a hard whack. The initial contact cut off her breath. Twisting her head, she buried her face and muffled a high, keening scream with a pillow.

"Present yourself. Ass up, face down," he commanded, his voice deep.

In short, jerky motions, she shifted onto her forearms and knees, and arched, leaving her rear twitching in the air. Craning her head over her shoulder, she stared at him. Without the usual laugh lines crinkling around his eyes, he looked stern and unyielding. He wasn't letting her get away with a thing.

Huh, perhaps he's a man I can trust after all.

With slow precision, his large hands curved over her butt cheeks, parted, and lifted them. She squirmed; goosebumps raised on her flesh. His thumbs pulled her inner lips open and subjected her to a thorough inspection.

"You have the prettiest, little cunt." He tutted softly. "Too bad about your attitude."

Head hanging down and palms clammy, she held herself still for his perusal.

Thwack.

A scorching blaze ripped through her. The impact of each spank scooted her forward on the bed until her crown touched the headboard. Greta blew air out as she absorbed the pain of his swats. Her mind gave shape to thoughts, but each jolt popped them like woozy bubbles.

Then, it happened. The stings receded and a dark, lusty warmth pooled in her belly.

"Your ass is getting flushed. Cherry red looks good on you. Wish you could see those cheeks bounce back after the paddle leaves its mark," he murmured.

Cutter pinched her clit, and her spine arched like a reed bending against a windstorm. Swirling a finger inside her, he chided, "Dirty, wet girl. You're leaking on my sheets. Tryin' to leave your scent in case another woman comes to my bed."

Her chest hollowed out. Fuck him for mentioning another bitch when she was in his bed.

Primitive growls emanated from her throat as she whirled around and lunged for him. He threw the paddle on the floor, caught her, and spread her legs open. She tried to buck him off, but he circled his cockhead against her soaking sex, and her hips betrayed her. Her inner muscles spread around his girth with a gratifying stretch as he worked himself into her slick channel, his abs tightening and shifting as he took her. Just as she began to adjust to his size, he drove into her all the way to the hilt. *Holy fuck!* The strength of his thrust tore into her.

Yanking her hair back, he withdrew on the command, "Tilt up more."

Once she angled her ass high in the air, Cutter notched his shaft and plunged back in. His hands flanked her, arms bending and straightening on either side of her. Good God, he was fucking her while doing push-ups. She crowed with glee at the filthy beast she'd unleashed.

"My cock in that tightness hurts, doesn't it babe?" he asked.

"Shut up and use me. Fuck me like an animal," she begged. Desperate, she was desperate.

Biting down on the slope of her neck, Cutter pounded into her. She rocked up against his bludgeoning shaft, dragging on the hot steel as he stroked in and out. The pleasure was building, higher and *higher*, when his shout rent through the air. Thick streams of his come jetted into her core, and she detonated. Shattered into shards and blew away like a flotsam of balloons into the stratosphere.

Over her shoulder, a glow haloed the outline of his head as he continued to move in a slow, languid dance inside her. Mindless, she drifted in a sea of light, gripping the sheets to keep from collapsing, and milked him for every drop he was worth. The mattress pitched, and she felt him crash beside her. Sheets rustled and drifted over her prone, wrung-out body, and she dozed off with an arm banded across her waist, weighing her down.

20

GRETA

"Shhh," a man whispered near her temple.

Greta jerked out of sleep to find Cutter fondling her between her thighs.

In the space between sleep and wakefulness, between unconsciousness and consciousness, it was Shadow parting her legs.

Shaking off the unwanted vision, she nestled back against Cutter's solid body. His hand palmed the inside of her thigh, his pinky caressing the edge of her sex. Molded against the curvature of his broad chest, she rocked her pelvis against his groin.

"My girl's got a greedy little pussy." He tried to withdraw but she trapped his hand between her thighs. Satisfaction glittered in his eyes. "It was meant as a wake-up call, princess. I didn't hear any complaints, but was I too rough?"

"Of course not," she replied.

None of her past partners, her right hand, or good porn drove her to the edge of her sanity, like he did last night. There was something about challenging Cutter, along with his firm and steady response, that sparked off a climax faster than a lit firecracker on Chinese New Year.

"Good, but I know I worked you over good last night. You've got to be sore. I'm gonna give you a bath." A light swat tapped her rear. "Depending on how you behave, I might give you a reward."

Raising up on her elbows, she griped, "Alright, I'll get into the shower."

He stopped her with a hand on her breastbone. "I said a bath."

Greta sat up and stretched her neck, dubiously eyeing his bathroom through the partly opened door.

She worried her bottom lip. "I'd prefer a shower."

One corner of Cutter's lips quirked up. "You worried it's not clean?"

"Pretty much," she confessed, meeting his eyes. She wasn't about to be embarrassed when it was his bathroom that was probably nasty as all hell.

"Male plus biker does not equal cleanliness. Is that it?" he rumbled.

"Correct," she chirped. His chuckle vibrated in the air around her.

"I'll try not to be offended." A smile split his face, but his somber eyes didn't fool her. "I take my responsibility seriously. Part of that is to tend to you. To wash you and pamper you. I chose this house with certain specifications. One, was security." He nodded toward her. "Your security to be specific. Two, was the square footage. My plans to renovate are detailed. We'll be spending a good amount of time here because this is where I plan to lavish my attention on you."

He was telling her to take him seriously, but could she really? The idea that he had a house, and had renovated it with her in mind, was preposterous. Not but a few weeks ago, he was living at the clubhouse, wallowing like a pig in mud.

"I'll believe it when I see it," she sniffed, lifting her nose up in the air.

Nonplussed, he pulled her up to standing and her muscles groaned. As if that wasn't enough pain, Cutter took the opportunity to palm the welts on her ass.

She hissed out, barely stifling a curse from the smarting pain. Following him to the bathroom, Greta stopped short at the threshold. She squinted her eyes and blinked.

It was large and freshly finished. In the airy space, the upper part of the walls were a mosaic of colors ranging from dark blue to turquoise, while the lower part and the floor were a warm, terra-cotta color. In a gritty corner of Poughkeepsie's urban center, Cutter had carved out an oasis, a Mediterranean cove of his own.

A huge bathtub took up an entire corner. Porcelain always sparkled bright, but this was no run-of-the-mill tub. It wasn't just clean, it was pristine.

On a low bench, downy towels were laid out. Her fingertips graced the fancy soap and the caps of what looked like fancy shampoo. She was not one to indulge in luxurious cosmetic products. He wasn't kidding about pampering her. A fluffy bathmat squished between her toes. It felt divine.

But thoughts, ugly thoughts, flittered through her mind. They left her standing there, hesitant to snatch up the gift he dangled in front of her. If he was to be believed, then he'd accepted her as she was: dark tempered, rebellious in nature, and above all else, a contrarian just for the hell of it.

Of course, aftercare was an integral part of a well-executed bout of power exchange, but this was far more than she deserved.

Cutter bent over and drew a bath for her. Saliva pooled in her mouth as she stared at the honed muscles of his boxer's neck and upper back, flexing and bunching as he adjusted the knobs to his liking. His torso twisted and she got an eyeful of his chest, covered with golden curls.

Dominance radiated off him like the haze steaming off the water filling the tub. Testing the temperature of the bath water, he glanced over his shoulder. His steady gaze suffused her with heat, and she finally released the tension she'd been holding onto.

"You're the first woman to step into this house," he confessed.

"So what?" she asked and winced at the jealousy lacing her tone. His reminder of the gaggles of women before her pricked her pride. Too soon, she'd be confronted with who *knew* how many other women, jumping out from every corner she turned. God, she was *such* a brat, but she couldn't help it. She'd likely scratch their eyes out just for having been with him, even if he was a reformed manwhore.

"Uh-huh," he replied with a knowing, half smile.

Satisfied with the water, he gestured for her to approach. "Come here. I'm going to bathe you."

Backing up a step, Greta shoved her arms over her bosom. *Oh God...aftercare. The smooth after the rough. No, it's too much. Too much intimacy.*

Caring for a sub was standard procedure, so to speak, but the intimacy it garnered was far more unnerving than if he walloped her ass or sank his cock inside her. Those, at least, were acts of primal lust.

She spun around and gave him her back, a sign of disrespect. Cowering behind hunched shoulders, her fingers curled into themselves. Nope, no way would she surrender to his ministrations. She simply could not do it. Inching her head up, she peeked over her sloped shoulder.

Cutter sat on the edge of the tub; legs splayed with his forearms resting on his sleek thighs. Sharp lines bracketed the corners of his lips.

"Don't you dare back away," he warned in a tone brooking no disobedience. "Approach me."

She shuffled toward him, her gaze bouncing off the mosaic of tiles. He pointed to the mat on the floor between his open knees. "You were bold in bed but seems to me like you're running scared."

If eyes could shoot daggers, she'd have sliced him to death.

"Kneel," he ordered, his tone dripping with dominance.

Her eyes dropped, but her knees couldn't quite drop with them. Her heart banged against her ribs as she wrangled with the jangling nerves prompting her to flee. Eventually, the sultry, warm steam and his steady gaze soothed her heart rate and swathed her in a light daze.

"Greta," he warned.

Eyes trained on his toes, she lowered herself to her knees.

"A firm hand," he approved. "That's how you do best. You've got fire, no doubt, but I'll bring you to heel."

He caught a strand of hair and twirled it around his finger. Tugging, he directed her to lean her temple against his thigh. His cock was at rest, but she drew in his earthy musk, laced with a hint of spice. Delectably bold, like him. The rich scent lured her tongue to dart out and rasp the crown of his shaft. His cock jumped and began to fill with arousal.

Cutter tapped her lightly on the nose. "None of that."

Her lips pursed in a disgruntled pout. "But I want *that*."

"Little one, you're trying to distract me. Trying to get me to fuck you raw instead of taking care of you." His fingernail scraped across her naked ass, and she winced. "See, you're sore. Antics won't distract me."

"I don't want you to take care of me," she muttered, hiding her expression in his thigh. "Must I repeat it again for the hundredth time? I'm a self-sufficient adult."

Grasping her by the arms, he brought her to her feet, leaving streaks where his fingers had wiped the humidity off her glistening skin. Leaving her standing, he dropped a bath bomb in the steaming water. Her eyes popped out. "What the hell is that?"

The marine blue of his eyes glinted with sparks of humor. "A bath bomb."

"Bikers aren't supposed to know those even exist."

"Stereotype much?"

"That's like, so unmanly."

He checked out his dick, stiff and erect as a staff. "Not worried about my manhood, babe."

Badly played. She had to own up to her unvarnished prejudice. Heat flamed from her hairline to her chest. "I apologize."

Unfazed, he ushered her into the tub. One foot, then the other, she stepped into the warm, foamy water swirling around her calves. "Sit down."

Jets of water bubbled around the contoured oval tub. She gripped the sides and slowly lowered herself into the hot streams rippling below the surface. Her ass skimmed the top and she hissed through clenched teeth. "Dammit, Cutter, this is blistering my butt."

Cutter's laughter echoed off the tiled walls. "It'll feel good once you're soaking in it. Give it a chance to massage that sexy pink ass of yours."

She scowled at him, not appreciating the commentary on

the color of her butt. Between locked arms, she lowered herself little by little. In her peripheral vision, a stream of liquid from a bottle plunged below the surface, and instantaneously, a mountain of bubbles whipped up around her.

"Bubbles!"

Peals of laughter escaped as she corralled swaths of them in her cupped hands. Her stinging ass forgotten, she played with the mounds of foam, shaping them at her whim.

Calloused knuckles ran down her cheek. "Better?"

She batted her lashes playfully and mustered a smile. "Yeah, better."

She laid her shoulders against the bath and sighed. After the initial shock, her butt was starting to feel better. "How were you able to afford a house and renovate parts of it in such a short period of time? I don't mean it as an insult, but this had to cost tens of thousands of dollars."

"Living rent-free at the clubhouse for years left me with money. Besides my bikes, I don't spend much. No old lady or kids to support. Those are the big expenses," he threw out casually, "like you." Greta averted her eyes. "The brothers helped. We renovated the clubhouse ourselves, so a few rooms was an easy job."

He picked up the bar of soap. A French-milled lavender soap, to be exact. Triple-milled, to be even more precise. Okay, so she knew a few things about soap. Hey, a woman had to indulge on occasion or else life wasn't worth living. Books had their own scent, but it wasn't exactly a sexy smell.

In his strong, masculine hands, Cutter lathered a washcloth with the soap. Veins bulged and swerved between the scrapes and calluses that were especially prevalent around his knuckles. She licked her lips at the memory of the magic his enchanted fingers wielded on her clit.

"Hoodie helped with the design," he sais.

"Hoodie? As in the young punk who patched in with Whistle? The quiet one?"

"He designs our merch, which we sell online. Not only does he design it, but he set up the website and runs it. The prospects take shifts to cover the orders."

Her jaw almost dropped but she caught herself in time.

"You know our website, right?" He cocked an eyebrow at her.

Obviously, she didn't know about their merchandise, or their website, or pretty much anything about how the club made money. She presumed that it involved criminal activity, although she had no actual proof.

"The club sells biker gear, T-shirts, key rings. Christ, the kid has us selling travel mugs and water bottles. Stickers, decals, posters. There's an inventory list a mile long. Makes the club a nice bit of change."

"I didn't know," she replied softly, somewhat humbled.

"You weren't lookin'. Assumed we're straight-up hoodlums, and that was the end of that. You judged us like a civilian and then kept on judgin'."

His statement was said without bitterness or anger, increasing a sense of shame that had been building during their conversation.

"The wall art? The paintings tacked up on the living room wall are Hoodie's?"

"Yep."

"The graffiti of the Squad's motto, brushed in oil paints, is brilliant."

"Rise and face the wall," he ordered. She did as he commanded and spread her feet wide. Her nails tore at the rough finish of the tiles as he washed down her flanks. He was a bit rough when he scrubbed her down, and she had to bite back a moan.

To distract herself from his delicious touches, she rambled, "It's incredible. He's so talented. Well, this bathroom makes much more sense now."

The lathered washcloth came up, circled her shoulder, and swept over her breast. The friction was like a concoction of chili peppers and ice cubes on her nipple, setting up a vibration in her body.

"You in my bath is what makes sense," he said.

She sank against the wall, bare breasts pasted against the tiles, eyes fastened shut as he gently massaged down her leg. Placing her foot on his bare thigh, he kneaded her calf. Her eyes drifted open, beads of moisture clinging to her lashes.

Cutter was bent over in concentration. She could watch him forever. The steel ropes of his arms, gliding and rippling with each movement. His massive chest covered in blond fur, a shade darker than the mane of his head. His mutable eyes, reflecting the colors of the walls and the water.

Every aspect of him filled her with a trembling urge to touch him in return. Her fingers twitched to feel the texture of his wide shoulders, the thickness of his chest and the tautness of his abdomen, ending in the springy hair surrounding his erection. But he'd reprimanded her, reminding her that she was his, not the other way around. As tantalizing as it was to bury her fingers in the curls at the root of his cock, she didn't dare interrupt him.

Cutter guided her down into the water, and ordered, "Tilt your head back."

He collared her throat while massaging slow circles down her chest. His nails scraped her dusky nipples peeking out of the foam. The pillows of her breasts shuddered with each nick. She arched her back, but he refused her unspoken plea for more. Instead, his fingers wandered down to knead her core muscles. "Ahh!"

The deep kneading of her belly was like nothing she'd experienced before. His breathing kicked up as his slick fingers eased into her pussy, massaging away the soreness. Greta wiggled, and he planted a strong hand to hold her down.

"Stop teasing me."

"Babe, you've got no idea what you do to me," he rejoined.

She struggled to rise but he captured her clit between two digits and gave it a hard pinch. Palming her nape, he slanted his mouth over hers and gave her a bruising kiss. Her hands ran up his chest and wrapped around his neck.

Abruptly, he broke their kiss.

Her fingers drifted over her puffy lips before dropping open on the lip of the bathtub. Dick swaying in the air, Cutter anointed her exposed chest with a fragrant oil until she was in a stupor.

"Receptive to my guidance. Submissive to my authority. I don't take your trust lightly."

Everywhere he touched her filled her with a humming energy, like spiced honey. Greta licked the sweat off her upper lip.

"Out," he commanded, in a husky timbre.

Water sluiced off her lithe frame as she stood up. Hunger burned in his gaze, chasing away her shiver and replacing it with sultry heat. Moisture seeped out of her sex and slid down her thigh.

He caught the movement and bent his head to catch the rolling stream, tasting her. His tongue reached the apex of her mound and circled around her clit. Lips suctioned around her nub, and he sucked it brutally into his mouth. She clutched his shoulders to stay upright.

Seating himself on the edge of the bathtub, he folded her in an embrace. It was a super-sweet gesture, but who cared when she was clenching a hot, empty pussy. A fact he damn well knew since said pussy was rubbing the thigh she was using as a seat.

Beginning at the dip of her throat, his knuckles ran down the center of her body, skimmed over her mound and landed between her outer lips. Her vagina gripped inconsolably at the lone knuckle, but to no avail because he dropped his hand away, leaving her bereft once more.

"Quit teasing me," she said.

Snickering, Cutter opened a large towel for her to step into and then rubbed her down languorously. She followed his directions, moving this way and that, until he'd dried every inch of her. He discarded the towel and prodded her back to his lap. Tucked under his chin, she melted into his torso. She lay pliant under the strokes of his fingers, her body and mind quiet.

She was almost dozing when he gathered her up and carried her to his bed. He dragged a blanket over them, and she nestled against him, in a cocoon.

"Why the birds?" he asked.

The birds. He was referring to the running theme of bird prints in her life. On the coverlet, sheets, and curtains of her bedroom, the wallpaper she had painstakingly molded onto the walls of her kitchen and the pj's she wore last night. "They represent freedom. I may not ride anymore, but I can hold a bird in my mind."

"I imagine you riding your own bike. Hot as fuck, decked out in a motorcycle jacket with my name stamped on the back." She snuggled deeper and his arms tightened around her. "You'll ride again, princess."

She smiled and dragged a faint kiss across his chest. "I don't miss it any longer."

A total lie.

But wrapped around the sexiest male alive, who cared about such things anymore? Greta draped herself over his torso and listened as their heartbeats fell into the same rhythm.

21

GRETA

Not only had Greta spent the entire night with him, but she had submitted to his care and woke up in his arms again.

It was the longest amount of time she'd spent with one person, in one uninterrupted block of time. Cutter was striking her shields down faster than a toddler faced with a stack of wooden blocks.

Around noon, he tugged her out of bed, wrapped her in a bathrobe, and settled her on one of the two chairs around his kitchen table. She peeled the price tag off the bare wooden slab and tossed it in the trash can. Besides a few appliances, there was nothing. No tablecloth. No curtains. Not a scrap of cloth that wasn't utilitarian. No vases, candles, or decorations.

Granted, he'd only recently moved in, but the simple, straight-shooting masculinity of the place was pure Cutter.

Raising a hand to shield her eyes, she said, "Wow. This is a special shade of yellow you have on the walls."

"Haven't had a chance to paint it. Surprised you're complaining," he smirked, "considering it's a perfect match for the yellow ducks on your pj's. Your favorite color, no?"

"Hardy har-har. First off, those were *cartoony* ducks, not real ducks, so they're exempt. The spanking-bright yellow of your walls was meant for birds, canaries to be exact." She lowered her voice conspiratorially, "Never, ever walls, unless they're part of an LSD research experiment."

Rummaging through a couple of drawers, he pulled out a pan and bowls. "What do you wanna eat? Bacon and eggs? Omelet? Pancakes?"

Drawing a hand to her chest, she breathed, "Be still my heart, a biker who cooks. And here I thought only bitches had kitchen duty."

Opening the refrigerator, he grabbed a carton of eggs, butter, milk, and bacon. "Ha, ha. Every day was kitchen duty in my household growing up. Food only got as good as I could cook it. So, I got good."

"Your mom brought you up right," she said approvingly.

His expression instantly shuttered. "She had to work hard to provide for me and my uncle. You gonna choose or am I cookin' them all?"

"Pancakes," she piped up. "I love pancakes."

His features softened and he gifted her with a lopsided grin. "Me, too, but I'm going to make it all. What can I say, I'm a growing boy," he said as he grabbed containers of whey and protein powder out of a cabinet, "who likes to box."

As he cracked eggs and mixed ingredients together, he asked about her mother. And because, with each egg he cracked, he cracked open another shield around her heart, she loosened her tongue. Tossing out a prayer that she wouldn't get dragged into an undertow, she answered questions about her childhood, starting with the one about her parents.

"My mom must've been around seventeen when she fell for him. Scorpion was much older, and a bad boy. I suppose he may have loved her, but who really knows. His love had hard limits."

He leaned down to wrap an arm around her, and her head lolled in the crook of his shoulder. Stroking her back, he laid a kiss on her neck and then bit down lightly. Then, he returned to prepping.

"The more I saw my father's rotating whore-door and my mother's helplessness, the more I was determined to save her. But, I was a kid so I really had no idea how."

Greta shook her hair like the mane of a horse dislodging gadflies biting into her hide. Gorging on her blood.

Cutter paused his mixing as he asked, "He ever touch you?"

She shook her head. "He never touched me, but he made sure to hurt her in front of me. In a way, I wish he *had* hurt me. It would explain why I only get off when I'm being dominated. If I'd been molested, at least it'd make sense to me."

Suddenly, Cutter was in her face, gripping her chin. "Don't say that. Don't even think it."

She cast her eyes down as he continued, "It hurt to watch your moms getting beat down. A child wants to help, no matter what. I know a bit about that myself. And when we can't save the ones we love from harm, we hurt. Bad enough that we grow up thinking we're fuckups. Don't wish the worst on yourself. By the way, you don't have to come from a fucked-up family to enjoy getting your ass tapped with a crop. That's Hollywood movie shit, not real life."

Silence stretched between them, punctuated by the sound of his whisk smacking against an aluminum bowl. "How did you and your mother get away?"

"With help from another biker, ironically. After all she'd been through, she went ahead and fell for a biker." A glimpse of a smile flashed on her lips. "Still, the day we drove away out of Camden was one of the best days of my life."

Cutter wasn't showing much in the way of sympathy, which she appreciated. An unexpected sense of relief washed over her as she revealed herself to him. She didn't talk about her past much, preferring to pretend it had never existed, but it felt unimaginably light to talk about it with Cutter. She felt as buoyant as a dove released from a cage. Sparkly clean, like after the bath Cutter had spoiled her with the night before.

"I remember every moment of that day like it was yesterday. Mom was on lockdown in the house and I was at school. It was after the last dismissal bell, and the stairs of the front entrance were flooded with kids running to meet their parents or to pair up to walk home together. I was going to walk home alone, like always. Except that afternoon, Trucker was there, waiting for me."

Greta closed her eyes and drifted back to the moment when she noticed him. He was leaning against a lamppost at the street corner, smoking a cigarette. Spotting her, he threw the butt down and captured her in a big bear hug. His truck was idling a few feet away. He boosted her up to the front seat, rounded the pickup truck, and jumped in.

"'Listen up,' he said, 'face forward and keep cool. Your mother's under the blanket behind you. We're leaving for good.' I peeked behind me and my mom smiled up at me, face bloody with another busted lip."

"'Scorpion's gonna kill you,' I warned him, and he said, 'don't worry about me, pretty girl. Worry about your mama.'"

Greta slanted away from Cutter, giving him her profile. "We went underground. Hooked up with a real, modern day underground railroad. Fled from house to house, crisscrossing the country like fugitives. But we couldn't run forever. Trucker's brother was a member of an MC in Vermont called the

Green Mountain Boys. They took us in, so we ended up there. Of course, Scorpion found us. The 'details,'" she air-quoted, "were hammered out between the clubs."

It stuck in her craw that her mother ultimately turned to an MC, another patriarchal organization, to save them from her father.

Turning from the stove, spatula in his hand, Cutter waited for her to continue.

"Scorpion agreed to let us go, but finagled one last meeting with my mother. I remember how she made him wait outside the house. She took a seat on the couch, watching the clock, as the brothers begged and pleaded for her to meet him. Exactly thirty minutes later, she stood up, and marched out the door." Greta's voice dropped low, "God, how I loved her for that."

Cutter slipped a plate of pancakes in front of her. She stood up to get silverware, but he pressed her back into her seat. Moving around the kitchen, he collected utensils, napkins, and a bottle of maple syrup.

Then he lifted her, sat down, and perched her on his lap. Greta leaned against him as he cut off a piece of pancake, swirled it in a pool of maple syrup, and brought it to her lips.

Her stomach growled.

"I knew my girl was hungry," he confirmed with a grin.

Greta opened her mouth and took a bite. Sweetness burst on her tongue, and her eyes fluttered closed as she savored it. He fed her several more bites before allowing her to continue.

"The brothers pretended to drink beer and watch TV while listening for sounds from outside. Pfft, as if they had a chance in hell of stopping Scorpion if he'd taken a knife to her."

Cutter swept a kiss against her temple. "If I were a guessing man, I'd say my brave girl didn't sit around, letting shit happen around her."

She flashed him a smile. "I crept out the back of the house, scurried around to the front, and dove underneath a bush. I overheard her saying, 'As stubborn as I was to love you and fight for you, I'll be just as stubborn to keep Greta away from you.'"

Greta fell silent. What she didn't tell Cutter was that Scorpion hadn't come alone. When she'd peeked out from her hidey-hole, she spotted Shadow by his side. She was about to jump out of the bushes when her mother flung out her hand and said scornfully, "Your boy's solid. You don't need Greta to keep him by your side, so you best leave her alone." Raking Shadow up and down with an expression of disgust, she said, "Bet he's relieved that he doesn't have to keep up the charade. You know, the one where he pretends to care for her."

The words thrust a spike of ice into her heart and blood gushed out like water through cracks in a damaged dam. All those times Shadow had shielded and comforted her—were *pretend*? Tears rolled down her cheeks, and she muffled her sobs in the dirt. His love had been a sham.

Greta shook her shoulders, as if shaking off the past, and finished, "A year later, I went away to college. The past was dead to me. I buried it and left."

Cutter's knee jiggled. It was so sweet of him to be upset on her behalf.

Stroking her hair, he mused, "He was a controlling motherfucker. He could've taken you no matter what your mother said."

Bile rose from her gut, disgust congealing on the inside of her mouth. "The thing was, you see, I wasn't male, so, no, he wasn't keen on taking me with him."

Shadow was a male. Perhaps it was as much of a blessing and a curse for him as it had been for her. After all, he wouldn't be shackled with a girl he didn't love.

THEY WERE CUDDLING in his bed, his powerful presence enveloping her like a warm blanket taken right out of the dryer. Every centimeter of her was safely encased in his aura. Greta never thought she'd enjoy lounging around, doing nothing, as much as she did, but Cutter was like a drug to her.

In a rumbling, seductive tone, he murmured, "Once a princess, always princess. I bet the bikers hounded you from the day you turned thirteen."

Greta snort laughed. "Is this your attempt at stopping me from brooding?"

Drawing back, he blinked his eyes in mock innocence. "It's a straight-up honest statement."

"Please, I was flat-chested. No ass, no hips, no curves. It would have been easier to pawn me off if I were platinum blonde, but I wasn't into bringing attention to myself back then."

"No brother wanting to keep his balls attached would've taken you on, except as an old lady. But it doesn't mean they weren't panting after you."

She sat up, a hearty laugh gusting out of her lungs. "My lack of sexy was the least of it. Sha—" Her lips clamped shut. Cutter tightened his hold on her, searching her eyes for more, but she wasn't about to say *his* name aloud. The last time she heard his name was the day she learned of his betrayal. The taste, like poison, still lingered on her tongue.

"Whatever. Since then, I've lived by a few simple rules. The most important one is no bikers," she declared.

"Never is a word meant to be broken. Never ride a bike. Never join an MC. Never go past 120 mph. Never, never, never," he teased.

"As much as I like fucking you, Cutter, that's a hard 'never' for me." She craved fucking him like his cock was dusted in coke. Hell, she'd dumped her plan to save Sage so fast, she'd gotten whiplash, but that didn't mean she was idiotic enough to fall for him.

"Anyway, you're interested in me because I'm a challenge," she went on matter-of-factly. "One you've found worthy. I'm flattered, for sure. A man like you doesn't go out of his way just for any bitch."

Dark blond lashes blinked slowly over steely-blue eyes. He gripped her forearms and brought her so close she could see the dark outline of his irises. "Have I once acted as if I don't know my own mind? Like a kid who's wet behind the ears?" he ground out.

Greta made a scoffing noise through her nostrils. "Bikers are all the same. You want me for what I symbolize. Besides being a bitch, I'm a challenge, an agitator. It's ironic considering you hold the prize for being the biggest mischief-maker."

A tick pulsed at his temple. Then, purposely, the corners of his eyes crinkled, and the icy blue melted, leaving his irises as crisp as pools of aquamarine. His growly chuckle vibrated against her, and she felt the grooves of his laugh lines against her throat. In a tone infused with 100-proof alcohol, he spoke, "I'm warning you, don't talk to me about other men."

Greta shoved against the hard edges of his ribs, but he cinched her wrists. A tinge of pain moved up her forearms and her pulse spiked. "You're hurting me."

"If I wanted to hurt you, there'd be no doubt about it, sweetheart. I'm in control of myself. Always." Pressing in closer, he warned her, "I'm the best tracker there is, and I'm on the hunt for your soul."

His promise flayed her, but he was a man who wasted his time entertaining himself and his brothers. True, he'd taken on a big job corralling Kingdom and Loki for the future of the Squad, but he was a biker. It was natural for the Squad to be his priority. A woman? *Not so much.* A niggling voice told her *that's not true*, but she forcefully stamped it down. She couldn't afford to believe and get her heart stomped on again.

His tongue flicked her bottom lip, then his teeth delivered a sharp nip. The nip turned into a bite, which was followed by a suckle. Euphoria went in through the puncture wound of his bite, like an opiate pulsing through an intravenous needle. *Drip, drip, drip.* Desire volleyed through her veins, rushed toward her heart, and stunned it.

"Brave girl, I'm not a fool like your father. I know what you're worth, and I'm gonna take care of you the way you deserve," he vowed.

He wants me, not like Shadow. He's not Shadow.

Leaning forward until the tips of their noses grazed each other, he begged, "Give us a chance, babe. Come on, princess. Give *me* a chance to prove you wrong. Yes or no?"

Her vision blurred. Despair was a gray blue, like his eyes, but pour on red-hot sex and her brain floated in a violet-colored subbie heaven. She could almost taste the heartache, but damn her, she would take the chance. He bought this house to have a place to bring her to, he got the brothers to help him renovate it, he'd bought the couch they were currently snuggling in. It wasn't right to paint him with the same brush as Scorpion or Shadow, simply because that was the foundation of her image of all bikers.

"Yes," she said, yielding to him.

She prayed she wouldn't regret her decision.

22

CUTTER

The chorus of the Cindy Lauper song "Girls Just Want to Have Fun" rang out.

Greta turned to him with a grin spread across her lips. "You have a Cindy Lauper ringtone?"

"My mom's favorite song," Cutter muttered as he reached for his cell. Motioning Greta to be silent, he answered, "Hey Mandy, what's up? Tommy okay?"

He strode into the living room, away from Greta, although his side of the conversation was still audible to her.

"I'm here with him. I think he hasn't taken his meds. His door is broken," said Mandy.

"Got it. I'm getting ready. Be there in two hours," he promised.

"I can stay with him until you arrive."

"If he's not hurt, go on home. I'll come over to your place after I see him."

"Are you sure?" she asked.

"Yep. I'll be there in a bit," he confirmed.

"Alright. I'll tell him you're coming and then go on home."

"Will do," Cutter concluded, before disconnecting. He

propped his forearm on the fireplace mantle and leaned his forehead into his palms. He didn't want to air his dirty laundry, but he'd have to explain the situation to Greta before sending her off. The scent of pancake, maple syrup, and Greta wafted off his fingers. Damn, he didn't want to leave her, but Tommy was his responsibility. Always would be.

Face set, he strode back into the kitchen. "Princess, sorry to cut our time short, but somethin' came up and I gotta head out."

His expression must have tipped her off that he was upset, because she came to him and wrapped her arms around his waist, rubbing her cheek against his chest.

"What's going on?" she asked sweetly.

"Remember I told you I have an uncle. I'm his primary caretaker and his neighbor called. I gotta go see him, yeah?"

He pulled on her arms to break her hold, but she clasped him tighter.

"I'm coming with you," she declared.

A humorless laugh burst out of him. "You don't want to do that."

The corners of her lips tilted downward as she peered up at him. "Why not?"

"Tommy's my responsibility. I take care of him, alone," he explained. Of course, he wanted her with him, but Tommy could be a handful. Not often, but he had his moments.

"I'm sure you do, but you don't have to. You're here for me and I'm here for you. That's how this relationship thingy works. Remember? The one I agreed to not five minutes ago," she reminded him.

His chest hollowed out. He'd never brought anyone to visit Tommy. Kept that shit under wraps, because, while it had gotten easier over the years, seeing Tommy pried open old wounds.

"I opened myself up to you about something that Sage doesn't know about," she argued.

He was officially screwed because he couldn't cut her off from his past after she'd generously shared her pain with him.

Resting his chin on the top of her head, he nodded. "Yeah, okay. We'll have to ride over to the clubhouse and get the Jeep. He lives on the side of a goddamn mountain, and the last part of the ride is off-road. Plus, we gotta get supplies."

"Sounds like he lives far out there," she noted.

"Tommy needs lots of space. He's done lots of therapy and interventions, but he's as good as he's gonna get. Anyways, he's happiest where he is. Not worth having him live with me to get additional services when he'd be unhappy and run away."

"Being a caretaker is extremely difficult. I'm certain you're making the best choices for him," she replied soothingly.

He grunted. "Don't be so sure."

"Oh, please," she scoffed, "as much as you like to pretend you don't care, you don't back down whatsoever when it's important."

CUTTER GLANCED over the console where Greta had settled in, wrapped in his jacket. They'd returned to her house and stopped by the clubhouse before heading out. The temperature dropped down to a bitter low further upstate. Since he ran hot, he'd stripped off his jacket, and she promptly snagged it and put it on. She looked goddamn gorgeous wrapped in his leather.

He handed her a bag filled with a few pounds of milk chocolate wrapped in tinfoil Christmas motifs. Santas, reindeers, and Christmas trees. Tommy was superstitious as fuck and he only ate children's chocolates. He tolerated Halloween candy and Easter eggs. Gold-covered chocolate coins would do, in a pinch. Had to have a piece after every meal. Never dark chocolate. Made that mistake once and it took him an hour to coax Tommy to finish his dinner.

"So...Tommy's your uncle," she began. Cutter's fingers flexed around the steering wheel and expelled a sigh. *Here goes nothing.*

"He's my mom's younger brother. Has several diagnoses and learning disabilities. After my grandmother's death, he came to live with us. Since my moms was a nurse and worked crazy hours, I took care of Tommy. Not that I'm complaining."

Greta shot him a side-glance of speculation.

"Should warn you that Tommy gets off his meds occasionally. Mandy, who is his closest neighbor, checks up on him once a week. I show up once a month."

"You're a good nephew, Cutter," she stated.

"I'm not," he countered.

She turned to look at him, "What do you mean? You take care of family," she said, in a matter of fact tone.

"Tommy is as good and as pure as they come, but he can be a handful and I'm not always patient with him," he admitted.

"I find that hard to believe. You're incredibly patient with me, and I can be a handful."

"Not the same," he replied with a smirk. Then he sobered and continued because it was important that she understand the situation, "Listen, I was eight years old when Tommy came to live with us for good. The moment he moved in, her attention and love was for Tommy. Nothing left for me."

He swallowed. "Sounds dumb as fuck to complain, but as a kid, I didn't understand what was going on. My mom bent over backwards to go to every doctor or therapy appointment, but never showed up for my school events. Before his meds got stabilized, Tommy would disappear. She'd go out looking for him and leave me alone for days. By the time I turned eighteen, I was done. Joined the military the same day."

Greta's hand slid over and grabbed his. Her thumb swept over his knuckles. "Where is your mom?"

"Dead. My last promise to her was that I would take care of him, again."

Once they reached Tommy's rudimentary cabin, Cutter jumped out of the cage, threw his head back and took a deep whiff of the brisk mountain air. Feet on the running board, he drummed the roof of the Jeep.

His head snapped forward and he looked off toward the door of the cabin, hanging by splinters. *Fuck, what the hell happened?*

Tommy's unruly ginger curls and ruddy cheeks peeped out from behind the twisted door.

Raising his hand in a salute, Cutter jumped down. He grimaced when his knee popped. Tommy came out from behind what was left of the coarse wooden planks he'd fashioned into a door and rushed toward him.

A blur of fur whizzed past his uncle and landed on Cutter's steel-toed boots. Grasping the scruff of a fluffy mongrel, he curled it into the crux of his elbow, and arched an eyebrow at his uncle.

"What in the hell is this?" he snapped. He let out a sigh for exhibiting his irritation at his uncle.

"A doggie. Duh." His face broke into a grin as he ruffled the puppy's fur.

"Snapper's the name," his uncle informed him.

The rough rasp of a wet tongue lapped the base of his thumb. Nothing snappish about this dog. He attempted to give Tommy a stern look, but his lips twitched.

"Snapper. Seriously, he looks like a fucking poodle," Cutter grumbled.

"It's a *she*, and she's vicious. She'll protect me from invaders," his uncle explained sagely.

"Tommy, we've been through this," he said gruffly. "There are no invaders. Even if there were, this little thing is a poodle. It's not savin' nobody."

Tommy's face fell. His uncle maneuvered the wriggling dog into his arms. His head snapped up as Greta moved toward them. A grin spread over his uncle's face.

Turning toward him, Tommy asked, "Who's this?"

Cutter motioned to her, "This is Greta. She's a friend."

"You've never brought a friend before." Tommy looked her over curiously. "Hi, friend."

"Hey, Tommy. Glad to meet you," she replied, bestowing his uncle with one of her rare, brilliant smiles. Hell, if he hadn't been balls deep inside her already and knew he would be again, he might be jealous of that smile.

He wrapped one arm around Greta in a side-hug, the puppy squirming between them.

She hugged him back and he nestled into her for a moment before stepping back and saying, "Nice hug."

Nodding a thanks to Greta, Cutter swung his arm around Tommy's shoulders and walked him toward the cabin.

At the entrance, he paused and nodded toward the broken door. "What happened here?"

His uncle looked back at him sheepishly. "Invaders."

"Were they trying to come in again?" he asked, defeated. They'd been over this, time and again, but Tommy couldn't understand that there were no such thing as "invaders."

"Nah. This time they wouldn't leave. Damned troublemakers. 'Hurry, hurry, hurry,' they shouted." Shrugging his broad shoulders, he continued, "I had to let them out and I pulled on the door too hard."

"Uh-huh," he replied. *More like ripped the damn thing off.*

"That's why Snapper found me. She knows about them and runs them off when they come visiting," Tommy explained.

Yeah, there was a story behind how Tommy got the dog, but it would have to be pried out of him another time. Although his uncle was tolerated in these parts, where people kept to themselves, Cutter sussed out any interactions he had with others. He couldn't afford to have Tommy taken advantage of or gotten rid of. Not everyone saw a six-foot-three behemoth as harmless.

Greta followed them in, holding the bags. He took them off her hands and dropped them on the table, which swayed on rickety legs. Handing a kettle to Tommy, he ordered, "Go on and get fresh water from the pump. I'll make coffee."

He scurried out the door with Snapper at his heels. Caressing Greta's jaw, Cutter asked, "You okay?"

"Really Cutter, being here isn't a big deal. Your uncle obviously adores you. His face lit up when he saw you," she observed.

Rummaging through a cabinet filled to capacity with canned goods, he pulled out a recently opened can of coffee. He breathed in the scent of dark roast. Then he found a can of evaporated milk and punctured a hole in it with a knife that was on the counter.

"Tommy built everything, but he hasn't gotten around to making drawers, so it's cluttered."

Ten minutes later, he poured the brewed coffee into three mugs and slid one over to Tommy, another to Greta. Settling down in a wobbly chair, he sipped the rich coffee as Snapper circled around before laying her head on Cutter's boot with a wuffling sound. He'd have to purchase dog food from here on out. Listening to the cracking and popping sounds of the lit fireplace, he chastised Tommy mildly, "You gotta be careful with the door. You'll freeze your ass off. Don't matter how big you make the fire, it's still cold at night in the Adirondacks."

"Sorry, Nephew. It happened last night, and I hadn't gotten around to fixing it. I didn't know you'd be coming today."

An old ache bubbled in his chest, but he stuffed it down. One day, he'd be able to return Tommy's open, honest love in kind. Greta turned her attention to Tommy and asked him questions, getting him to laugh in a way Cutter didn't try.

"Tommy, seems to me that the invaders come when you forget to take your meds," she explained in a gentle tone.

Forget my ass.

Greta shined an easy smile at his uncle. "If I forget to take my medication, I start feeling sad. And I don't like to feel sad."

"You take meds, too?" Tommy inquired in surprise.

"For sure," she replied nonchalantly. "Otherwise, I don't feel my best."

"I don't like them because they make me tired."

"Do you like the invaders?" she asked.

"I *hate* the invaders."

"The invaders are worse than being tired," Cutter interrupted. They'd been through this time and time again.

Greta kicked him under the table and resumed her conversation. "I hate being sad. I remind myself that if I miss more than one or two days, I'll start getting sad again. I'd take feeling sleepy over feeling sad any day."

Tommy tilted his head. "You would?"

"Oh, definitely," she said with a resolute shake of her head. "I have a calendar and every day I take my medication, I cross off the date. You should try it. It's fun to draw a line across a square for every day that I do it right. Maybe we can get you a calendar. And stickers for you to put on it."

Popping off his seat, he said, "Stickers are for kids. I like to use markers."

Opening the carton of sugar, she poured some into her spoon and swirled it into her coffee mug. "Do you draw or color?" she asked.

"Yep. I went to an arts day program for years. Painting, watercolors, collages...things like that."

Cutter quirked an eyebrow. *News to me. Sure, Tommy went to a day program, but I had no idea what he did there.*

"I bet you're pretty good," Greta commented.

Tommy puffed up his chest. "I won an award once. My sister, Ellen, sent it in to a competition."

Again, news to me.

"Cutter and I can go and get you art supplies. We could make a calendar together." Bending down to rub Snapper's head, she suggested, "What about a calendar with dogs?"

"Sure!" Tommy relied excitedly, his eyes lighting up.

Catching Cutter's eye, she said, "We passed a drugstore in the last town."

Facing Tommy, he asked, "You think a calendar would help?"

"Greta says it works for her. It'll work for me because she's like me in that way."

"I have another idea," she interjected. "If you take your medication every day, then you should get a reward. How about if you paint Snapper for the following month and show it off to Cutter on his next visit."

"Will you come, too?" he asked shyly.

Tommy's and Greta's heads swiveled in Cutter's direction at the same time. He wasn't convinced it was for the best, but she'd already met Tommy and didn't seem put off, so he'd allow it.

Fidgeting with excitement, Tommy demanded, "Yes, yes! Cutter, invite her!"

She did seem to have a way with him. Humbled him a bit, 'cause she seemed to enjoy herself despite the fact that she was sitting on a shaky chair and was slurping coffee out of a chipped mug, made with water pumped from the backyard and milk from a tin can.

"If Greta comes, we won't be able to stay the night," he warned.

"Yes, we could," she instantly contradicted him.

Cutter raised his palm to silence her. No way in hell was she camping out in a one-room cabin with no central heating or running water.

Monitoring Tommy's reaction, he declared, "Not up for discussion."

Tommy beamed at Cutter. "I don't mind!"

Cutter stood up and dragged a toolbox from the floor onto the table. "Alright, it's settled. We'll fix this door and then Greta and I will go buy you supplies to make a calendar. How's that?"

Tommy stood up with his empty mug and dropped it into a bucket of soapy water by the entrance. While his uncle's back was turned to them, he leaned over the table and murmured in Greta's ear, "You're a smart girl. I haven't forgotten you, little one. You'll get your own reward."

A pretty blush reddened her face, and he gave her a lingering kiss.

23

GRETA

Greta lounged among the overstuffed cushions of the couch, appreciating Hoodie's paintings, in Cutter's apartment.

She'd won the fight over the material and color of the couch, but she'd lost over the size. The thing was humongous. As if it wasn't enough that it was a sectional sofa, there was a fold-out sleeper unit. For the brothers, he said. Heaven forbid they had to drag their butts out of the house after imbibing too much liquor. But no, the brothers should have a place to crash if they needed it.

Earlier in the day, Cutter had texted her, giving her exactly thirty minutes to wrap up her work at the office and meet him at his place. Sage's giggles still rang in her ears, upon hearing that Cutter got his own house. Although she remained poker-faced at Sage's gleeful display of hilarity, Greta was secretly giddy herself. They were coming along.

Greta heard him ride up, shut down his motor, and thump up the stairs of the stoop. At the rattling of his keys, she dropped the pretense of reading her book. By the time her gorgeous man prowled toward her, her pussy clenched and thrummed in anticipation. She gobbled up the vision of him, windswept blond hair, cerulean-blue eyes, and strapping chest muscles encased in a leather cut.

Eyes glittering with mischief, a smug smile played on his lips. A smile of her own tugged at her mouth in response. *Cutter the trickster is out and about, ready to play.*

Lifting two bulging shopping bags from his fingers, he dropped them by the couch. Shrugging off his cut, he threw it down beside her, and commanded, "Change."

Alrighty, then. *Joker out, Dominant in.* Normally, he'd take off his cut, hang it over the back of the chair placed by the door, and *then* grab her. Melt her with a hot kiss or two. Draw her over his lap for a cuddle. But fuck if her heart rate didn't quicken at his bossy tone. Which was exactly why she wouldn't do what he demanded of her.

Lounging back, she slid her feet to the ground and lazily let her thighs drop open. Sliding her skirt up, she exposed her thong, the gossamer white fabric barely hiding her arousal. His gaze didn't stray below her chin, so... *In for a penny, in for a pound.*

She cocked an eyebrow and drawled, "Excuse me? Did you leave your manners at the door?"

The muscle of his jaw began a rapid-fire ticking. Oh, he did not like that one bit.

Bending down, Cutter thrust the cushions away from her, lifted her up by her butt, and then dropped her. Her heart skipped another beat at his display of strength.

Dubiously eying the bags by her feet, she raised her crocheted sweater over her head, and threw it away from her. She paused for confirmation.

Standing, legs braced apart, he swirled his finger for her to continue.

She wiggled out of her skirt, letting it drop to her feet.

Then, she caught the ends of her shirt and seductively rolled it off, slowly exposing her lace-clad breasts. Under his heavy-lidded gaze, she unhooked her bra and let it drop halfway down her arms.

Hugging her elbows, she stopped, brazenly facing him.

His expression was impenetrable, but the bags sprawled open, spilling out clothes, and she became concerned.

"Down," he directed.

The lines of her forehead puckered.

"Hands down," he elucidated.

Dropping her arms, the bra slipped off.

Rubbing the back of his nape, a smirk touched his lips. "What do you think comes off next?"

Oh, she knew. She knew, but she hesitated anyway. It wasn't to disobey him, exactly. Rather, a sudden wave of shyness swooped over her, swathing her from head to toe.

"A woman has the right to some privacy," she quipped.

Teasing the band of her panties lower, he replied matter-of-factly, "Not when it comes to me."

Soft shivers rippled down her limbs. Hooking the thin scrap of cloth in the crook of his forefingers, he shimmied it down her legs. Her face flashed in a hot, cold, hot, cold pattern. It was one thing to lie down in the bedroom with the lights low, and quite different thing to stand in the living room with bright light showing all her imperfections.

"I should have shaved myself bare," she whispered.

Cutter's gaze zeroed in on her pussy with a forbidding expression. "Fuck no. I didn't order you to shave. I want something to tug on when you're being bad. Like right about now."

His praise cooled down her urge to bolt. Nevertheless, she almost swallowed her tongue when he commanded her to turn around. Balking, she crossed her arms tightly around her chest.

One of his eyes squinted. "Wipe that stubborn look off your face." He released a breath of frustration, but his tone softened a touch. "Woman, you're fuckin' hot. I'm an exacting man, as you damn well know, and I expect perfection from you. I don't expect less than you can deliver, Greta."

She hesitated for one more moment, but ultimately held out her arms and bared herself to his gaze.

"Better. Now present your ass to me," he demanded.

Greta's nostrils flared, but she complied. Bracing her hands on the seat of the couch, she spread her legs and pushed her ass out. He muttered more nonsense about her being perfect, but she felt like her hair was going up in flames. The bastard could see each dimple of her jiggly ass. She shuddered as she continued to suffer under his unyielding gaze.

"Back around," he ordered.

Relief whooshed out from her constricted lungs. Facing forward once again, she shied away, and her gaze dropped to a spot on the refurbished floor.

His eyes burned a path down her body. "Greta, I'm done with you hiding. I want you showin' off those sexy legs of yours when you're in public with me." The side of his lips twisted up. "And, it goes without sayin', those bouncy tits and that thick ass."

Her head snapped up, eyes wide in panic. She clutched her shoulders to cover herself. "Why?" she croaked out. She hated, *hated*, showing her body.

"Bring your fuckin' hands down before I tie them behind your back," he growled low.

Thorns of humiliation prickled against her skin while, God help her, her pussy wept helplessly. She quickly dropped her arms.

The deep lines bracketing his tightened mouth smoothed

out and he clarified, "Because I want show off my woman. Because I want easy access to your tits, pussy, and ass."

Sure, it was easy for him. He was gorgeous, from top to bottom, with his thick mane of messy, blond curls and two bright blue stars for eyes. He spoke in a businesslike tone, as if he was ordering a fucking birthday cake at a bakery.

Gut churning, her fingers curled into tight fists.

"You're out of your fucking mind," she spat out.

She reached down to grab her clothes, but his boot stomped down on them, forcing her to release her grip.

His eyes had turned from pretty blue to the hue of dead granite. "I've put up with your long skirts and hippie shit long enough. It ends today. I got you clothes, and this is what I want you to wear. You're a biker bitch, *my* bitch, and you'll wear what I say."

"Well," she cocked her hip, "here's a news flash, Cutter. I'm not an object to be displayed solely for male sexual desire and satisfaction. To ogle and bid on me like a broodmare at a horse auction."

His knuckle dropped down and dragged along the cleft of her pussy, and she had to bite down on her bottom lip to stop from whimpering.

"Babe, if we're getting into horse terminology, I'm the stud and you're my filly," he clarified. "You're a willful one at that, which is why you require a handler with a firm grip. We come back to the same lesson, again and again. Your primary goal should be to please me."

He pressed in deeper, and her thighs began to quiver. His persistence was giving her a serious headache. "I'm the only one who sees you for who you are, who knows how to take care of you. Completely, and even in ways you don't yet understand."

"I'll be the first to admit that I'm particular, but"—she

clasped his wrist and thrust it away from her—"I'm a feminist, and feminists everywhere would have conniption fits if they—"

Her thought was interrupted by his knuckle, which had returned to her mound. It slipped down to her pulsing clit and rotated. Her heart stopped, her jaw dropped open on a groan, and she began panting.

"They're not in our bed or our heads," he finished, in a sexy rumble.

She blew out a puff of air, and the pink fringes on her forehead shuddered. "One thing I learned from Scorpion was pride. Pride in your club, of course. Before the Dark Horsemen, he had the pride of his Native tribe, the Lenape community he grew up with. See, I have an American Indian grandmother. She died before I met her, but that quarter of honor was enough to fill my entire being."

"I'm with you so far. Go on," he encouraged.

"Well, I..." she struggled for words, "I didn't grow up like he did. As a member of a tribe or with an extended family. My pride found its rightful place in being a woman, and I have to maintain my self-respect as a woman, at any price."

His brows drew together, and his jaw tensed. Two telltale signs of an imminent, good ole-fashioned whupping.

"Hold up," he growled. "You think that you're disrespecting yourself because you do what I tell you to do. You think that because your my little sex toy," he raised her chin with this index finger, "my skin-flick star, my sexiest wet dream, that you're less of a woman? Am I gettin' it right?"

Heat tinged the tips of her ears and her shoulders rose in an itsy-bitsy shrug. Standing in front of him naked, with his hands on her made her so hot she was about to fan herself.

A filmstrip of expressions flickered over his features before they settled into a harsh, chiseled countenance that was for her and her alone. The kind that had her wanting to roll over on her back and beg him to fuck her.

"Christ." He swiped his hand down his face. "Women."

"Well, one woman to be exact," she reminded him smartly, with a wan smile.

His churlish gaze dragged over her and paused at her pussy. "Don't remind me. I'm thinking I'm better off sharing myself again."

Drawing herself up to her full height, her fists slammed on her hips. "Oh, hell no, you won't."

"Why not?" he shot back. "You think you're less of a woman because I have the balls to pry off the choke hold you've wrapped around your throat. Shit, I'm nothin' compared to the noose you strangle yourself with. Your poor body's grateful for—*fuck that*—desperate for my commands and restraints. What you are is a little brat, not less of a woman."

Humiliation gurgled into a boil, but his reprimand flamed her nipples, raising them to diamond-hard peaks. He moved fast. Her vision spun as he whipped her flat on her back, knocking the wind out of her. Straddling her on the couch, his broad chest encompassed the whole of her world.

"There are no *shoulds* when it comes to desire. People read books or watch bullshit movies and think the magic between us is twisted or abusive. Hell, they can't begin to wrap their heads around the idea of a male submissive."

She punched his shoulder and teased, "Are you sure you aren't one of those? It would sure make my life easier."

A low growl emanated from him, and she clamped her lips together.

"You don't need a sub, you need a dominant, and if feminism is about freedom and power, then it includes getting your sweet ass spanked." The tenor of his voice dropped to a sexy growl. "And loving it." His fingers cupped her neck in a snug hold. "Your desire to please me runs deep. You can send all your time shaming yourself over it, but ain't nothin' about that gonna change."

She swallowed around the pressure, and he eased up around her throat. "Understand?"

She nodded.

"Now," he resumed, moving off her. "Back to the business at hand. In the world *we* create for ourselves, other males do not exist. Your attention must be trained on me. At all times. Me and only me because I won't guide you wrong."

The slivers of his eyes turned as sharp as the steep granite outcrops of the Gorges around Ithaca. "Greta, you have to trust me to know what's best for you. I've been doing this for a long time. Been in the life for a long time. I may be easy-going in everything else, but I take my job here seriously."

Cutter overturned the bags and shook them. Clothing poured out, and she caught glimpses of leather, of netting, of a Harley logo. She craned her neck to get a better look and poked at them with her toe. *Spandex? No fucking way.*

Greta slumped down into the cushions with crossed arms over her chest with a pout on her face. He tutted, and she immediately pushed herself up.

Gesturing grandly, he offered, "Choose what you want."

She licked her parched lips and gritted out, "Fuck this. I don't wear biker gear."

24

CUTTER

The she-devil said she doesn't wear biker gear.

Cutter stared up at the ceiling. Could he have found himself a better bitch to spar with? It was in her nature to struggle against him. His lips spread in a devilish grin. Fine by him. Lifting a pair of skintight leather pants and a slinky shirt, he thrust them toward her. "Wear these."

Holding them up with an outstretched arm, she scrutinized them as if they were filthy. The woman would soon *be* filthy if she didn't dial back the brattiness. She should be thankful he bought her a shirt with a bra inside, even if it might be practically see-through. Hell, he didn't do it for himself. He'd rather have her go braless, but he'd relented for her modesty.

Angie, a new hanger-on at the clubhouse, had been enlisted to help him choose Greta's clothing. She was into kink, and so, didn't require explanations. Fuck knows, he didn't focus on what women wore, but rather how fast to strip them out of it. Browsing through the lingerie section, he'd had no idea the choices vanilla females had to deal with. No wonder, they were confused. They were given too much freedom.

Greta fussed with the clothes. "Where are the panties?"

He gave her a belabored sigh and looked up at the ceiling. "Access, Greta, access."

Inspecting them critically, she said in a shaky, soft timbre, "You know my size."

He barked out a laugh. If she had any idea how much he knew about her, she'd run for the fucking hills. Tearing off the price tag, she shimmied into the leather pants and tugged on a shirt that left little to the imagination. His mouth watered at her tits, plump and firm, begging for him to suck through the stretched material showing off her large, firm nipples. They were already beaded tight from their earlier sparring. Saliva pooled in his mouth.

Pleased with her look, he laid back to enjoy the view. That was, until she donned a jacket that concealed her chest behind leather. His saliva dried up. God*damn*, they had just finished talking about this. Although her ass, in those tight pants, would be on display for anyone to see, she still felt the need to hide from him. The fact that the material was identical to his favorite crop did not lessen his ire. Struggling, she yanked at the two sides of the tight jacket, but they didn't join over her chest.

Realizing the futility, her eyes began to roll around her head, like a panicked horse.

Splaying his feet wide, he pointed to the floor. She collapsed and hid her face in her hands against his thigh. Her back racked with silent sobs.

His long fingers sifted through her hair. "Girlie, I know this is hard for you, but you can't keep hiding yourself. Especially from me. I won't have it."

"You want to degrade me," she mumbled from between her fingers. He grazed her cheek with his knuckles.

"You're a warrior princess. A badass bitch. You should be decked out in shiny black leather, wearing thigh-high spiked boots ready to kick some fucker's ass. Tits hanging out of a harness. Nipples jutting out, bold and proud, for men to drool over." His grin turned wolfish, but he spoke in an austere tone. "Hiding your assets is demeaning. It doesn't do you justice and it's a damn pain in my goddamn ass."

Greta swiped a forefinger under her nose and sniffed loudly, "Where do you come up with this stuff? Warrior princess, like Xena."

"Babe, you gotta rise up and take your place by my side," he warned her. "The bitches will tear you apart if you dress like a cross between a hippie and a damn librarian."

Greta growled low in her throat, and he smiled inwardly. She was a competitive, possessive little thing. Time to set her straight about his expectations. Again.

"Get used to the fact that I display what's mine. If I'm in the mood to have men panting after what's mine, wantin' to fuck my woman, then that's how it's gonna be. Don't you dare cover your fine ass with skirts dragging to the floor. No more. I'll tear them in half until they barely cover your pussy," he threatened. "You're under new ownership, baby."

"I'm not an old lady in your club. Anyone in the Squad can touch me, mistake me for a hanger-on, a new girl ready for anything and anyone. Or a seasoned biker bitch that likes getting touched or grabbed."

He snorted. As if he'd ever let that happen. For a brainy woman, she was fuckin' clueless. He chucked the bottom of her chin and promised softly, "How about we take it slow. We'll go to a club party for members only. It's the birthday of one of the kids. Rated PG. But, to make sure you understand your role...," he trailed off as he reached inside his cut and took out a fancy square box. Balancing it on his knee, he nodded, giving her permission to take it.

Reaching for it like a feral cat, she clutched it greedily to her chest. Slowly, she unclasped the lid and raised it.

"A collar," he stated.

He'd taken his time, searching until he found one with the right width and thickness, because the compulsion to attach a collar around her slim neck had been riding him hard for a while.

Clack. Her palm slammed down on the wooden lid. The sound echoed between them, like a crack across a cheek. He pried her fingers off the box and creaked it open. Eyes bulging, Greta fixated on the brushed silver metal.

"No, no, no," she pleaded as her head jerked from side to side.

Keeping his tone even, he said, "Chill out. Collaring a female is not something I take lightly."

It was a contract, as definite as slicing a cut for a blood pact. Sure, he'd collared women dozens of times. It was the way it went in his bed, but he had rules. For one thing, he never flaunted a woman wearing his choker. It wouldn't do to signal the brothers about ownership toward one particular bitch. Until Greta.

In an instant, she was up on her feet.

"Nope, nuh-uh, *no way*," she sputtered as she spun left and right, looking for a getaway route.

Before she made a move, he grabbed her by the hair. Struggling, she screeched loud enough to break glass, but, through a volley of shouts and curses, he hurled her face down onto his lap, her tits hanging over his thighs.

She reared up, but he laid a hard, staying hand on her lower back, until she collapsed. With her head down, her hair polishing the floor, the hellcat squirmed on his thighs. Which was doing little to help his raging, insatiable hard-on.

Cutter landed a smack on her rump. She took a swipe at him with her claws, but he grabbed a fistful of hair and pulled her head back. Neck arched; she hurled another ear-piercing scream.

Yep, her scalp was on fire.

"Every part of you is mine to do with as I please. You'll do as I say," he grated out. He ripped her pants off and walloped her butt cheeks like a battering ram. She writhed and bucked, but he kept his palm steady, lacerating her ass until it was nice and hot. To add an extra layer of awareness, he dragged his nails across one red cheek.

"You think a collar is a prison, but it's a safety net. It reminds you that I am your provider." He began to knead her abused flesh.

In a smooth, alluring tone, he murmured, "Don't I pleasure you, baby girl? Don't I make you scream when I have my mouth on you, tongue-fucking that sugar pussy of yours?"

"You know you do," she whimpered, wiping tears that tracked down her cheeks.

"Do you pleasure me?" he queried.

Her plump bottom lip pushed out. "I hope I do."

His cock, pointing north, dug into her belly and he made a grinding motion with his hips. "You damn well know you do."

He propped her up on his lap, callously scraping her bottom against the rough denim of his jeans, before maneuvering her until she straddled his waist. Couldn't wait to see the horizontal indentations of his jeans cutting across her rump.

Cupping her jaw, he continued, "You wear my collar long enough and it'll trigger muscle memory." He held up the choker and brushed it with his thumb. "It will strain the tendons of your neck, reminding you of who owns you. Wherever you're at, whatever you're doing, your attention will be on me. When someone compliments your necklace, it will be a compliment to your surrender to me. Make no mistake, brave girl, your surrender is the hottest fuckin' thing in my life. It brings me the deepest pleasure." In his throaty baritone he finished, "The pleasure of the man who owns you."

He purposely spoke of her as his plaything, weaving the language of dominance and submission between them. Spreading his thighs stretched open her heart-shaped ass and gave him access to massage to her pussy. He wet his fingers in her sweet cunt before moving between her buttocks.

Humming, he worked a digit between the clenching muscles of her tight hole.

"Cutter," she moaned, her forehead thumping against his chest. His name on her lips was like honey dripping on his cock, waiting for her to lick it off. A deep breath of satisfaction expanded his ribcage. Planting her hands on his chest, Greta bowed her spine back and rubbed her tits on his chest.

In a wobbly voice, she said, "These clothes will expose me. People will see my tattoo. They will know who I am. Where I came from." Her eyes dropped to his. "Don't you understand?"

Finally. He let out a breath. *Note to self: It takes a finger up her ass to get her to spit out her fears.* Her dark secret wasn't the sole reason behind her refusal, but it was a very real one. Deserving a small reward for her courage, he dipped his other hand between her quivering thighs and brushed the lips of her sex. As his fingertips continued to pet her, the gap of her thighs widened.

His balls grew heavy, but he took his time, flexing his fingers inside her pussy until her hips bucked and ground down on his hand. He gave her what she needed. Greta's head slumped on his shoulder, the pink ends of her tresses brushing against his chest.

"No one's going to see it," he assured her.

"They will if you parade me around half naked," she countered.

Damn, his bitch could wear a strong man down. He pulled slippery fingers out of her clenching pussy and gripped her chin.

"I'll allow you to cover the tat," he compromised. "But you'll wear the collar."

"The clothes are about the tat," she gritted out, "but the collar... Damn it to hell, I'm not wearing a collar like an animal."

"What's the difference between an animal and a pet? Because you *are* my pet," he growled possessively.

"Like hell I am," she snarled.

Before she could wiggle off, he threw her, belly-down, over his thighs. He didn't care how many times it took, but he *would* tame her in the end. "If you'd listen, I wouldn't have to do this. But you need more discipline, don't you?"

With perfect aim, his hand cracked against the bubble of her ass and left a white handprint. She propped one knee on the sofa, arched her back, spreading her pussy for him, and looked over her shoulder. Lust dominated her expression.

That was it. His cock needed in.

"On your fuckin' hands and knees. I'm going to give you the fuck of your life. After, you're still gonna wear the collar."

GRETA

The main reason Greta and Cutter decided to meet her mother and the Green Mountain Boys MC at Bike Week in New Hampshire was because it was safe. The Dark Horsemen avoided the state like the plague after a run-in with a local MC.

Rolling down the last stretch of highway, the mid-June heat warmed her shoulders and back. Meanwhile, chills ran down her arms, and her belly buzzed like a hive of wasps in anticipation of going to her first rally in years.

Cutter turned into the grounds, and she was graced with the sight of rows and rows of perfectly angled parked bikes. Flamboyant, ostentatious, shiny bikes. *Hell, yeah.* Nothing trumped the sparks reflecting off polished chrome on a line of bikes.

A motorcade of bikers, wearing helmets and sporting ink on exposed skin, roared by. The riot of colors displayed on their cuts and engines was a glorious show, indeed. Rounds of boisterous engines resounded in her ears and she almost let out a giggle, feeling the giddiness she felt as a kid going to rallies.

Rolling into a parking space, Cutter's eyes cut to hers. "You alright?"

In the midst of roars and rumbles, she flashed him a glowing smile. "I haven't been this relaxed in years."

Cutter cocked an eyebrow and corrected her, "Besides in my bed, you mean."

She playfully swung at him, but he caught her fist with ease.

"Show off," she grumbled, with a wide grin. Dragging her close by her fist, he took her jaw, and devoured her in a searing kiss. He tasted so good, musky with a hint of tobacco and mint. An audience of bikers cheered them on. Another thing she loved about any public gathering; bikers relished public displays of affection.

"Better believe I'm showing you off." Molding his palm between her thighs, he said, "By the end of the day, every biker up in here will know this pussy is mine."

Smacking his hand, Greta threw her head back and laughed. She couldn't remember she'd laughed so freely.

They roamed around, and Cutter bought her an ice cream. She licked it luxuriously, while giving him fuck-me heart eyes, until he pushed her against the side of a stand and kissed her soundly.

Finally, they made their way to the entrance, where they were meeting her mother. Seeing her, Greta swayed her hands above the throng of people. Dropping her cone, she forgot Cutter and swam through the crowd until she landed in her mother's arms. Ahhh, the familiar mommy scent wrapped around her like a cocoon. She draped her arms around her mother's worn leather jacket, fingertips brushing the patch with the words "Property of Trucker" printed on it.

Suddenly, she felt waves of heat roaring against her back.

Casting a worried look over her shoulder, she heard her mother mumble *yikes*.

Oopsy, she hadn't meant to stray.

"Greta," Cutter's low, growly tone vibrated above her head. Her mother's neck strained above her shoulder as she tried to pull away, but Greta clung to her. Her nerves were already strung tight from the imminent meeting between her mother and her man. Throw in one pissed-off biker and she was prepared to bury herself inside her mother's chest like a newborn babe.

She also needed an extra moment before introducing Cutter to her mother. Granted, he had the ability to charm anyone, but Marianne was no ordinary woman. She was First Lady of the Green Mountain Boys, and she didn't take any shit. Not anymore. Heart pumping, Greta dodged his gaze and cautiously stepped aside.

Fists clenched and expression stern, Cutter briskly tugged her to his side and slipped a finger under her choker. A pair of vivid green eyes, identical to hers, were trained on him.

Marianne asked, "Greta, are you going to introduce your man to us?"

"Yeah, sure...um..." She swallowed. "Mom, this is Cutter. Cutter, this is Marianne."

Cutter extended his hand and said, "Glad to meet you, ma'am."

An excruciatingly *looong* moment later, her mother broke into a wide grin and gave him a half hug. The sudden shift in Cutter's stance caused him to practically choke her. He instantly released her collar, and she rubbed the chafed spot on her neck while Marianne's arms wrapped around his burly torso. "I see you have my daughter well in hand."

"Mom!" she gasped.

"You told me you were coming to Bike Week for my birthday. You didn't tell me you were bringing along a man." Her gaze flicked to his cut. "And a brother at that. From the Demon Squad." She gave Greta the stink eye. "You've been holding out on me," she accused.

"It was supposed to be a surprise," she fibbed weakly.

Hands perched on her hips; her mother tapped her foot impatiently. Trucker came up and, assessing the situation, stepped in between mother and daughter. He jutted out his hand toward Cutter. "Trucker's the name. This sure is a special birthday present for Marianne. I can barely believe my eyes."

"Cutter," he responded curtly.

Shaking Trucker's hand with a hard grip, Greta barely contained an eye roll while the men went through the mandatory, macho hand-wrangling ritual. Because that was no simple handshake. Bikers. It wasn't even midday and she was already worn out from the testosterone.

Finally having reached some sort of truce, Trucker wrapped an arm around her mother's shoulder and said, "Marianne's my old lady. Greta here is the daughter of my heart."

"Really, Trucker, that is so cheesy," Greta said with a tiny sniff. His hand came out to ruffle her hair, but it didn't reach its destination. Cutter's hand stayed his wrist midair. Her breath stalled as the men stood there. Add another tense moment, and she was about to tell them to knock it off, when Trucker's hand returned to his side. Lucky for them, Trucker was as easy going as a biker could get. He only wiped his mouth to hide his grin. He was enjoying this, the bastard.

She checked on her mom and saw her mouth gaped open. *Just great.* Marianne's gaze found Greta's and stuck there, bleeding with questions. Oh boy, she was gonna get it. A massive inquisition was in her near future. Greta skewered Cutter, that asshole, with a mean look for his possessiveness moves. Cutter placed a finger under her mom's chin and gently closed it.

Now her own mouth dropped open. Greta's eyebrows hit her hairline. Trucker threw Cutter a warning look and Cutter lifted his hands in apology for touching another man's old lady.

With a chuckle, Cutter suggested, "Let's drink some beers and get to know each other. I know of a good place about five miles down the road. Called the Red Pool Ball. Has a shingle falling off to the side that says Open for Bikers Only."

"Yeah, I know it," replied Trucker. Her mother pecked her on the cheek before turning away and disappearing into a horde of bikers.

The instant they were gone, Greta shoved him in the chest. "You embarrassed me. I thought you were going to behave yourself and act like a gentleman. I'm going to get enough smack from her as it is. Your he-man act just tripled the amount of shit I'm going to get."

"Count yourself lucky that I'm so laid back and that I was the one to teach her old man who I am to you. Saved you a smacking for running away from me in a fucking crowd. We talked about the rules of engagement, and you already slipped up big time."

Color drained from her face. She had forgotten about him when she'd seen her mother and he was right, she shouldn't have run away from him. Not that she was about to admit any of that out loud.

Instead, she turned away from him and grumbled, "You and your damn ego. Always needs more stroking."

A hard swat to her butt made her jump. "Owww!" she cried out as she glared at him while rubbing her butt.

"You're lucky you even have a mother to bitch about. Keep

complainin' and you'll end up with stripes covering that sweet ass of yours," he lectured her.

Her heart cracked at his words. Especially, when he fixed a solid hold on her nape and drew her into him as he led her through the swarm of people to his bike.

26

GRETA

Trucker had somehow hustled a couple of bikers out of their table and was holding down the fort as Cutter and Greta entered the bar. Standing on a chair, he waved them over.

With an arm around her waist, Cutter plunged into the throng of people and carved a wide swath of space for them. Dread curdled in her belly because her mother's eyes sparked like a boxer sparring before his opponent entered the ring.

As usual, any discomfort in her life made her want to take a swing at Cutter. Eye twitching, she threw another death glare at him. She was close to spitting with fury, but he didn't so much as flinch when he caught her expression. Although, he got his point across when he gripped her shoulder and pressed her firmly into a chair. He wasn't going to tolerate any disrespect in front of her mother and step-father.

Cutter got her mom's and Trucker's drink orders but left without asking her what she preferred to drink. Pressure pulsed at her temples. He could've at least had the decency to at least *pretend* in front of her mother. Instead, he stroked her collar with a hot look and sauntered off without a word.

Her spine hit the chair. She crossed her arms over her chest and huffed out a curse, but sobered when she found her mom and Trucker leaning over the table with intent expressions on their faces. Sheesh, they might as well have been sitting on her lap.

"Do you know what I'm thinking Greta?" her mom questioned her. "Do you have any idea? Hmm?"

Nerves rattling like a cracked brake pad in a broke-down car. She slunk down into her chair and shrugged. "Dunno, but I see you're about to explode."

"Explode?"

Before her mother could begin her lecture, Greta cut her off, "I know, I know. I don't ever bring a guy around, and then I show up with a...a biker." Ducking her head, she picked at the lacquer flaking off the edge of the table.

Her mother placed her hand over Trucker's and said, "Babe, why don't you go help Cutter at the bar?"

Trucker dutifully got up and ruffled Greta's hair as he passed by, muttering about how he didn't care for bikers who didn't let a man touch his own daughter.

Once alone, her mother declared, "I never said that I didn't want you with a biker."

Greta shrugged. Her mom might be a strong woman, but sometimes she acted like she had Stockholm syndrome. Why else did her world still revolve around a club after what she'd been through with Scorpion?

"I figured you wouldn't want that future for me. Trucker's a gem, so of course you kept him around." She attacked the polish of the chipped table with her thumbnail. Waves of hair rained down around her face, but that didn't save her from her mother, who reached across the table and stroked the pink tip of an errant braid.

"Sweetie, I don't keep him around just because he's a good

man," she began with a light chuckle. "I've loved him for as long as I can remember. Even when I was firmly under your father's thumb, I noticed him. He always went out of his way to do something nice or sweet for me. It touched me. Every single time." Her mother's mouth softened with a nostalgic smile. "You know how he is. So gentle and loving."

The scraping fingernail stilled, and she leaned in to hear better over the din of the bar.

"Trucker and I got together long before we left. Yes, he plotted our escape and saved us, but I wouldn't have stayed with him if I didn't love him. It wasn't about the biker; it was about the *man*."

Her mother's eyes held hers, frank and steady.

"I suppose I came to my own conclusions," Greta acknowledged.

Her mother laid a comforting hand on top of hers and squeezed. "I figured it was best to leave the past alone, so I didn't bring it up. You hightailed it out of Vermont like a demon was up your ass, and you'd made the right move. College. Paralegal studies. A professional woman. You're a success, and I'm proud of you. Sure, you never brought a man around, but I took comfort in the fact that you had a social life. Trucker often shows me your Facebook page."

She choked and pounded on her chest as she wheezed. Curse Facebook! Thank goodness, her mother hadn't seen her other social media, where she posted more, *uh-hem*, risqué bondage pics.

A man at a table near them rose to his feet and bellowed to get the attention of a guy near the entrance. Greta flung a look over her shoulder at the same time as Cutter's head whipped around to check on her.

His gaze snapped around, taking in their surroundings, and then his attention turned toward the biker who yelled.

The brutal displeasure drawn on his face crossed over the ruckus of the bar and burned through the biker's drunken fog because he promptly shut his mouth and plunked down on his seat. Cutter stared right at her for a moment and must have decided that she was safe enough because the grooves around his mouth relaxed a little. He winked at her and then returned his attention back to getting the drinks.

"That's one mighty fine biker you have there," her mother noted approvingly. "Very protective."

Squinting through the dusky light, she scrutinized her mother's expression, then cocked her head in suspicion.

Her mother burst out, "What are you thinking? That I'd hate if you were with a biker? I love the life with all my heart. I wanted the same for you, but you deserved the freedom to follow your own path. I accepted that you wanted a normal, civilian life. Seems like I should have made myself clear."

"I did find my own path," Greta insisted. Her lips pursed and her forehead puckered. "At least, I thought I'd carved out my own path, but that path did *not* include a biker. Then, Sage had to come and fuck it all up. Hooking up with Kingdom. Dragging me to parties." She flung her arm out at the bar. "Look where it got me."

"I don't see anyone forcing you to do anything," her mother teased. "You were a tough little thing from the get-go. Had an emergency C-section because you had the umbilical cord twisted around your neck and feet. When the nurse held you in her arms, you belted out so loud it almost pierced my eardrums." Her mom gazed off into the distance. "If you're here with him, then this is where you want to be. Problems have a way of solving themselves. All that matters in the end, is what the two of you have together."

"Mom, I'm not saying that this is going to...last." Okay, that was a big, fat lie, but she was barely handling this conversation as it was.

"You're young. I was younger than you when I met Scorpion, and I was in far worse shape than you will ever be. One good thing came out of that hell and made up for it. You. Walking free on this earth, with your eyes wide open. You've seen the worst side of life, you survived, and it made you the strong woman you are today. I never thought you'd come back around to the life, but here you are. At a bike rally," she motioned to Cutter, "with him. It's proof that you've moved beyond the past."

Greta's eyebrows shot up. "Moved beyond the past?" she spluttered. "What the hell are you talking about? I mean, I know you're happy with Trucker, but be serious."

"I'm dead serious. Trucker was part of it, but I stayed on my terms. I carved out my place. With him. With the club. With myself. I've been praying for years that you'd come to terms with Scorpion."

Greta's lips curled back. "That's never going to happen. Hearing his name makes me want to vomit."

Her mother's head snapped back. "Greta!" Her eyes narrowed into slits. "Be sure you work out your issues," she nodded toward Cutter, "or they will come back and haunt you."

Her chest rose and fell quickly, and pain hammered her like a thunderclap. Suddenly, a hand was gripping her nape, tilting her over the back of the chair and Cutter's visage swam before her. Nostrils flaring, Cutter whirled her around so quickly it took her breath away. Hauling her to her feet, he attacked her mouth. Her brain shut down and she met him, thrust for thrust, twining strands of hair between her fists and clinging to him. Whoops and cheers broke out around them.

His hot breath blew across her cheek. "Can't leave you alone for a damn second."

Slipping a finger under the metal of her collar, he sat down, pulling her along with him. Her favorite IPA beer sat on the table before her. He hadn't asked her, but, turned out, he was paying attention.

"Drink up," he ordered. "I give your people half an hour. Then we go back to the motel. I don't know what the hell happened, but you can be sure that I'm gonna fuck the pain out of you."

27

GRETA

Greta loved spending time with her mother, but her nerves were legitimately fraying.

Although she hadn't verbalized her stress, Cutter noticed and decided it was time to return home. New Hampshire didn't mandate that bikers wear helmets, so Kingdom was on babysitting duty, making sure the brothers didn't get themselves killed. Greta would take over the office, giving Sage the chance to join Kingdom, who was about to lose his shit without her.

Cutter stopped at the motel's front desk to check out and waved her outside with an order to relax and soak in the sun. Lounging on a wooden Adirondack chair on the tiny motel lawn, Greta played with the buckle and metal rings on her thigh harness.

Face lifted toward the sun, she absorbed the warm rays and drifted into drowsy contentment. The night before, Cutter had given her a full-body massage before tucking her in early. Said he didn't want to overtax her. She'd grumbled a bit under her breath until he slipped in beside her, and she got to rub herself against his blissful nakedness. Exhausted, she fell asleep.

A soft smile played on her lips as a parade of bikers came up the road. Her one last chance to see them en masse. The bright sun shot into her eyes; pinpoints of colors dotted her vision as she squinted at a dark figure at the tail end of the group. He was dressed in black leather from head to toe. Strange gear for such a warm early summer day. His bike helmet, paired with sunglasses and a long, shaggy beard, hid his face.

But when his head swiveled in her direction, a blast of heat charged through Greta, leaving behind a cold, clammy sweat. The stance of his body. The way he rode his bike. They were too familiar. As he passed by, she recognized the braid of jet-black hair draped down the back of his cut. How could she forget? Underneath the balmy sunlight, an icy draft smacked her across the face.

Gripping the wooden arms of the chain, her breath stuttered.

Shadow.

She quickly scooted forward to get a better look, teetering on the edge of her seat. Blinking, she craned her neck, but he was already gone. As she scrambled to her feet, her calves scraped against the wooden slats of the chair and she tumbled back, landing heavily in the seat. Clutching her knees, she sat there, stunned.

No, no, no. Not possible.

Her breath sawed in and out of her lungs, and she screwed her eyes shut. A Dark Horseman would never show up here. Although the similarities were eerie, this man was larger and bulkier. Maybe it wasn't him? Maybe she was dreaming? Then again, Shadow would've changed from a sleek nineteen-year-old to a hardened thirty-year-old. Blood drained from her face as the spike of adrenaline rushing through her blood plummeted, leaving her feeling light-headed.

Think. Could it really be him? Scorpion was bold, but even he wouldn't dare push Shadow into enemy territory. Not his golden boy. Supposing Scorpion had a brother watching her, he wouldn't choose a man so easily identifiable because not only she, but her mother would recognize him immediately. There was also Trucker, his brothers, and the other club from Vermont that the Horsemen had beef with. There were tens of thousands of people at the rally. Someone tailing her would have to get close, and even if he continued to wear leather and sunglasses, he couldn't spend entire days and nights in a helmet. No matter how much he changed, no matter how much he disguised himself, the risk was too great. It couldn't be him. But the *braid.* How many bikers wore braids? She twisted her lips wryly. *Well, many, actually.*

Let's face facts, there was no way Shadow wanted her. If he was here, he was acting as a henchman for Scorpion. Hypothetically speaking, if it was Shadow, why now? Not only was she under the protection of the Squad, but Scorpion had chosen to leave her alone long ago. There was no good reason to approach her. In addition, why take the risk of antagonizing her mother, because if she got a whiff of the Dark Horsemen, she'd strike them down without mercy.

Just because a random biker reminds me of Shadow doesn't mean it's him. Her vision may have been impaired because she'd been far away. Maybe the sun was blinding her. It had been a split second, not long enough to confirm it was Shadow.

Greta cast her gaze up and nearly shrieked. Cutter was standing over her, brows knitted and pulled down.

A finger brushed down her cheek and tipped her chin up. "Something wrong, highness?"

Clasping his wrist, she stroked the pulse point. There was no way she was going to bring up Shadow, especially since she wasn't sure it was even him. Batting her eyelashes, she licked her lips and replied, "No, sir."

His pulse quickened, and a low warning growl originated from the back of his throat. The warm, languid sensation that always surrounded her when she was around Cutter returned and shook off her worries.

"Best behave yourself, or I'll get our room back and fuck you into oblivion. I'm not riding back to Poughkeepsie with a hard-on. You, riding with a burning ass and sore pussy behind me, would satisfy me, though. We clear, girl?"

She sprang out of her chair. He made to catch her, but she slipped past his outstretched fingers and dashed toward the bike. She was about to swing onto the seat when two solid arms wrapped around her and slammed her against an unyielding chest.

He breathed into her ear, "You can try to run from me, but I'll always catch you, babe. Never forget that."

GRETA

Greta's cell phone wouldn't stop ringing. Rolling over, she reached across the empty bed and checked her alarm clock. 1:54 a.m.

Fumbling with the phone in the pitch-black darkness of her bedroom, she managed to swipe it open, and croaked out a hello.

Sage's tense tone came through the speaker. "Cutter's been arrested."

She toppled over the edge of the bed and crashed to the floor, facedown.

What did she say? No, please, no.

Greta had sworn to herself that she'd never be on the receiving end of a call like this. Yet, here she was, thrown back into the same recurring nightmare. A flashback of Shadow's face, spotted purple and yellow with bruises, swam in front of her vision, blinding her with a surge of rage.

Her cell phone had flown off somewhere. Rubbing her throbbing nose, she wrestled out of the bundled bedsheets wrapped around her ankles and scrambled for the cell.

It was by her ear in time to catch the end of Sage's

sentence, "—brothers were celebrating. The ink hadn't even dried on the contract for the bar. A bunch of steroid-pumped college boys wanted to test their mettle against a crew of bikers. Toxic masculinity at its finest," she seethed.

He was supposed to be out of town, riding up to Canada. Wiping a sheen of sweat along her hairline with shaking fingers, she asked, "Is he okay?"

"Yes," came the reply.

A whoosh of relief swept through her, quickly followed by another burst of fury. "Seriously? Cutter got caught up in that kind of stupid, infantile shit?" It was unlike Cutter, but then again, he could be as ridiculous as any biker when it came to the pride of his club. "Where's Kingdom? He get arrested as well?"

There was a slight pause. "He was with me."

"Good to know someone was intelligent enough to stay in bed, instead of gallivanting around like an idiot and getting into pointless fights," she said bitterly.

"Sweetie don't do this. It could have happened to anyone. You know just as well as I do that if Cutter got involved, something must have gone wrong. He's not a hothead."

"He's not, but that doesn't mean he has the maturity to back down from a challenge, regardless of the consequences. He didn't need a college course to graduate from Hyper Male Posturing 101."

A weary sigh came through the phone. "I hear you. Listen, I've got more to do on this. They're staying overnight until I can get them out on bail tomorrow. At least they're together," she muttered. Shuffling of papers crinkled in the background. "They'll be arraigned and have a bond hearing in the morning. Will you be there?"

"Of course I'll be there. I need to make sure he gets out so I can kick his ass. I'll be wearing my sharpest stilettos for the occasion because if he thinks I'll put up with this, he's a pure-bred idiot," she raged.

THE INSTANT they'd stepped inside her house, Greta stepped into Cutter and wrapped her arms around his neck, breathing in the unique combination of leather and male. Specifically, the male who brought her to her knees with his scent alone. *Damn him for making her so weak.* This would have to last her a lifetime because she couldn't continue down this path. This path was littered with pain and heartache. It would end in agony. Last night's phone call and this morning's court hearing were proof of that.

She'd gone through this scenario one too many times and was well acquainted with the full extent of its misery. The waiting and fretting. The handwringing while waiting to see your loved ones. The last time Shadow was arrested, she'd made him promise that if they got together, they'd transfer to another club. Not only to get away from Scorpion, but also because she couldn't knowingly be part of a criminal enterprise that would drag the man she loved to jail or worse.

Although this arrest was over a simple bar fight, it was a harbinger of things to come. Hell, if he couldn't control himself over something silly, how was he going to survive something awful? She'd broken lots of promises to herself on behalf of Cutter and been okay with them.

Until now.

Cutter cradled her head in his hands, gazed into her eyes for a long moment, and kissed her forehead. "Babe, you were scared."

Scared didn't begin to express what she felt. Panic swelled around her throat like a steel band, cinching tighter and tighter, leaving her short of breath. He'd thrown her into a roiling whirlpool of dread and abandoned her to drown in it. She couldn't live through this craziness. Not again.

Stiffening, she pushed off him and stomped away.

Whipping around to face him, she snarled, "You're. A. Criminal."

His eyebrows slammed down; expression shuttered. "Watch it," he warned her.

Arms straight as planks, hands clenched to her sides, she forged on, "I know too much. I've seen too much." She smacked her thigh with a brutal slap. "It's etched on my damn body. And you fucking know it better than anyone. The second you put yourself in a position to get arrested, this relationship morphed into a situationship."

Acid flooded her tongue, but she continued. "Putting Scorpion aside," she slashed one hand in the air like a rapier, "I've attended funerals of fallen brothers. I've heard the whisperings about cigarette burns and saw bashed faces. These were men I loved, fathers and uncles who replaced Scorpion as my father figures. Dammit, I have PTSD over the lives that were lost over a fucking club. How can a sane man be loyal to a twisted organization that demands that they sacrifice life and limb? What happens the day you come home, your body bruised black and blue, your face unrecognizable?"

Cutter reached for her, but she motioned with her outstretched palm for him to stay put.

"How many brothers have been in jail for shit the club has done, Cutter?" she demanded.

His hand froze midair.

"A few," he answered in a careful monotone.

"How recently?"

"Besides Whistle? A brother in the Poughkeepsie chapter. For a nickel."

"A nickel. *Five years.* Five years of his life gone, rotting away in an overcrowded jail in the middle of fucking nowhere." She heaved out a long sigh. "Would you leave the Squad for me?"

"What? No! How could you ask some shit like that? It was a fucking fight, not a five-year prison sentence. You're overreacting," he said, his voice low and controlled.

"Do what you must for the Squad, but I won't be the one abandoned," she stabbed her finger toward him, "at your gravesite." Her voice cracked. "I've changed. My new normal is you, but you've dragged me back down to the gutter and I won't stay there. I can't."

Her throat clenched up, halting her rant, but it was the unvarnished truth. Born in the club-life, she knew the methods clubs used to earn a living, but he was hers as much as she was his, and he wasn't supposed to get harmed. Same as he demanded of her. Either way, she couldn't do this any longer. Her fears lashed her inside out, flaying her skin. Stampeding like panicked horses, tossing her among their kicking hooves like a rag doll. Shattering her.

Greta opened her mouth to continue, but he stymied her with a scathing expression. Heat flared up the back of her neck. Crossing his arms, he regarded her like a petulant child. Damn him for making her feel like she was being ridiculous.

"Calm the fuck down," he cautioned, his voice hard and dominant.

Her stomach pitched. If she got too bratty, she'd be over his knee in a heartbeat. And if that happened, she'd be lost. This clusterfuck required level headedness. Gritting her teeth, she dug deep to reclaim a modicum of self-restraint.

29

CUTTER

His sight zeroed in on her left thigh, the one marked with her Dark Horsemen's tattoo. He rammed his jaws together, the muscles ticking away.

She'll mourn me till the last, and she'll mourn me the most.

Cutter ached to turn away from the pain darkening her eyes. He hadn't considered what his life might mean to a woman. He hadn't expected to be with a woman, care for her, fall for her. Because, yes, he'd fallen for Greta. She was sexy and sassy, but oh so sweet when she melted in his arms and on her tongue. He didn't just own her. She owned him; she was the sole proprietor of his heart.

Greta's love was undying—unless he was harmed or died. Her flaming spirit would curl up into itself, leaving her to roam the world like a ghost. Tilting his head toward the ceiling, he stifled the roar building in the back of his throat.

"Look, I get it," he gritted out. "Shit got out of control when those pricks came looking for a fight. It shouldn't have gone down the way it did. I misjudged the situation, and by the time I got involved, the first punch had already been thrown. After that, it was a free-for-all."

"Wow. Over a barstool. I'm speechless," she said with derision.

Christ, Sage had spouted off that the fight started over a dumbass barstool.

"There were only three things I expected from you, Cutter. Don't fuck with my head, don't cheat on me, and don't get arrested. My rule used to be 'no bikers,' but I amended that for you, and look where that got me," she pleaded.

He threw up his hands. "I'm a real fucking biker. Bikers don't follow laws, and that can get us arrested. For fuck's sake, one of the founders was named Riker because he and Prez met in Rikers Island, the prison complex down in the city."

"You don't think I know what that is," she snapped. Yes, bikers get arrested. And hurt. And killed. That doesn't mean I have to stand around to watch that happen to the man I live and get my heart ripped out of me."

Fuck. She'd declared her love for him for the first time and the eyes to her soul were boarded up like an abandoned steel-mill town. He'd just gotten out of jail and was ready to blow a hole through a fucking cement wall. Normally, he scaled walls and landed smoothly on the other side, as agile as a cat. But he was filthy and tired. He hadn't expected a welcome-home party, but son of a bitch, he deserved a get-out-of-jail fuck. Instead, she retreated behind a blank wall without a foothold for him to mount.

He cracked his neck from side to side. It wouldn't be right to coerce her by fucking or dominating her, although he was jonesing to do both. At this point, his best bet was to step away. Give her time to calm down while he figured out how to avoid a repeat.

It was his responsibility to protect her properly, including blowback from the brothers and their antics. Damn, he was about to turn into Kingdom, constantly stressed out over

Sage's well-being. Thank fuck they were working hard to turn the Squad away from its more criminal activities. The final piece was about to fall into place with the boxing gym. Afterward, Kingdom would ensure that the remaining holdout of brothers flipped, and the club would be fully legit. Christ, nothing felt as urgent as it did now, but he wasn't gonna front and divulge anything to Greta until it was a done deal.

He approached her slowly, hands out, so as not to rattle her any further. "I'm gonna do right by you. I'll give you three days to settle your ass down. Then, we talk. I gave an oath to take care of you, and that's what I'll do."

Tension vibrated off her as she crossed her arms and tapped her foot. Lines of disapproval bracketed her pursed lips. Any other day, that attitude would have ended with her in restraints and a crop to her ass. Goddamn, did his fingers itch to reach for a paddle or anything to smack her tight ass.

He placed a finger on her lips as she was about to respond and cautioned her, "Hush, before your mouth gets you into trouble. Ya know, I could easily fuck you into submission, but I'm not going to do that. I want you clearheaded so you can think about what you want to do."

She'd admitted that she loved him. She was just scared and he'd give her a little time to calm down on her own. She'd come back around.

He traced the line of her cheekbone. She swiped at his touch, but he dropped his hand in time to avoid her nails. He'd have to start clipping them his damn self.

"This is a concession on my part," he stated. "I'm trusting you not to abuse it."

Cutter cupped her jaw. She recoiled slightly, but then raised her eyes to meet his. Pain was there. Fear, as well. Yet, she didn't shy away from him. Thank fuck, their connection was intact. They'd survive this and come out of it stronger.

"Three days," he repeated.

She turned away from him, staring at the far wall, and gave him a curt nod.

Good enough.

He rolled his shoulders, shrugging off the unease weighing them down. Without a last backward glance, he stepped across the threshold.

SHE'D GHOSTED HIM.

Cutter had blown up her phone, but two days later, still no word from Greta. The Fourth of July party at the club was poppin', but he ignored everyone as he combed through the clubhouse and raked through the crowds in the front and back yards. She was a no-show. Shit got real when your woman was a no show for the Squad's notorious Independence Day bash. He wouldn't have taken her for a runner. Red haze distorted his vision as his fingers balled up into fists, itching for a pound of her flesh.

He barely contained the fury poking at the surface of his mask when he cornered Sage by a table laden with food.

"What's with Greta?" he asked tightly.

Sage searched his expression, and being Sage, laid a gentle hand on his arm. Worry laced her tone. "Why? Has anything happened?"

"Nothing," he lied.

"Our client didn't show up at one of her designated meeting sites. She was distraught so I suggested she take time off and visit her mom." Pausing briefly, she went on. "You didn't know."

He felt like the wind was knocked out of him, like he'd been sucker punched in the gut. Finding out from another source that she'd gone out of town, without his permission, was a blow. The urge to jump on his Harley, track her down, and strap her over his bike to bring her back rode him hard. The arrest was raw, but he suspected that she got spooked for more than that reason alone.

Grabbing his nape, he rubbed a crick in his neck. "She seemed alright the last time we were together."

Not a total truth, but truth enough.

Canting her head to the side, Sage's gaze roved over his face. "I see."

Yeah, she wasn't buying his bullshit one bit. She looked around the party, her lips turned inward and pressed flat as she contemplated something.

Finally, she said, "Greta is one of a kind. I would say the same about Marianne. When I stayed with Marianne, I learned more about Greta than she ever revealed to me on her own. She's kept quiet about how far things have progressed between the two of you. I'm not sure if it's because she's ashamed about her sexual preferences or because you've burrowed in deeper than she's comfortable with."

Sage took his hand into her clasp. "But I will tell you this, Cutter. She has many reasons for being distrustful, reasons she likely never told you. She likes to keep things close to her chest, but bad things have happened to her, and your arrest triggered something from her past, I'm sure of it. Promise me that you'll be patient with her."

Sage's gaze cut to her left, and a blush bloomed across her cheeks. Cutter rotated in a semicircle to find Kingdom glaring at them from across the room. Sitting on a worn couch as if it were a throne, his eyes were glued on Cutter's hand, enveloped in Sage's.

Sage quickly released him, but Cutter called out exasperated, "For fuck's sake, we're just talking!"

Kingdom hollered back, "You're done talking."

His harsh gaze swept over Sage possessively, then he turned away to speak to Puck sitting beside him.

"The man is pussy-whipped," said Cutter.

"He may not be the only one," quipped Sage.

Cutter grunted, causing her to laugh.

She waved a delicate hand in the air. "Never mind. My point is that behind her perfect face and bitchy attitude, Greta is a sensitive soul," she said, defending her friend.

"Yeah, I got that," he rejoined.

"Perhaps, but I suspect there's more involved than you're aware of. You're a good man, Cutter, and you've changed in the past few months. Despite the posse of women who follow you like trained puppies, I believe in you. My advice is to tread carefully because she won't take to being controlled like the women you're used to hanging around you."

He nodded grimly, gritting his teeth. He knew she meant well, but he didn't take kindly to being lectured about his woman. Sage knew about Greta's kink, but she didn't know how things worked between them. Yet, he had to grin and bear it when it came to the vanilla.

Sage stepped away but turned back toward him for a moment. "Oh, and one last thing. If you hurt her, you're a dead man. If I don't kill you, Kingdom will. He may not show his feelings, but Greta has become like one of his own."

She gave him a quick peck on the cheek and joined Kingdom, who captured her roughly, hauled her onto his lap, and buried his muzzle into her throat. Cutter sighed. They had a ways to go before Greta was in such a familiar position with him, in public.

As bad as he wanted to run her down—and he *badly* wanted to—a man had his pride. Getting talked down to by Sage, even if she hadn't done it intentionally, hadn't helped.

Christ, he was a biker. He had an image to protect and it sure as fuck did not include roping in an old lady. While bitches dropped to their knees at his command, she'd betrayed his trust. It stung like hell, but he wasn't gonna let any bitch tear him down. She left him, like his momma had, so fuck her.

Bending over the bar top, he snatched the nearest bottle-neck. Without checking the label, he twisted off the cap, and tipped it to his mouth. Cheap vodka flooded his tongue. He almost spat it out but forced himself to swallow the liquor down his gullet.

Stalking through the crowd, he reached the dance area and snatched the closest female to him. She spun around and smashed into his chest. Fingers slapped away strands of sweat-plastered platinum-blond hair and revealed a pair of baby-blue eyes. Blinking up at him, a smile spread over her red-lacquered lips.

Angie. *Young, submissive* Angie. She'd do fine as a replacement. She was bent, like Greta, but not salty or defiant. His soul howled in rejection, but fuck if he cared. His soul is what got him into this fucking mess of a situation.

Angie was a biker bitch, through and through. She'd never stray from his word. Never contradict him. Never make him doubt her. Why? Because he was a biker, and she knew to respect that.

Digging into her narrow hips, he smashed his mouth down on hers.

30

GRETA

The verdant fields of the Green Mountains of Vermont were alive with the riotous colors of wildflowers, surrounded by dense evergreen trees. From her window seat on the Northeastern train, Greta watched the scenery pass her by, her heart thumping with pain as each mile whisked her farther away from Cutter.

She was wearing leather suspenders beneath her oversized, button-down, short-sleeve shirt, the kind that attached to a belt around her waist. Her bare nipples chafed against the leather, keeping them erect through the journey.

She had no idea how she was going to survive the aftermath of Cutter, but she wasn't going to watch helplessly while his life went down the drain. As silly as the bar fight may have seemed to him, his arrest had triggered fears deeply steeped in her past. Knowing the Squad's illegal dealings, it was only a matter of time before brothers showed up at the clubhouse beaten or dead. She couldn't handle that.

Thankfully, Trucker and the Green Mountain Boys had the wherewithal to stay clean. It had been a prerequisite to joining the secret network to help DV victims.

The train slowed down and eventually cranked to a halt with one last screech. Greta hauled her duffel bag over her shoulder and staggered down the metal steps, almost tripping over the strip of bumpy treads wrapped around the edge of the platform like a yellow ribbon. She quickly moved aside for the passengers behind her to disembark, dragged her bag over the wet pavement, and into the station. She plunked down on an ancient wooden bench and texted her mother that she'd arrived.

Moments later, Trucker breezed into the station, dressed in faded jeans and a tee topped off with his Green Mountain Boys MC cut.

Whimpering under her breath, she stood up and flew into his arms. He hugged her tight and kissed the crown of her head.

"Hey, kid," he murmured in her hair.

They stood in the middle of the near-empty station until Greta got her bearing.

Sneaking a hand up to dry her tears, she sniffed and said, "Geez, what took you so long? I've been waiting around for, like *hours*."

Chuckling, he checked the large circular clock above the ticket counter. "You haven't been waiting more than ten minutes."

"Sure, sure, easy for you to say, but it felt long to me," she argued.

Trucker pulled her in for one last hug, and said gruffly, "Good to see you, too, sweetheart."

Spotting the duffel bag on the floor by the bench, he lifted his chin. "Good thing I brought the truck. You do this shit on purpose. Bringing bags too heavy to strap onto a bike. Lucky I know your ways already."

She gave him a woeful smile. Yeah, no riding for her.

"You know me too well," she conceded.

Teasing was his way of commenting on her unspoken rule. A few days after they'd settled in this town after escaping Scorpion, Trucker asked her to hop on the back of his bike for a grocery run. Greta stood numbly, rooted to the ground. The only sound she heard was her pulse going *ba-boom, ba-boom, ba-boom.*

Edging away, she turned tail and took off. He raced after her, caught her and held her until she stopped struggling. In an incredulous tone, he asked if she was afraid of riding. Incredulous, because no one loved riding more than she did. With the Horsemen, she'd constantly pestered the brothers to take her on rides. It got so bad that Scorpion had to intervene. Her father propped her up on his bike, slid in behind her, and taught her to ride himself. He refused to have her wear a helmet because, as he once told her, he'd never let her come to harm. Not on his bike. Not on his watch.

Greta took to it immediately. Their mutual love of riding was one of the few things they'd shared in common.

"Anyway, I'm not a kid anymore," she defended with a sniff. "A woman has needs to blow dry her hair. Do you think this hair," she held up her tresses for his inspection, "does itself? Yeah, no. So, I'm not putting a helmet on my head and ruining hours of hard work to get on some bike."

To fit in with the natives, she'd teased her hair within an inch of its life. After learning that Shadow never loved her, Greta stopped fixing up her hair. She took to dying it instead, hoping she wouldn't recognize herself anymore. *Yeah, good luck with that.* The tat stamped on her leg, like a branded heifer, proved that she'd always be owned by the devil himself.

Great settled into the cab of the truck when Trucker's quiet timbre interrupted her stroll down memory hell. "What you been up to?"

Greta dipped her chin and hunched her shoulders forward. "Nothing much. You know, the usual," she lied.

Trucker didn't respond, but the silence that settled between them gave her solace. Trucker had always taken her as she was.

The engine of his truck was almost as loud as the pipes of his bike, so by the time they reached the cabin, her mother and several brothers were waiting outside. Around these parts, the MC was as respected as the famous American Revolution patriot militia they were named after.

Jumping out of the truck, she was greeted with hugs and whatups. Her mother elbowed her way through the men and bitches who'd circled around her until she was on top of Greta.

Grabbing her, she snuggled into her mom's chest and confided, "It's good to be here, mama."

Taking hold of her shoulders, she pivoted Greta toward the entry of the cabin, hollering over her shoulder, "For Pete's sake, don't stand around like lumps of wood. Get Greta's bag already!"

The aching tension banded around her heart like a belt eased.

With a shrug, Marianne quipped, "What else are they good for? With the amount of time they spend here, I should be charging rent. Only time they go down to the clubhouse is for business and women. Time they earn their keep."

The sun began its descent behind the mountaintop, dimming the light of day, and darkness fell like a swath of curtain. Once inside, her mother unburdened her of her jacket and marched her into the kitchen. Her domain.

Hands on her hips, she scanned Greta with a critical eye.

Greta spun away, suddenly hot under the collar, and chided, "Mom, stop staring at me."

One of the prospects popped his head through the swinging door of the kitchen. "Where do you want Greta's bag? It's heavy as hell."

Greta blew out a quick breath of reprieve from her mother's attention.

"Upstairs!" her mother directed.

The door swung on its hinges behind him as he called out, "Alright, you don't gotta shout!"

Marianne yelled out in response, "If I don't shout, you don't hear me."

A moment later, another familiar voice came from the doorway. "Hiya."

It was Bolt, a brother about her age. He stood with his hand wrapped around the molding of the door, his eyes drinking her in with greed.

"Get out of here, you," said her mom with a wave of her hand. "Track her down later. This is mother-daughter time."

He opened his mouth as if to say something, but Greta's mother pointed to the door and cried, "Out!"

He raised his hands in surrender. "You don't need to bust a man's eardrums."

Undaunted, her mother raised a spatula and waved it at him. "This one's metal and it'll sting like hell, so don't make me use it."

Greta slapped her hand over her mouth, but he heard her laugh anyway.

Throwing her a cocky smile and a wink, he said, "Check you later, babe."

A chuckle rolled out of her. Man, she hadn't laughed since the arrest.

Sobering, she responded, "Yeah, for sure."

"You're done flirtin' with my daughter. Now, out," her mother griped.

GRETA

Greta stared at her mother wielding the spoon in her hand. To think this was the same woman she once found buried under blankets, hiding from Scorpion. Here, she was a queen. Although she may not be the oldest of the old ladies, she was by far the mightiest. She had years of silence to make up for.

She lost her smile when her mother reached over and swiped a thumb over the circles under Greta's eyes and observed, "You're tired."

Greta tore herself away gently, and said, "We've had an uptick in clients, and we've begun working on DV cases. A client vanished on us. It's been rough."

"You mean the domestic violence cases. You don't need to sanitize it with an abbreviation. It is what it is," her mother replied casually.

Lines of tension slid off her mother's forehead. At the sideboard, she lifted tops off plates of food. Plucking out a few pancakes, she added different toppings and smothered them with maple syrup, the way Greta liked it.

She deposited the loaded plate in front of her, but Greta

stared down on them, remembering the last time she had pancakes with Cutter. Her heart pounded a dull ache in her chest.

Her mother prodded her with an elbow. "Eat. You look like you've been eating about as well as you've been sleeping."

Flashing her a gentle smile, Greta said, "Thanks."

Removing her apron, her mom hung it on a hook near the sink and sat down. Greta sank her teeth into the spongy pancake and the burst of blueberries in her mouth was divine.

Between munches, she complemented, "So good."

Relaxing back into her chair, Marianne beamed down at her. Trucker waltzed into the kitchen for a refill of coffee and kissed her mother on the cheek. Greta paused midchew, and her throat closed up. Trucker treated her like gold. The same as Cutter, except he added a dollop of discipline to the mix. Swallowing the lump of food halfway down her constricting throat, she clasped the glass of orange juice and guzzled until the obstruction was cleared.

On his way out, Trucker ruffled her hair. All she could do was nod in return.

Wearily, she said, "I love that guy, even if he is a biker."

"I love him too, and being a biker doesn't factor into it." Her mother gave her a pointed look. "I don't hold fear in my heart anymore, so I'm not prejudiced."

"There's a lower percentage of good men in MCs," Greta claimed.

"Three women became old ladies in the past year, and their men are loyal to them," countered her mother.

Looking down at her favorite meal, she stabbed her fork into the top pancake and forced another mouthful between her teeth. "I doubt it."

"Hold your tongue, young lady," her mother warned in a tone brooking no backtalk.

Greta coughed up a chunk of food. Grabbing a paper napkin from the table, she spit it out.

"You're making judgments about couples you haven't seen together," her mother continued. "I taught you better than that. What about Sage and Kingdom?"

Her shoulders drooped, and she pulled her chest inward. Apparently, Marianne wasn't pulling any punches today. Greta tossed the napkin down and slapped her hands on the tabletop.

"You saw what Sage went through," she seethed.

"What I saw was a woman in love. What I saw was a woman processing her pain. What I saw was a woman deciding her man was worth the work. The choice was hers. Only hers."

"How could you want that for her after what he did? Sage was a broken woman. After everything you've been through, you seriously wanted Sage to go back to that cheating bastard?"

"She healed. They love each other," she argued. "And he didn't cheat on her. That bitch tried to twist the truth to break them up and it almost worked."

Trembling, Greta grasped her silverware and blindly cut into the pancakes. "He didn't deserve her. He got a second chance, but he didn't deserve it."

"Why? Because he's a biker?" her mother rebutted. "Not that your opinion counts. Kingdom cares for her. He fell for her and freaked out when she disappeared. He got scared off, like you, right now, but he quickly learned that he'd acted like an idiot and he repented."

Greta's fingers flexed around her fork and knife. She was going to throttle her mother. Between clenched jaws, she replied, "I am not running from anyone."

"You sure about that? I didn't think my daughter would scare so easily."

Drawing herself up, Greta threw her shoulders back and glared at her mother.

Marianne rose from her seat and said, "I'm going to leave you and check in on our guest. Yes, we have someone here. Get off the pity-pot because she's staying for a few days, and I don't want her getting spooked. She's scared enough as it is. You remember that, don't you? Having life-and-death problems?"

Oof. That was a hit to the chest. The swishing of the swinging door brought Greta halfway out of her seat, ready to grab her bags and leave. Sometimes, she hated her mother. Seriously. Hated. Her. She was shoving the chair back with a screech when Tack, Trucker's nephew, sauntered in.

Seeing her, he swept her into a bear hug. "Hey, how's my favorite girl doin'?"

Swallowed up in his bulging arms, Greta dug her nails into his wide chest, unshed tears stinging her eyelids like fire. She sucked in a breath; the scent of leather and motor oil coiled in her nostrils.

She grabbed the man bun knotted at the crown of his head and shook it. "Just because you happen to be Trucker's nephew does not make you family. Now that your dad retired and made you president, you're getting too big for your britches."

His guffaw riffled through her hair. "My pops is Trucker's brother and Trucker's married to your moms so I'd say we are, little cousin."

"Hmph. Don't get fooled by a marriage certified by some two-bit clerk in a two-bit town," she joked.

He tossed back his head with an unfettered laugh, and she trembled at the reminder of another man who laughed so freely. Holding her by the waist, Tack pulled out a chair and sat her down over his thighs. The long metal keychain hanging off his jeans chimed against the leg of the chair.

Patting his cut, she relented and asked, "How's it going? How are you? How's the shop?"

"It's going. Can't complain. Winter's the slowest season, spring was better, and with summer comes more business. Shit's lookin' up, woman."

"Mom told me there's a new batch of old ladies. Were you behind that little development? I know how sneaky you are beneath all that biker gear you wear," she teased.

"Nope, I ain't that smart. But I will tell you that my men are happier. One went through a bad accident and he met his girl in a rehab center. Came back a whole new man with a bride in tow."

Brushing back wisps of hair from her brow, he inquired, "How's your man?"

"Meh," she said with a shrug.

"Ya know, if you weren't family, you'd have stolen my heart." She laughed as she shoved him. He broke into another easy grin and went on, "Smiling looks good on you. You hate dirty bikers like me, so I've got no chance with you, Ms. Thang."

Squeezing him tightly, she replied, "No, I don't, Tack."

"Sure, you do. I'm okay with it, little cousin, but it's not good for you. Hatin' on your own people."

Her voice came out strangled, "I love you. I love the brothers. How could you doubt me?"

He pulled her against his chest and clucked, "Don't worry, babe. I know you have your reasons. It's too bad is all, 'cause love it or hate it, we're family. We love you no matter what you do, and we don't need you lovin' us back. That ain't how love works."

Greta's nose stung and began to run. Sniffling, she uttered, "I don't hate you, Tack."

Pain was tearing at her heart, ripping off pieces like a cannibal gnashing into thick slabs of flesh. Loving Cutter, leaving him, running to her mom, and then getting this undeserved love from a Green Mountain Boy was more than she could handle.

Rocking her, he reassured her, "Try your damnedest, but you don't have that much hate in you. You're hurting is all. My bets are on you, babe, because Scorpion didn't break you. After that bastard, you can survive anything."

She threw her hands up to hide her face and broke into sobs.

"Hush there, what happened to my strong girl?" he crooned.

Shaking her head, she couldn't stop crying. His body tensed under her.

Pulling her hands away, he lifted her chin up until they were eye to eye. "He hurt you?"

"No, nothing like that," she hurried to answer through her tears.

"Then why do you look like it's the end of the world?" he asked, his tone gentle.

"I fell for him, and he's a biker!" she wailed out.

He eased her head back down and nestled it against his beating heart. "Yep...I know, that's like the end of the world to you."

32

CUTTER

Cutter's nose tickled from the dust motes spinning in the air as he sauntered into Prez's old office. Back from chemo and radiation, Prez was too tired most days to move off the couch on the main floor. That was his new office. However, privacy was needed for the next step in Cutter's plan so he asked Prez to meet in his office.

Hey, if he couldn't get his shit together with Greta, at least he could fix his club. Time to get to the bottom of the Loki situation. Figure out where his head was at and lock him down. His gaze moved to the man in question, who hung back against the wall like a caged wild animal.

Kingdom came in behind Cutter. Glancing over his shoulder, he registered Kingdom's hard eyes and tight mouth.

As they took positions around the room, Prez locked the door and pocketed the key. No one was leaving until he was done. The tension in the room was as deafening as a jackhammer on a construction site.

Prez stalked behind the desk and, bending over it, placed his knuckles on top.

Cutter braced himself on the edge of Prez's desk,

crossed his legs at his ankles, and cut through the bull-shit by addressing Loki, "The four of us are the core of the Demon Squad. We'll either make or break this club. We care too damn much and worked too damn hard to let it go to hell so we want to know, where do you stand, Loki?"

"Worked too damn hard? Hell, since when have you worked for shit?" retorted Loki.

Cutter ground down on his molars. He held his hands behind his back, gripping his left wrist, and argued, "I'm workin' for it now."

"Maybe, but that doesn't mean you've got what it takes to bring this club together. Brothers aren't gonna follow you just 'cause you want it to be so. Didn't know you had ambitions, but you're not using me as a guinea pig to show Prez you've got what it takes."

"I get that you're defensive, but this meeting ain't about me," he shot back. Cutter forced a smile and fought to contain his frustration and not curse Loki the fuck out.

"The fuck it isn't," Loki challenged. "Don't know where you get the right to drag me in here and confront me like this, Cutter. You want a kumbaya moment between me and King-dom, but you don't have what it takes to get anything serious done for the Squad so fuck you."

Cutter dropped his smile. Fuckin' Loki, always a pain in his ass. Kingdom and Prez remained silent, curiosity gleaming in their eyes as they studied him.

"Fair enough," he conceded. "I haven't worked hard for the club until recently, but it's only the beginning."

"Fuckin' understatement of the year," Loki rumbled.

"Give me a fuckin break, Loki," he snapped.

"There isn't a break to give you. Prez is out, and we gotta drag our heads out of our asses. You wanna man up, but your track record is shit, unless you count the number of bitches you've tapped," Loki replied with a snicker.

Cutter clenched the wrist of his fist tightly behind his back. "I'm in this till I die, don't you ever doubt that, *brother*. We'll crash if we don't strengthen our loyalty to each other, and I can't stand by and allow that to happen."

"You talk a good game now about loyalty, but when was the last time you've proven yourself to the club," he taunted. "You've never committed to more than a bitch for one night."

That was a fuckin' lie. He'd committed himself to Greta, but he couldn't bring that up after she'd abandoned him, like his mother did. His mom might not have abandoned him physically, but she was too wrapped up in Tommy to pay much attention to him.

"'What ifs' aren't helping," Cutter continued with bared teeth. "The past is dead. Move the fuck on. I know I have. And the biggest barrier to our future is you, not me." Loki bared his teeth. Christ, the brother was as prickly as Greta. "You and Kingdom, that is. I showed initiative setting up this meeting. What do you bring to the table?"

The question hung in the air, whirling above them like a buzzing drone.

Sitting, Prez tapped a pen on his desk, and said, "Fair's fucking fair, Loki. What do you have to say?"

"You questioning my loyalty?" he demanded, his tone dangerous.

Prez clucked his tongue. "Stop shootin' from the hip, son. You're smarter than that."

Loki took them in, one by one, his gaze sharp and suspicious. "I'm loyal."

Cutter gave a snort. "If by loyal you mean you're not strangling the life out of Kingdom, then, yeah, it's an improvement. You gotta do better, bro."

A growl boomed from Loki's chest. Cutter harrumphed. Prez slashed his hand to shut him up. Locking in on Loki, he asked, "What's gonna make this right?"

"Nothing can change the fact that Kingdom failed in his duty to protect Chopper," Loki spat out.

Kingdom hissed.

Loki was dragging up the past by blaming Kingdom for Chopper's suicide. It had taken Kingdom a year of hell, and falling for Sage, to dig himself out of guilt and grief. But if they were going to move forward, together as band of brothers, then this had to be dealt with once and for all.

"Chopper had PTSD. No one could've saved him," stated Prez. "Thought the last fight you had with Kingdom settled that shit."

"It squashed enough to breathe the same air as him," clarified Loki.

"But not enough to show up for the Squad completely," finished Cutter. "Christ, you say I don't have what it takes but look at you. Callin' the kettle black, much? You've got to lance the boil of poison destroying you, brother. The Squad aside, you can't continue like this."

Mutiny weighed down the corners of Loki's lips. "You think you can fuckin' fix me with an exorcism?" he barked, eyes crackling like a blitz.

"It's about Sage, too," Kingdom pronounced, glaring at Loki.

Loki shifted on the balls of his feet, like a kid about to piss his pants.

Cutter's head snapped up and he fixed an incredulous stare on Loki. "Hot damn. Is it *still* about Sage?"

Loki had hit on Sage a while back, but everyone assumed his only reason was to get to Kingdom. What in the actual fuck? Was Loki legit jealous? *Bitches, man, the bane of a man's existence.*

"Like hell it is," Loki denied, vehemently. He reared back as if he was about to spring on Kingdom, when Prez, with surprising alacrity, stepped into his path and bumped chests with him.

"Settle down. It don't mean you're in love with Sage," he announced.

"But, you were," Cutter pushed. Prez gave him a scathing look, but he wasn't gonna back down. "This shit has to be dealt with. He'll continue to resent Kingdom, and it will destroy us."

"I will resent him till my dying breath," Loki confessed.

Cutter threw up his hands. "For fuck's sake, we're at an impasse, then."

His gaze flicked to Prez. "Do we gotta choose between them?"

Loki made a move toward the door, but Prez planted a hand on his chest. "No. Loki ain't going anywhere. I wouldn't have him here unless I believed in him. Loki, what do you say?"

Eyes lifting and locking on Kingdom, Loki said, "We have a long history, you and me. Last time we had it out, I gave you my word I wouldn't hurt you or your woman, and I haven't. I'm not a fuckin' animal, for Christ's sake."

"True," Kingdom confirmed. "You've backed off, like you said you would."

Prez scrutinized them both, and then asked, "We good, then?"

Cutter waved his hand in front of Prez, as if he were blind. Normally he didn't show any disrespect, but there was no way a "we good" was satisfying enough. "No, we ain't good," he jeered.

"Will you stop trying to wring blood out of a stone?" accused Prez. "Loki's not going to change, and if he does, it sure won't be because of us. What do you want, a group hug? Want us to swap tampons while we're at it?"

"I'm not gonna let his envy come back to bite us in the ass," Cutter fired back. He squinted at Loki, searching for a sign that he wasn't on the up-and-up, but as usual, the bastard was stoic as fuck. "Kingdom, back me up on this."

Kingdom scrubbed his chin, his eyes locked on Loki. Loki stiffened further but maintained his gaze. They stared at each other in a way they hadn't done in a long time.

Finally, Kingdom said, "He belongs with us."

Cutter spoke cautiously, "You sure? Because Prez kept the peace, but once you're on top, there won't be a buffer."

"You said you could handle anything, Peacemaker," Loki said drolly. "Won't you keep the peace between us?"

"Not likely," Cutter scoffed. "I might be a peacemaker, but I'm not miracle worker."

"Loki's one of us," Kingdom cut in. "He's a man of his word and he hasn't strayed once."

Personally, he'd kill any man who touched Greta, but who was he to contradict Kingdom? The brother was no fool; he'd worked through every angle before making his final decision. Loki hadn't been with a bitch since Chopper died. Lived like a monk, and Cutter didn't see that changing anytime soon, so he supposed that was why Kingdom wasn't worried about Loki moving in on his woman.

Prez grabbed Loki's hand and placed it on top of Kingdom's, holding them both in his large fist.

"This is a blood pact. The sacrificial blood being mine 'cause I ain't long for this world. At least I'll leave knowing I took care of the Squad's future, but if you fuck up, I will rise up from my fucking grave to hunt you down and kill you fuckers with my bare hands." Grinning like a loon, he clapped them both on the shoulders and said convivially, "Let's go. Time to get drunk."

The men followed their leader out the door.

Halfway down the corridor, Loki slowed his step and seized Cutter's arm, holding him back. "You're gonna be vice president."

"The hell I am," Cutter sputtered.

"That's my condition," he pronounced.

Cutter bit back a slew of curses. Loki had the upper hand, and they both knew it. "Back there, didn't sound like you had faith in my abilities. Why you pushing me for the position?"

"'Cause, I said so. I'll protect him with my life, but I'm not babysitting his ass. That's gonna be your fucking job."

"Babysitting him? He's the most capable brother I know."

"He's not going to have time to fight every fight. I'll keep him alive. Sage will keep him human. You keep him free to take care of the big picture," Loki elucidated, revealing his reasoning.

Cutter groaned. Just the thought of overseeing the nitty-gritty details of the club, day in and day-fucking-out, was a close second to having his fingernails yanked off one by one. "Changing your tune, huh? You want Sage to support King-dom, but last year you were running her down."

"I'm leaving her alone for the good of the club. We'll be crushed with responsibilities and I'm not letting you off the hook, *brother*."

"You're a miserable cocksucker," he complained.

"I don't give two fucks what you think about me. You're the one wanting us to play nice together, so it's on you to ensure it sticks."

Cutter's hands flew up and shoved Loki against the wall of

the corridor. Hearing a loud thud, Prez and Kingdom glanced over their shoulders.

"Playing nice, boys?" asked Kingdom with a smirk.

"Fuckin' hell," he gritted through his teeth. Loki straightened up, swept Cutter's hands off his cut and flashed his teeth. "No backsliding or slacking, either. Otherwise, I'll gut him myself."

The glint in his eyes revealed how much he was enjoying himself. Making a point in that asshole way of his. Loki's smug expression set his teeth on edge. Cutter would figure out a way to get out of it.

"Message received, you extorting motherfucker," he snapped, "but don't make a habit of threatening me."

"Don't make me have to," Loki shot back.

Loki bumped his shoulder as he moved past him. Cutter's hands twitched at his sides, itching to handle a leash. Greta's leash to be exact. He could almost feel the smooth leather in the palm of his hand, almost hear the *clink clink clink* of the swinging chain. A shot of yearning struck him in the middle of his chest.

If he had Greta, he'd be speed-dialing her right the fuck now. Ordering her to go home, strip, and play with herself until her cunt was primed and ready for him. Torturing her clit for hours would've been a perfect outlet. He'd take his teeth to it and keep her to edge before pushing her over.

Eyeing the erection straining against his jeans, he fell back on the wall, the sound of plaster cracking behind him. Of all the fucking days to miss her, this had to be the worst.

33

CUTTER

Cutter swallowed the black and tan, the dark malt sliding down his throat with thick smoothness.

He lightly squeezed Angie's hip. A faint whistle called to him, from behind the bar. Semi, who was tending bar, slanted his head toward the clubhouse door, and Cutter swiveled around to get check out what he was referring to.

His fingers stiffened around his frosted pint glass.

Greta stood in the doorway, arms crossed, eyes shadowed. Her defiant stance both challenged and aroused him in turn. A faint smile played on his lips. She was upset because he was with another woman. Fuck yeah, she deserved it.

Angie had noticed Greta, but being a good bitch, didn't question him. Didn't even sneak a peek his way, unlike the woman who was casting him the evil eye from across the room.

He nudged Angie off his lap and took his sweet old time sauntering over to her. He rolled his shoulders and stretched his neck from side to side, preparing himself for whatever bullshit she came to throw down.

Easy. Cool. Controlled. Outwardly, he was cool, but inside, his nerves crackled like a wildfire. As he got closer to her, he sucked in a quick breath. Goddammit, she was as stunning as ever. Her damp raven locks were tousled from the wet wind outside. Her pupils were dilated, dancing with emerald flames. Her lips were moist and red, as if she'd just bitten them. And the sweet scent wafting off her...*Christfuck*. Fucking mouthwatering memories of going down on her pelted him like hail.

As she clutched her arms, the sleeves of her raincoat fell and revealed the oxblood leather bracelet with buckles that he'd given her. She wasn't aware, but that choice signaled that she was his. Always and forever his. Fuck, his dick was blowing up in his jeans.

Leaning against the door jamb in a lazy pose, he inquired, "Whattup?"

Her mulish expression didn't change, although the pulse along her delicate neck buzzed away like a coil tattoo machine. As sexy as she was, she was trippin' if she thought she could show up whenever she felt like it and give him grief. Arrest or not, he'd *trusted* her. He didn't trust just anyone, and especially not a female, but he'd given it to her and she'd failed him.

"What's up?" she ground out. "You're asking me what's up? You haven't responded to my texts and I come here to find a bitch on your lap."

Sure, he'd gotten the texts, the ones about *having a talk*. His answer to that was a silent *hell motherfucking no*. She ran out on him, torqueing his heart and grinding it into the dirt. Pulling a cigarette from behind his ear, he tapped it against the heel of his palm. A cocky smile appeared on his lips, and he ruefully shook his head.

"You're smiling. You think this is funny?"

His smirk vanished. "Watch the salt in your tone."

"I came here alone, and believe me that wasn't easy, because I was terrified that something happened to you. Look, Cutter, I got spooked and needed time to work through my feelings. See," she poked him in the chest, "this is the reason we broke up."

He stiffened. Fucking hell, the nerve of her to blame *him*.

"I don't owe you fuck-all. You didn't show me the same courtesy the day you ghosted me. If you had told me you needed space, I would've given it to you. As for coming here alone, don't throw that in my face. None of the brothers would've hassled you," he said.

"This isn't my club." She lifted her chin. "I came here alone, looking for you."

It was true that in the club she came from, an unaccompanied female was open hunting season. Although brothers wouldn't hound her, in their eyes, she was just another woman he'd thrown to the curb and they wouldn't think twice about steppin' to her. Crinkled paper dug into his palm. He opened his hand to find his cigarette crushed with tobacco strands clinging to the sweat of his skin. As much as they may be hatin' on each other, nothing came between him and her security.

Wiping his hands clean, he said, "Why are you here, Greta? You made your position loud and fucking clear. No *criminal* bikers."

She remained silent, staring over his shoulder, most likely on Angie.

"No answer? Alright, then. You came. You saw. Since you didn't get my message, here it is. I'm alive, I've moved the fuck on, and I'm not your booty call."

"Excuse me?" she sputtered.

"I'm done serving my balls on a platter to you. You're the woman I wanted. I motherfucking *owned* you, feel me? I could've pressured you to submit, but I left the decision in your hands. You made your choice, and that choice wasn't me."

"I'm not your chattel," she sneered.

"And that there's your problem. When I say I owned you, you damn well know what I mean. I would've taken care of you in every way. Protected you, cared for you, slapped you the way you liked, fucked you the way you craved. But you, sweetheart," he tapped a finger to her cheek, "you don't get to fuck with me."

Her expression crumbled. Caving into herself, she stooped over, and clutched her belly. He yearned to reach for her, but he held himself back with clenched fists. He refused to be made a fool of himself over this chick yet again.

"I wanted to be out of the club world. I wanted to be strong and independent, to be equal to my man, but I fell in love with you and did everything in my power to make it work. I thought I was as important to you as the club, but you proved me wrong," she finished with a crack in her voice.

Normally, that would have hobbled him, but he couldn't forget how she'd tossed him aside at the first sign of trouble. "Bullshit. I made *one* mistake, and I promised it would never happen again."

"You've certainly gotten back on your feet," she scoffed, eyes fixated on something beyond him.

Cutter slanted his head over his shoulder and caught sight of what she was looking at. Or rather who. "Jealous?"

Her gaze lashed his, fury snapping like hissing cobras in her eyes. Her jealousy ignited his own spark of anger. This whole fucking mess was on her. *Her.* Yeah, he'd fucked up and had gotten arrested, but he was ready to fix that.

"Tell me, Cutter, how long did it take you to sub me out?" she asked, tone laced with pain.

"Not long," he countered, briskly. He was being hard, but he'd been soft and that had gotten him nowhere. He wasn't about to be a doormat for her. "You got somethin' to say, then say it. I'm all ears, but careful how you speak, 'cause you're the one who took off."

"I see, you're putting this all on me, then. Nothing on your part," she said tersely.

His blood boiled over into a torrid whirlpool. Wrenching her arm, he dragged her until they were inches apart, and growled, "I was willing to do whatever it took to make this work. I didn't fucking abandon us. That's on you and you alone."

A hysterical laugh slipped out, and she shoved at his chest. "I explained that I needed time. Yes, maybe I should have told you first." Cutter grunted, and her eyes slitted in response. She went on, "I came back, ready to deal with what happened between us, only to find you with *her*." She flung her arm out in Angie's direction.

Oh, she felt betrayed? Perfect, 'cause that's exactly what she'd done to him. Betrayed and abandoned him, like his moms. He had no idea a woman could make him feel that shit again. It'd hit him in a place that hurt deep. He wasn't about to let someone get away with hurting him again.

"God, you're such an idiot. I was foolish to run away, but the real foolishness was thinking you'd still be here a week later and we could work it out. Instead, you're with another woman. Typical fucking biker love." Tears sprang from her eyes and she swiped at them furiously. "I should have known better," she murmured to herself, bitterly.

Fuck, this time the tone in her voice cracked the ball of resentment lodged in his chest, and his heart gushed with self-recriminations. Instead of trusting her to come back to him,

he'd lashed out, and struck where it would hurt her the most
—in her possessive, little heart.

Cutter lunged for her, but she tore out of his grip and fled,
the door slamming against the exterior wall. A gust of rain
whipped in, soaking him to the bone.

34

GRETA

There was a tingling at the base of Greta's skull as she drove to her date with James.

It was her first outing since her breakup with Cutter. James was a brilliant criminal attorney, ambitious, but dedicated to social justice, like she and Sage. Greta swerved sharply to the right and ducked into a narrow alley. Squinting through the deep shadows, she zigzagged through the streets of downtown until she lost the car following her.

It might be Cutter, because, even if they hooked up with other women, bikers were notoriously chauvinistic. Her lip curled. *Angie*. Little submissive bitch. She hated her on principle alone. *Gah*. Or it was a Dark Horseman, but she didn't have the energy to wrap her mind around that possibility. At any rate, she knew how to lose a tail, and the idiots were either drunk, high, or both.

An irritated breath blew wisps of hair off her forehead. It was time to stop wallowing and get back out there. Hook up, rebound, or better yet, meet a man. A man who was nothing like Cutter. She'd messed up by running, but she never imagined he'd toss their relationship away in a matter of days.

Her fingernail worried the raw patch of skin on her wrist. She itched from how badly she missed him. Meanwhile, Angie's ass was probably getting slapped at this very moment. Slamming her palms against the steering wheel, she expelled a low screech. *Stop it, stop it, stop it. Stop thinking before you go insane. Focus on moving forward. God knows he has.*

Last week, James had taken time out of his busy schedule and stopped by the office to ask her out. Speechless, she searched for an excuse to decline when his expression grew stern. The longer she made him wait, the sterner he got, until she was squirming in her seat, under his hawkish stare. Although, she'd vowed to stay far away from dominant men, it was that touch of Cutter in him that pushed her over.

After parking, she entered the upscale restaurant and approached the hostess, who gave her a long once-over after she mentioned James's name. So what, she'd worn a corset? Sheesh, so judgmental. At the bar, she shimmied onto a high stool and ordered a whiskey neat. The lamp suspended from the ceiling above her was an upside-down wooden barrel, which she found interesting. The place had a cool, hipster vibe. Hopefully, the food was good.

Swirling the whiskey in the glass snifter, she kept her eye on the entrance. James entered and instantly scanned the area. The hostess touched his sleeve and leaned into him to whisper in his ear, but James brushed her off and crossed the busy floor straight for Greta. More than one pair of eyes followed his elegant, trim figure as he confidently strolled over to her.

He looked good, walking toward her. James was a golden boy with warm hazel eyes, but she couldn't help comparing them to Cutter's mutable blues. She couldn't help noticing that although he was slim and fit, he didn't have the same broad-chest and large-frame of a certain biker-that-shall-not-be-named.

Kissing her lightly on the cheek, he took in the burgundy wraparound dress that showcased her black lace corset. Classy, but with an edge of raw sex. She crossed her legs, her slinky dress slipped off her knee and bared half her thigh.

"Good evening, Greta. Love the dress," he said, as he thumbed the material. James peered down at her drink and gave her a luxurious smile. "You're a woman who knows what she wants."

A laugh bubbled up from her throat. Yep, that about summed her up. With a light touch to his sleeve, she said, "I'd applaud your astuteness, but not all women are quite that easy to read."

"True. Some women are far more intriguing than others," he mused.

"You should steer clear of such women," she counseled.

His gaze slowly caressed her again. "I think not."

"Ahh, a man who knows what he wants," she joked.

The hostess approached them and hovered by James's shoulder. Gaze to the floor, she murmured, "Your table is ready." Then she cleared her throat and finished with a sultry "Sir."

Greta's eyebrows shot up. *What in the hell was that?*

Ignoring the hostess, he took Greta's elbow and assisted her off the stool. Plucking her whiskey glass from the bar, he placed a guiding hand on the small of her back until they reached the table. With a flourish of his hand, he pulled out a chair for her, and dismissed the hostess with a nod.

She settled in, slipped the pristine cloth napkin on her lap, and teased, "Why James, are you wooing me?"

She liked saying his name. It was so timeless, so proper, so unlike road names.

"You noticed. Finally," he replied.

Before she could respond, the waiter came over and took James's drink order. It was a Campari, which seemed to fit him perfectly.

Eyes on the menu, he commented, "I've been solicitous for quite some time. In fact, I asked Sage about you a while ago, but she suggested that you were unavailable. Recently, she mentioned that your schedule cleared up so I decided to make my move. A woman like you doesn't stay single for long, I imagine," he suggested.

"I didn't realize Sage was acting as my pimp," Greta answered pertly.

Holding the embossed menu at an angle, he tilted his head to the side and gave her a penetrating gaze. "Aren't you a defiant one," he said softly.

The steel in his voice gave her pause. *Oh, crap.*

As if hearing her thought, James spoke quietly, "Oh yes, you've guessed correctly. I'm a Dom. I was curious how long it would take you to figure it out, but you're as intelligent as you are beautiful. Although, your radar needs a bit of polishing."

Greta closed her menu and slid her trembling hands beneath the tablecloth. Twisting her napkin, she focused on the votive candle in the center of the table. "You've known since the beginning?"

"I've been in the lifestyle for quite some time. It's second nature to me. There was one specific moment that told me for certain," he revealed.

"Is that right?"

James leaned forward and opened his palms. "Give me your hand."

After a moment of hesitation, she placed her hand between his. His thumbs drew circles on her skin. "There is no need to be afraid. I have no intention of hurting you."

She exhaled the air wedged in her throat.

"There's little that shows you're a sub, so don't concern yourself." He squeezed her hand. "But I couldn't kick my fascination with you."

"Oh, please, you were after Sage in the beginning," she scoffed.

He chuckled darkly, "Just because I may be attracted to a woman doesn't mean that she's able to meet my specific requirements."

He drew her closer and murmured against her temple, "I saw you on the street with a biker. He was gesturing to you with domineering mannerisms, and you, my dear, responded with remarkable alacrity." Greta's heart spiked at the word *biker*. He released her hand and leaned back. "That told me everything I needed to know."

If she could, she'd curl up into a tight ball and roll right out of the restaurant, regardless of whether it was four-star or not. Cringing, she asked, "Was I that obvious?"

"To me, yes. As to others, I wouldn't know. I tend to be quite discreet, whereas your friend seemed to be visibly demonstrative." With a light shrug, he concluded, "There isn't a right or wrong way to do this. To each his own."

Swallowing, her spine hit the back of the tufted dining chair. She shuddered to think of how many people had witnessed her playing lapdog to Cutter.

"Don't look so devastated," he said, soothingly. His tone changed when he ended, "You have greater things to worry about."

Her eyes flared wide. "What could that possibly be?" she asked with surprise.

James gave her a long look until she dropped her eyes. God, she was so predictable.

He gripped her chin, lifting it firmly until their eyes held.

"Why, your satisfaction, of course. A beautiful, intelligent submissive like you is priceless. If you were auctioned, you'd have billionaires vying for the highest bid."

Her brows hit her forehead. Greta escaped his hold; her elbows dispersed the silverware as she rushed to cover her face. Grasping her wrists, he pried her hands away and enfolded them in his own.

"Take your menu," he instructed. "You will dine on the sole with capers."

He gave a short nod and a waiter appeared immediately. She bowed her head while James ordered. Thankfully, he'd chosen a bottle of wine. After the waiter left, she scraped the utensils over the tablecloth back to their proper places, gnashing her teeth. *Grrr.* If she kept this up, she'd soon need a mouth guard.

The waiter returned with the bottle of wine, gracefully twisted the cork off, and gave James a taste before pouring a sizable amount in each wineglass. After a large gulp, Greta turned the bottle around and read the Argentinean label.

"Interesting choice," she said, praying to take his full attention off her. She could barely stand his intensity, as it was. She didn't know how she'd get through an entire dinner like this.

"My knowledge of wine comes from my mother, who, despite growing up on the wrong side of the tracks, developed a passion for this particular fermented beverage. She became a consummate connoisseur of French wine. Only French wine. For hours, she drilled my brother and me about various strains of grapes and the regions where they originated. The fermentation process, the bottling, the storing. Etcetera," he finished with a little flourish of his hand.

Her own memories included stories as well, of spirits that flittered about her like butterflies, as if they were living beings. Told to her by Scorpion, on breaks during long bike rides they took when she was a kid, and then later, when he taught her to ride.

"My brother followed in her footsteps," James continued. "He's even delved into our family genealogy and found that one side of our family came from the Languedoc region, in France."

Their conversation paused as the waiter brought the main course. The sole was delicious, it's flavor mild and delicate, but after a few bites, her throat closed up. She fiddled with her fork and knife, the silverware feeling heavy in her fingers.

"I spent my summers in Buenos Aires, with my maternal grandparents, and drank a prodigious amount of table wine, at dance halls. My judgment most definitely comes from drinking the cheapest wine I could get my hands on at the age of sixteen," he disclosed with a soft chuckle.

Greta laughed despite herself. She had to hand it to him, James was extremely charming.

"Unlike my brother, I've explored South American wines. Delicacies can be found in the more underappreciated places." His gaze lingered on her. "As long as one is curious enough to search."

The waiter gathered their dishes and placed a cheese board before them. James was clever. He'd come on pretty hard, but then he'd backed off and was easy to talk to. He petted her hand while they exchanged stories over dessert and a final digestif.

By the time she rose from the table, his hand instantly found her lower back, guiding her between tables that glided by in a bit of a blur. He held her coat for her and closed it for her, even tying the belt around her waist. Good grief, but the man was the epitome of sensual.

The hostess glared at her with brittle eyes, but no amount of cattiness could burst her bubble. Not while she walked on a cloud nine of good food, superb alcohol, and a sexy Dom tending to her. James cajoled her into letting him drive her home. He promised to have her car parked in her driveway before morning if she gave him her keys. While waiting for the valet, he fingered a tendril of her hair, twining it around and around in looping curlicues.

"You seem in a better mood," he observed.

She broke into a soft smile. "Yes, I am. Thanks to you." She really was. A shape darted across the parking lot, and her heart faltered. She canvased the entire area but saw nothing. Maybe it was a figment of her imagination. "I am better. At least right now. I sort of...kind of...ended a relationship."

"Sort of, kind of. He was a fool if he permitted you to slip away," he said resolutely.

"He didn't permit anything. I walked away," Greta corrected.

He brushed the back of his knuckles against her cheek and tucked a loose strand of hair behind her ear. "You have a lot to learn about men. I have a strong sense that it's not finished."

"Oh, but it is finished," she assured him.

"It's the biker, isn't it?" Peering up at the night sky, he intoned, "It's rare to have what I witnessed between the two of you. I had it once so I know how much it's worth, but being young and stupid, I allowed it to fall away and haven't found it since." His eyes cut to her. "Love, that is," he elucidated.

"Love," she snorted, derisively.

"Take my word for it, Greta, he loves you. To find someone who reciprocates what you feel for them, with the additional Dom-sub layer intact, is extraordinary. Believe me, that's not something you want to relinquish easily," he counseled.

"It doesn't matter. We're over," she said, between gritted teeth. Hadn't Cutter made his position crystal clear at the clubhouse? *For fuck's sake, he's probably banging Angie as we speak.* She couldn't seriously think there was anything salvageable between them.

James searched her face for a long moment. "Well, if you're convinced that that's the case, then you might want to continue your education. I can assure you, I'm a very good teacher."

She smiled vaguely. Damn him, they'd been getting along so well up until now. If only he hadn't brought up the subject of Cutter and love.

"Hmmm, I don't like the look on your face." He took a step away from her as the car slid to the curb beside him. "Don't respond tonight. Think about my offer."

He opened the door for her, and she slipped in. Ohhh... leather seats. Definitely a sign in his favor. She wiggled her butt in pleasure. Holding the top of the door, he bent over and brushed his lips against hers, tasting her with a featherlight flick of a touch.

Moments later, they were gliding away in his Porsche. Side-eyeing him, she observed the angular cheekbone and firm chin of his profile. His tongue had left a sweet, spicy taste, and his cologne coiled in the air delicately.

Leaving the car idling in front of her house, he eased her out of her seat and accompanied her up the stairs. At her front door, he took hold of her keys and opened it, sweeping his hand for her to enter. "Goodnight, sweet Greta."

She pressed her lips against his briefly and said, "Goodnight, and thank you."

After she locked the door, she heard him linger for a moment longer before tripping down the stairs with light footsteps.

In her bedroom, Greta undressed and paused in front of the unframed mirror leaning against a wall. Tilting her chin from side to side, she dissected the features men frequently commented on. Bright green, upward-slanting eyes. Warm skin. Sleek, dark hair. Pink tips.

"I'm cursed," she breathed out. "Cursed."

There was no other explanation for her string of bad luck; a lecherous, deadbeat dad, a farcical first love, and now an irresponsible biker.

Bedding down, she fluffed her pillow a few times, switched off her bed lamp, and pulled her bedsheet up to her chin. Her leg swished from side to side. Like an amputee who felt their missing limb, Greta felt the ephemeral warmth of Cutter's hot, delectable skin against hers.

She had a sneaking suspicion that she'd made a colossal mistake. The knowledge of it twisted up her spine like a coiling snake.

Kicking her feet out, she threw off the suffocating sheet. James was incredible, but he couldn't match up against Cutter. Not one bit. If anything, the fact that she'd had a perfect date with a perfect man was proof of that. She should be falling for someone like James, but instead she was pinging for Cutter's delicious body. Memories of him writhing on top of her, pummeling his thick cock inside her inundated her. But it was more than sex. The emotions he elicited from her were unprecedented. It's what had made her run so fast when he'd gotten arrested. If she could feel that strongly for a man, and he disappeared, where would that leave her?

Running from Scorpion had saved her so she ran again, but she felt lost instead of saved. Tossing and turning through half the night, she eventually fell into an exhausted slumber with the ghost of his hand collaring her throat, like a caress.

35

CUTTER

The Jeep windows were cranked down, and fresh air had finally dispersed Angie's cloying perfume after Cutter dropped her off before heading out to visit Tommy. Mile after mile, he traveled country roads heading toward the mountains lined with impenetrable rows of evergreens. The early morning fog had dissipated in the summer heat.

Tapping his fingers against the doorframe, a cigarette clung between two blunt digits, the tip long extinguished. On the passenger side laid a carton of donuts, to make up for Greta's absence. His gaze flicked over to his right, the memory of Greta's slim ankle propped on the seat, the tiny silver chimes of her ankle bracelet glittering in the sunlight. His cock hardened at the recollection.

Before Greta, dominance was, in and of itself, enough. Since her, he ached for the spark—any kind of pushback— that he got from being with her. He wasn't getting that hit from Angie, the meek. It had the markings of a problem. Scrubbing his eyes with the heel of his hand, he muttered, "Fuck, the donuts aren't gonna do the trick."

If he couldn't get Greta off his mind, how could he expect Tommy not to feel the sting of disappointment.

Bumping over the rutted and rock-studded dirt road, Cutter guided the Jeep close to the cabin and put it into park. Snapper bounded up his thigh by the time he stepped down into the overgrown grass. Tommy wrapped his arms around him in a bear hug. No man-hug or slap on the back from his uncle. No, it was a full-on body hug.

Pulling back, Tommy peered around him and inquired, "Where's Greta?"

Cutter suppressed a sigh. *Rip the band-aid off.*

"She won't be coming again," he pronounced in a gruff tone.

"Why not? Been takin' my meds. See, I've been good." Tommy held his calendar in front of his chest, showing off a new watercolor of Greta as he bent down to ruffle Snapper's coat. Christ, this was gonna be harder than he'd thought.

Clamping a hand down on Tommy's broad shoulder, he steered him toward the cabin.

"It's got nothin' to do with you. Come on, let's make coffee." He held up an empty, lidded paper cup. "I had an early start. Need a refill."

Crossing the threshold, Tommy dropped into one of the two chairs, shoulders slumped and head down. "She's mad at me. Thought I was doin' good."

"You are," Cutter assured him. Ever since his mother died, Tommy didn't have a constant female presence, and he knew his uncle missed that warmth in his life.

"Greta wouldn't stop comin' here unless I'd done somethin' wrong. She's loyal, like your mama." Tommy asserted.

Cutter slammed the tin of coffee beans on the wooden counter and gripped it hard between his hands. "Like mom, she can also be a judgmental bitch. Like mom, she can abandon you. Reject you for how you choose to live your life."

Deeper creases formed on Tommy's lined forehead. "Ellen never abandoned anyone in her life."

Cutter stabbed a large spoon into the can, measured out several scoops of beans into the coffee grinder, and pressed down. Hard. Loud grinding noises shook the air in the cabin. Why did people insist on digging up family nonsense that should stay buried?

"Blame me for the times your mother left, not her," his uncle said.

"I blame you both." *Fuck, hadn't meant to say that out loud.* Shaking the finely ground coffee into a large tarnished, old-fashioned percolator, he placed it carefully on the top of the wood-burning cookstove.

"It was my fault. She'd done the best she could."

Humph.

"Blame me, nephew."

"Done blaming anyone a while ago, Tommy," he rumbled out.

"You shouldn't have stopped. I was the reason your father left. It was a bad year, and Ellen took me in, but your pops said he couldn't take it no more and took off."

"He didn't come back once you went back to grandma, though. That was on him. He was a deadbeat motherfucker. Wasn't just about you," Cutter said gruffly.

"Your mother thought it was her fault. About my problem, I mean," Tommy said.

Although his back was firmly turned away from Tommy as he concentrated on the percolator, his head whipped over his hunched shoulder. "Why are you bringin' up the past? They're dead. What's the point?"

"Greta leavin' isn't the same as Ellen leavin' you to search for me."

Cutter's eyes narrowed. "How do you know Greta left?"

"Not the same thing at all," Tommy plowed on. "Ellen had her own demons. Guilt, especially. Blamed herself because she triggered my first psychotic break. We were kids, and there were already signs from when I was a baby that I wasn't normal, but she took it on herself anyways. It wasn't me she failed in the end, was it?"

Ignoring his uncle, he demanded, "Answer the question, Tommy. How do you know I didn't dump Greta?"

Tommy stared down at his fidgeting hands. Shrugging, he muttered, "You love her, and… you don't ever leave people."

"I left you and moms for the Army," Cutter grunted out.

"You came right back when Ellen called you. And you wouldn't have gone in the first place if it hadn't been for her. And me. You're loyal to the bone, nephew. One thing I know about you is that you're loyal to the bone. You'd never be the first to walk. Never," he finished emphatically.

Not totally true. He'd let Greta walk away from him when she'd come looking for him. Not that she didn't deserve it. Still, it was a leaving, of sorts.

"Happened a long time ago," Cutter muttered. "Stop dredging up old family shit, already."

"There's no way I can make up for the sacrifices you made for me, boy. Buyin' this piece of land so I can have enough space." His arms spread wide to encompass the cabin. "Watching over me these past years, but also leaving me in peace…" he trailed off. "Your mother did so much, too, but she was always pushing me to do something more to fix me. She stressed me out. Got so bad that I had to get away."

"She was obsessed with you," Cutter added.

"That she was. Took care of me way too much, and of you, not enough. Wasn't fair to you."

Gurgling sounds came from the coffee pot as it shook slightly on the iron cooktop. Praying to cut off the discussion, Cutter turned back and held onto the handle as the final spurts of hot water gushed into the upper part of the pot. He set it aside to cool down before pouring the coffee.

"The look on your face when you told me that Greta wasn't coming was the same look you got as a kid. Difference is that whatever she did wasn't the same as Ellen," Tommy said sagely.

Exasperated, Cutter swept up two chipped mugs with one hand, the coffee pot with the other, and plunked them down on the table. "She's as judgmental of the Squad as Ellen was."

Tommy shook his head, and greater irritation sprouted in Cutter's chest. "For fuck's sake, Tommy, she left because I got arrested. Shittin' on the Squad as much as moms did."

"Not Greta," Tommy denied vehemently.

"She's no angel," he gritted out.

"She's no Ellen, either," he fired back. "Ellen had a mental problem, too. Not as bad as mine, so it never got talked about. Anxiety always made her criticize everything. Greta's not like that. If she got upset, there had to be a good reason."

"Greta wasn't an easy woman to satisfy," he groused.

Tommy snorted, and muttered, "I'm not gonna pretend that I know anything about how to satisfy women, but I knew your mother inside out. More than you because, no matter what, she was your moms and you looked up to her. Don't confuse the two of them. Plus, Greta's in love with you."

It was Cutter's turn to snort through his nostrils. "That so?" he scoffed. "She sure has a funny way of showin' it."

Shaking the last dregs of evaporated milk from an opened can, he tossed it into an overflowing recycling bin. Time to bring the recycling down. Although Tommy composted and brought a small trash bag down to his nearest neighbor once a week, the recycling was up to Cutter. Greta had helped last time, but he wasn't bringing Angie for a visit, no matter how much she begged. Hell nah.

Tommy meant well, but every visit for the next year was gonna be a repeat of this conversation.

36

CUTTER

Cutter was chillin' beside Puck at an impromptu party after a long-ass, burn-the-midnight-oil kinda Church.

Kingdom had succeeded in uniting the brothers to convert the Squad into a legit enterprise. After Greta's visit to the clubhouse, Cutter had explicitly told Sage to keep her away, but, fuck his life, Greta was back. As Kingdom's old lady, Sage had a lot of leeway, but she was getting too big for her high-heeled lawyer shoes.

He scowled at her for a good solid minute before she noticed. Her smile wobbled, and she mouthed "I'm sorry."

Seething, he turned his gaze to Greta and drank her in like an alcoholic on a bender. As usual, she was covered, but that sexy, tight-fitting dress of hers left nothing to the imagination. His gaze bored into a group of brothers milling near her. Bet they were sporting raging hard-ons, just like he was.

On the other end of the bar, Semi was yakking with Greta, who threw him a cock-teasing smile. Swear to God, she was fucking with him on purpose. Balling his hands, he suppressed the urge to snag his brother by the scruff of his neck and take him outside for a beatdown. As for anyone who actually dared touch her, there would be hell to pay.

Fuck, I gotta get rid of her before I outright kill someone.

Angie sashayed over and wrapped herself around him like a damn boa constrictor. Acid churned in his gut. Her fawning was grating on his nerves, but she was loyal, and the green-eyed woman down the bar had recently taught him the value of allegiance.

Greta's gaze periodically lingered on him. There was a high flush to her cheeks, and her smile was too broad and stiff to be real. *Jealous, again, baby?* He whispered into Angie's ear, and instantly, Greta got up and crossed the room to chat up one of the prospects. Alright, two could play this game. He plastered Angie up against the bar. She released a high-pitched squeal and her legs swooped around his waist. Flexing his fingers around her butt, he groaned because, mother*fucker*, even her ass felt different from Greta's. If he was holding Greta, his cock would be punching out of his jeans.

Roughly, he took Angie's mouth. Her taste was all wrong. Bland. Vanilla. Meanwhile, he had a sweet tooth for a pair of honey-glazed lips just beyond his reach. Angie slobbered over his mouth and chin; frustration snorted out his nostrils. Despite his instructions and training, she couldn't get it right. His eyes popped open and Greta was locked in on him, eyes bleeding pain. He almost gagged, but he had to get rid of Greta. *Right?* Right.

Snapping his eyes shut, the liquor in his stomach curdled as he went to town on Angie. He dry humped her until her moans were loud enough to turn heads. Once satisfied that he didn't see Greta anymore, he dropped her to her feet, gave her a swat to the ass, and dismissed her with a wave.

"Go," he ordered her away. He couldn't take much more of this.

Angie air-kissed him and swayed those narrow hips of hers away from him. He needed a smoke before he threw up. Bracing his boot against the wall, Cutter drew out his tobacco pouch and rolling papers. A rich, woody odor bloomed, tantalizing him with a scent reminiscent of Greta's pussy. The musky endnotes began to pump blood into his cock, double time. *Fuck me.*

Glancing up, he found Greta before him, bolted to the floorboards. Her fine skin was stretched taut over her cheekbones. Bastard that he was, he licked his lips, smeared with another woman's taste.

A subtle shaking took hold of her. It was the shattered look in her eyes that broke through his defenses, though. Dropping the pouch and rolling papers, he hauled her against him. Her panting breaths fanned over his jaw.

She clutched his arms tightly before thrusting off him, turning on her heel, and barreling toward the exit. He seized her just as she reached the door, swerved her around, and backed her into a corner. Stepping in front of her, he hunched over her to shield her from prying eyes. She smothered her face into his chest, tears flooded his cut like a deluge. His lungs were about to collapse from the crush of remorse.

Wedging her tighter in his hold, he rumbled, "The fuck is wrong with you?"

"I tried staying away. God knows, I tried. How many times I broke down and drove over here. Waited outside for you, only to see you walk out with Angie. Sage told me about the vote, and I had to come."

"Wasn't her business to tell you," he said.

From the corner of his eye, he caught Angie approaching them. He shook his head. A few clicks of high heels later and they were alone again. Him, her, and their shared pain. Fucking hell, this was why he never wanted to see her again.

Catching her by the nape, he rasped, "Follow me."

CUTTER STRODE AWAY, and Greta drank in the sight of his thick boxer's neck and powerful shoulders encased in his cut. His jean-clad ass muscles rippled with every stride he took. He was a thing of beauty. Sheer *fucking* beauty. God, she hated herself for what she had done to them.

The moment he'd caught her staring at him and Angie, he smiled lewdly, and she lost her shit. She should've known better than to brashly show up at this party. It was a bold move, and she was going to pay for it, because after one command, she trailed after him like he was the pied piper.

By the time she arrived at the threshold of Cutter's new office, she'd broken out in a fine sweat. Lifting the hair off her nape, a breeze slid over her skin, but it gave her no margin of relief. Cutter took a seat and sprawled his legs wide across a brand-new sofa. She was all kinds of nervous, but she forced herself to walk in, head held high.

"Girl, don't pout at me. You came to me. Too late to back out now."

A soft mew slipped past her lips. His intent gaze scoured over her, from the crown of her head to her ankles. A matching pair of scarlet-colored leather harnesses were buckled at her ankles. He let out a short growl, and pride washed over her. Lifting her skirt, she admired their daintiness. The seam of his lips pressed tightly together. He liked what he saw, and she couldn't help preening.

"Coming here, wearin' those, tells me you're begging to be restrained," he mulled. Sounded like a great plan to her. Pointing to the spot in front of him, he ordered, "First position."

A wave of relief crashed over her. A turmoil of emotions merged at the tip of his finger motioning her to her spot. It was still hers. Angie might have a special "position" as well, but for the time being, she was claiming hers.

Raising her skirt, she dropped to the ground and advanced on her knees. Between his legs, she arranged her hands neatly on the top of her knees. Cutter was poker-faced, but for an overt, heavy-lidded stare. Inhaling and exhaling deeply, she catapulted into the safe zone she'd missed like a second skin. The steel tips of his boots, scuffed up and caked with dry clay, almost touched her knees. He'd been out tracking. Her breathing faltered; she was no longer privy to the way he spent his days.

After she drove by and saw Cutter help Angie onto his bike, she was determined to salvage her pride by never approaching him again. Sage had told her about Kingdom and Cutter's intensive campaign to clean up the Squad, and she'd called tonight, insisting Greta come to the club. Hearing about the vote crushed her resolve to stay away. But there was more.

Her face twisted, and she fixated on the far wall as she wrung her hands.

Sensing her disquiet, Cutter tensed above her. "Something's wrong. What is it?"

She swallowed audibly, her mouth going dry. He captured one of her braids and yanked until her gaze slid to his. "Spit it out. You don't deserve a fucking after the way you behaved, so talk."

"I...I couldn't stay away. I can't sleep, I can't eat," her voice dropped to a whisper, "I can't breathe."

"You shouldn't have come here," he warned with a defeated sigh.

Hope fluttered in her belly at the thought that he was

suffering as much as she was, despite the show he'd put out there for her. Nodding stiffly, she gulped out, "I know."

Suspicion crept in his gaze. "Why now? I know you almost as well as I know myself. You have little tells, and something in my gut is saying something is wrong. What is it, Greta?"

"Now that the club has voted, I won't live in fear that you'll be harmed or taken away from me," she began.

Forgetting his grip, she instinctively jerked her head, and whimpered when her hair was pulled by its roots. Nervous, she broke their gaze. His Adam's apple snaked up and down his throat. "There's more you're not telling me. I don't have time for your games, Greta. Go on, spit it out."

Shaking her head, she steeled herself. How could she tell him when she barely wanted to acknowledge it herself? All she wanted was to burrow into him like an animal. Even sex, and God knew she wanted to fuck him, came second place.

She gulped in a breath, shut her eyes, and confessed, "I saw Shadow."

A bite of pain stung her scalp as he wrenched her head up.

"What in the *actual* fuck?" he seethed.

"I thought if I didn't tell anyone, then it wouldn't be real," she hurried to explain. "I thought I could handle it, but I'm not sure I can anymore."

Cutter's expression made her tremble. She crumbled to the floor, her forehead slipping down to the cool cement, and she took hold of his ankles. The intensifying fear that she'd carried with her since the bike rally escaped, and she burst into tears. Her palms slid up his stiff calves.

A FULL-SCALE NUMBNESS ASSAULTED HIM. Even his hands tingled. He'd let his woman, *his* woman, hang out to dry. His fists balled at his side, palms sweating from the urge to punch something. The moment she tugged against her leash, he should've yanked harder, placed a fucking halter on her and put her through her paces. Instead, he let her fear take control of him, of them. And look what kind of shitshow it'd turned into.

"What did he do?" Cutter choked out.

"He hasn't approached me, but I've seen him again. And...I feel him around me," Greta stated, and he could tell that it was a hard admission for her. His woman didn't like to feel like weak, like she was a prey in someone else's sick game, especially Shadow's. And where there was Shadow, Scorpion wasn't far behind, slithering on his belly like the snake he was.

And his woman shouldn't be *feeling* any man. Especially that motherfucker. Only man she should be fucking *feeling* was him. The pressure in his chest collapsed his lungs. He replayed the words she'd just spoken in his mind, and caught on to the most disturbing word of all.

"Again?" he croaked out.

Greta's gaze skittered away, and he barely kept his temper in check. "Yeah. Twice. Maybe more."

"Christ!" he exploded.

She flinched, and he quickly placed a steadying hand on the crown of her head. The act of soothing her drove back the demons battering his ribs to escape. He'd already lost her once by allowing a combination of her fear and his pride to get in the way.

Lesson learned. From now on, Greta was truly his. Nothing would get in his way again.

Caressing her velvety black braids softened her stiff neck muscles and she dipped her head forward. His fingers and thumbs kneaded the tendons of her exposed nape. Then, he enfolded her in a fierce hold and rocked her. Her tears fell, and he swept them off with the flat of his tongue. Swallowed them down. Made them his. Because they were his. He owned every one of her tears, just like he owned every inch of her, every cell in her body. She was his. His. HIS.

"Baby girl, you're back where you belong. By my side and under my rule," he declared.

Limp, Greta brushed her wet cheek against his arm. "What's going to happen?"

He'd brief Kingdom on the situation. The Squad didn't need another MC covertly treading on their territory. First things first, he needed her safe, in his bed. "I want you in my house."

"What about Angie?" she instantly asked. He felt the jealousy flaring up in her, but Greta had nothing to be worried about.

"What about her? She can wait," he replied.

"She can, but I can't," she muttered.

Indulgent, he chuckled, "Baby girl, don't you worry about Angie."

"I do."

Women. In a whole heap of trouble, and her concern was about another chick. "We'll table this conversation for later. That's not my priority right now. You are."

Shifting her on his lap, he reached behind for his key chain. "Enter the house, lock it behind you, strip and wait for me in bed."

Opening her hand, he placed it in the center. Gently, his fingers folded around hers, and holding her gaze, he promised, "I'll be there as soon as I'm done."

37

GRETA

"I wanna wrap your throat in a collar," he intoned.

A voice, more like a growl, floated over her. Eyes flickering open in the dark, Greta stiffened and curled her fingers into claws. She was about to slam her head against the man on top of her when he spoke again, "Baby, it's me. Cutter."

The breeze from the open window tapped the cord of the venetian blinds against the windowsill. Her body went slack, and she swiped a shaking hand over her eyes. She hadn't immediately recognized his voice in her half-asleep state.

Once her vision adjusted, she found him crouched over her like a rapacious beast. In the semidarkness, she peered into his indigo eyes, reveling in the luminous fever shining through. Inhaling a ragged breath, she instantly recognized Cutter's scent. It entwined around her, swaddling her in reams of gauzy warmth. Her pulse slowed down to the speed of sluggish lava. Wetness gushed out of her core, slicking her inner thighs.

"I missed your heat," she confided in a rush, as if in a confessional stall.

"Not my sparkling conversation?" he teased.

Gripping the taut sinews of his shoulders, she arched and rubbed her breasts against his molded chest. "You're a furnace."

"Ah, so that's why the bedsheet is on the floor," he replied in an amused tone, as he ran his thumb across her bottom lip. She wanted to take it between her teeth and lick it like a lollipop.

"Sure it's not my cock you miss?"

"No question on that front," she affirmed with a throaty laugh. She stretched out like a cat, basking under his gaze.

"Reach up and hold on to the headboard. Don't take your hands off for any reason."

She latched on as he'd ordered.

"Spread your legs."

The lamp sitting on the nightstand clicked on. A splash of bright light blinded her, but she didn't remove her hands to cover her eyes. Cutter rummaged around leisurely. With a cluck of approval, he turned around, a black satin blindfold in his grip. The delicate fabric contrasted with the grooves of his calloused knuckles and scarred fingers.

Her smile faded slightly. A blindfold meant surrender, whereas a punishment would have been easier and a quick form of release. He draped the blindfold on the pillow beside her temple.

Standing above her, he languidly sucked on his index finger. There was a popping sound, and then the moist digit was dragging along her jugular vein. Her thumping heart boomed in her eardrums. He stroked the dip of her throat, slipped between her tits, over her belly, and lodged deep inside her pussy. Her hips shot off the mattress and she buried the side of her face into the pillow.

He speared her until his finger was drenched and then

thrust two more fingers inside. By then, her hips moved in tandem with his fingers. Propped up on his elbow, he gave her a rough finger-fucking while he watched on leisurely. She seized his head and crashed her lips against his.

Brusquely, he twisted away and removed his fingers. She bit down on her inner cheek to suppress her cry and tasted the tang of blood. Returning her hands to the headboard, she fisted it through gritted teeth and stared up at the ceiling.

The sound of shoelaces being tugged piqued her curiosity and she peered over to see Cutter hauling his shirt over his head. His back muscles bulged out, ridges on either side of his spine, and tapered down to his waist. Her tongue darted out. The top of his ass was exposed by the dip of his low-riding jeans.

Gripping the wooden frame above her head, she fought the urge to drop open mouth kisses on his lower back and then tug his jeans down to lick the crease between his butt cheeks.

She was about to move, when he cut her off, "Don't do it."

Cutter turned around, holding a utilitarian collar. Her body was on a hair trigger. Endorphins had been activated, inundating her brain with the natural drug. Leaning over her, he tied the blindfold around her. One thing she could say about the lack of sight was that it made her more attuned to him. There was the whisper of denim as his jeans slid down his legs, the creaks of the floorboard as he kicked them off. She heard a popping sound as he cracked his neck from side to side.

Blindfold be damned, a warmth cascaded over her chest, bathed her belly, and then slipped over her thighs.

The bed pitched, and a heavy weight settled alongside her.

"You're mistaken, you know, you didn't leave because of my arrest. I was unforgivably careless, but the truth is that you hadn't worked out your shit about the way I fuck you. It was an easy out, you took it and you ran with it."

He placed a soft kiss on her lips, and she chased his mouth, but he gently pushed her back down.

"After you left, I took up with Angie, but I couldn't go back to the way I was before you. Only a strong bitch will do for me now. Are you that strong bitch, Greta, because I can't be lookin' over my shoulder every time something goes down. Either you're here to stay, and I put the collar on you, or I take the blindfold off and you leave for good."

Her eyes popped open, eyelashes brushing satin. More than anything, she wanted to see his expression. "I'm here to stay. I swear it. I'm ruined for anyone else."

Disdain coated her tone as she spat out, "Speaking of Angie, I want to tear her apart. You can't imagine how badly I wanted to rip her arm off when she touched you. I envisioned slashing her to shreds. What are you going to do about her because she's not going to let you go. No woman would do that, but if she doesn't stay away from you, I'll end up killing her."

A smooth chuckle rolled over her, his breath feathering over her cheek. "Gotta admit, jealous is a good look on you."

He untied the blindfold. She blinked a few times before her vision cleared, and she swallowed at the earnest, grave expression he wore.

"Don't concern yourself about Angie. She'll bounce back with another man. She's a kid, and not real picky."

Greta shot him a dubious look. "I don't see how she's going to let you go, and she's not much younger than I am."

"She hasn't gone through what you have. You grew up fast. I'll tell you this, you're not the only one who's learned somethin'. My ego took a hit when you left. Instead of bringing you to heel, I turned my back on you."

His frustrated sigh shuddered through the room. "I should've done better by you."

"Don't blame yourself," she replied softly. This was her fault, not his. It was her fear that got the best of her.

His stark eyes fell on hers. "I blame myself," he confessed. "Your moms and the Green Mountain Boys wouldn't have done a damn thing if I'd gone to claim you. But I didn't even show my face."

Shaking his head ruefully, he said, "Next time I see Trucker, he and his boys are gonna give me a beating I'll never forget."

"I won't let them go too far," she promised.

"Highness, what's gonna go down is gonna go down. Fact is, another MC took care of what was mine. The brothers won't allow that to go unpunished. Any club worth their salt takes care of their women. And with your mother in the lead, those men are ruthless."

Shame vaulted through her like an electrical power surge, but she had to get one more thing out of the way. "There's one more thing we need to talk about." She gulped audibly. "Your arrest."

"We've squashed that. Believe you me, I ain't getting arrested again."

"Please, let me say my piece," she insisted. "I shouldn't have reacted the way I did. As a kid, I'd seen what the Horsemen went through for my father. The beatings and incarcerations. Even death. Men with families sacrificed themselves for a leader that didn't have their back. I witnessed what the girlfriends, baby mamas, and old ladies went through, left to pick up the pieces and take care of fatherless kids. But that doesn't mean I was right to dump my old baggage on you and ruin our relationship."

His roughened hand cupped her cheek. "Baby girl, your

worries were legitimate, and although I hated what you did, it pushed me to work harder for the lub. The Squad has started a new chapter. A legitimate one."

Greta nuzzled her cheek against his open palm and brushed her lips over it. "I know, but even if the Squad had stayed the same, nothing would stop me from loving you." Her fingertips caressed the stubble of his jawline. "I love you so bad."

Grabbing her fingers, he kissed the tips. "Babe, you ain't tellin' me anything I don't know."

He went up on all fours and boxed her in, his stiff cock dragging on her abdomen. Greta had the pleasure of watching him prowl over her like an alpha beast with his mate.

"Angie won't stop, you know," she predicted.

"Babe, not every woman is like you. She's loyal, but not caring. She's nothin' but a kid and the world is a candy store of cocks to her. Now, let it go, wrap your sexy legs around my waist and spread that pink cunt for me."

Her thighs gripped his sides, and the movement notched his cock against her opening. He teased her clit for a bit and then slipped his crown into the embrace of her plump lips. One hard thrust later, he rooted himself in deep. Circling her hips to accommodate him, she relished the burn of the stretch.

"Did I tell you to move? When I want you to change position, I'll do it my damn self," he warned.

She froze in place, only her inner walls pulsating around his shaft. Every shift elicited a flurry of shivers. Her pussy was a vessel, and this was a lesson on how to serve him. She was so primed that a few strokes put her on the cusp. His fingers circled her throat, a habit of his when he fucked her. Swallowing, she gauged the pressure of his fingers, and moaned.

"You're pussy's so fucking hot and wet. Sucking my cock so good," he rasped out, his rhythm increasing forcefully.

"Suck it deep." He slammed his hips forward on a hard stroke.

"Yeah, like that," he rasped as he pulled up short, before penetrating her tight heat once again. "Greedy little pussy, won't stop clutching on me."

Cutter rode her hard, until his rhythm got erratic and jerky. Withdrawing, he brushed his slippery shaft over her lower belly. The muscles of her abdomen fluttered in anticipation. Her shoulder muscles ached, and her fingers were numb, but she retained the lift of her hips for him to bury himself back inside.

Cutter's fingers slicked over her curls, pulled the hood back and strummed it while he stoked the fire in her pussy. "That's right. Feel it?"

"God, yes"

"Say my name."

"Mmmm."

"Say my fucking name, Greta. Who owns this pussy?"

"You," she croaked out. Her vision detonated. She was thrown down a rabbit hole and came with a blinding lightning-white climax.

Throwing her head back, she keened, "Cuuutter!"

She pumped upward, striking her clit against his pelvic bone, causing more sparks to fly. Her entire body twitched, while his tempo steadied, slow and precise.

Babbling mindlessly, she begged him to stop but he built her up again until she shattered a second time. A recurring sucking sound echoed in her ears, and she realized that it was her pussy. She'd been riding her orgasm like a surfer chick going for gold. Throat parched; she licked her cracked lips.

"Ready for me?" he asked, his question more of a warning than anything else.

She managed a wobbly nod.

"Good," was all he replied. Face contorted, Cutter hoisted her legs over his shoulder and bludgeoned her pussy.

"*Don't stop, don't stop, don't stop,*" she begged like a mantra. Driving high, his powerful thrusts reached an upsurge until he tumbled over the edge. Rigid above her, droplets of sweat fell as he shot his load over her. Ropes of come gushed out, slipping out of her pussy and painting her thighs. For a split second, she wished that she wasn't on contraception.

Cutter heaved above her, gripping his cock until it was empty. Settled in between her thighs, he grasped her hands and unclenched them from the headboard.

His fingers curled around her nape. "We're never gonna be separated again."

Dread snaked around her heart. "Cutter, I'm trouble, and I'm bound to mess things up." She inclined her head away from him and expelled a weary sigh. "To disappoint you."

He barked out a laugh. "Only way you'd disappoint me is if you weren't trouble." Two fingers entered her pussy.

"Not again," she breathed out. They'd just finished. How was he ready to go again?

He loomed over her again, the length of his cock thickening. One of his eyebrows arched and his lips quirked into a lopsided grin. "Get back in the ring and brace yourself for another round."

38

GRETA

G reta was lounging on Cutter's chest, dozing in front of the TV as a game played. Amid the sounds of roaring crowds emanating from the TV, she heard a loud rap at her door.

Rat-tat-tat. A short pause. *Rat-tat-tat.* And a third time. *Rat-tat-tat.*

Her heart stalled. The rhythm of the knock belonged to one man, and one man only.

Shadow.

The muscles bracketing her spine locked up. Unwrapping herself from Cutter's embrace, she strode toward the door. She flung it open and blocked Cutter's view of the entrance, praying to get rid of Shadow before all hell broke loose. She cast a glance over her shoulder and groaned inwardly when Cutter got to his feet.

Face carefully blank, she acknowledged her visitor, "Shadow."

"Greta," he replied soberly. His sharp gaze took in every detail, pausing at her chest and hips.

With a curled lip, she gave him a thorough once-over as well. He had gotten bulkier. Not one iota less sexy, but there was no "boyness" left in him whatsoever. His smoky eyes and shock of black hair were still as striking as ever against his pale skin. Above his beard, his features were composed of dark, flat planes that matched the flatness of his pupils.

Cutter came up behind her, his gaze snapping back and forth between them. His chest was a roaring fire against her back. "Who the fuck is this?"

"Who the fuck are you?" Shadow returned, in a deadly tone. His eyes had turned into hard narrow slits and his brows slashed down over them.

From the corner of her eye, she caught Cutter's jaw ticking, his expression downright murderous.

An arm snaked around her waist, and Cutter's open palm splayed over her belly, exposed by her cutoff tank top. His pinky finger caressed her mons. Shadow's fists tightened before he deliberately loosened them again. A sign as obvious as Cutter's pulsing jawline.

Cutter's free hand moved toward her breast, but she caught it in time and secured it over his other hand. Unfortunately, he was not about to be contained. Making a greater show of his ownership, he sucked on her throat, and bit down, giving Shadow a stare-down while his incisors sank into her. The bite spiked lust in her bloodstream. Sweat gathered in her armpits and the small of her back.

Meanwhile, Shadow's glare could singe the hair right off her arms. He had no right to say a word to her, but there was no point in poking the bear. Carefully, she tilted her head away to dislodge Cutter's teeth. A deadly growl shook against her throat.

Wrapped around her, pulsing with possessiveness, his

presence was an electric jolt to her system, his tightly laced violence was as hot as a branding iron. She wanted nothing more than to slam the door on Shadow and lose herself in Cutter. Shove him to the ground, pull out his cock and suck it deep to the back of her throat. *Reel it in, girl.*

"You're daddy know you're here, Horseman?" Cutter demanded.

Shadow was in Demon Squad territory, and the idiot was about to get himself hurt. She pressed her weight against Cutter to force him to take a step back. Nope, no luck.

"Quit with the pissing match," she snapped, eyes boring into each of them. Elbowing Cutter in the gut, she smacked his hands until his hold slackened enough for her to move out of his reach. It stretched her heartstrings taut, but she had to keep him in line.

Motioning to Shadow, she said, "Come in."

This was her way of returning the favor of her first kiss. His smooth lips on hers, his quick fingers playing along her ribs and skirting her budding breasts. That moment meant a hell of a lot to a thirteen-year-old girl. A quick side-glance toward Cutter and she almost squeaked. *Yikes.* Menace roiled in his eyes, and he was snorting like an incensed bull. Instantly, she returned to his side and wrapped herself around him.

WHO THE FUCK was this pussy showing up at *his* woman's door? In *his* territory? Wearing a Horseman's cut, the mirror image of the ink on her skin. Cutter's fingers clenched and unclenched, seconds away from crushing the fucker's windpipe. The son of a bitch wanted her bad. It was stamped on his face like a botched tattoo. He'd let it play out for a bit, but he was going to murder the bastard the second he stepped out of line.

Frowning down on Greta, he gave her a questioning look.

She answered it. "He's the Horsemen Sergeant of Arms."

Which meant he made it his business to kill, in cold blood. Before he realized it, his fingers were prying her jaw open, his tongue plundering her mouth. She gave her usual whimper, but an instant later, she was snatched from his clasp.

His face whipped around, and Shadow stood before him, holding Greta behind him.

Red fury swarmed his vision, and he thundered, "Get your fuckin' hands off her or I will end you, motherfucker!"

"I'll take you down if you hurt her. I don't give a fuck who you are."

"Hands. Off. Her," he gritted out.

Greta swooped out from under Shadow's outstretched arm, shook off his grip, and stomped her foot. "Fuck you both! I'm not anyone's property."

Fucking hell, he didn't need Greta goin' on a rampage.

Rounding on Shadow, she spat out, "I haven't seen you in a decade, so don't you dare act like you care. No need to pretend anymore, remember?"

The asshole's face went slack.

"Say what you came to say and get the hell out of my house."

Then his little spitfire wheeled around and skewered him with a look that could kill. "And you! This is none of your business."

Dead silence.

Heat scorched his skin like he was covered in burning sand. Once this was over, he was gonna collar her and torture her for days. He may have lost his cool for a moment, but there was a limit to his tolerance.

The timbre of his voice dropped to an intimate level, "Greta, you mouthing off ain't gonna work out for you. You want me to show him how I trained you to use that cheeky mouth of yours?"

Fire and ice fought for dominance, but smart woman that she was, she got hold of her temper and lowered her gaze. In a somewhat deferential tone, she said, "If this is too much for you, then maybe you should leave, because I need to hear him out."

Swear to God, he was going to take his largest paddle to her ass. This asshole wasn't spending a fucking second alone with her. Unwittingly, her tremoring hand slinked around her throat like the collar she was craving. Fuck, his woman was straight-up scared.

Greta swallowed and pleaded with him wordlessly. As much as he hated to relinquish an ounce of control, he had to trust her to deal with this scum, because he knew next to nothing about their dynamics.

Fuck me. This is what I get. Should have gone public with her long ago and slapped a jacket with my name on it on her back.

"Make it quick," he growled. Greta slumped against him. "I'm making a compromise, but don't give me an ultimatum."

Her gaze slanted up toward him, and she shot back, "Riiight, because this is your home."

Christ, his woman could trigger a temper tantrum in a saint.

Gesturing to the other biker, he warned her, "Last warning, woman. Provoke me again and I will strip you and fuck you in front of him. Then, let's see who has a claim."

He took the long chain hanging from his wallet and shook it. It was a chain he'd refashioned from one of her collars. Color drained from her face, because, yeah, she knew he had no qualms about lashing her wrists behind her back and using it as leverage while mounting her from behind. She may not want to acknowledge him in Shadow's presence, but in the end, the Dark Horseman would know who was boss.

Turning her in his arms, they faced Shadow together, and he ordered grimly, "Talk Horseman. You have five minutes."

39

GRETA

Greta collapsed on the sofa in Sage's home.

Shadow crashed through her life, wreaked havoc like the spawn of the devil he was, and then ran his ass back to whatever hellhole he'd come from. Once Shadow had driven out of sight, Cutter took out her collar, cuffed her, and dragged her to the floor. Then, he fucked his anger out on her.

Greta was in the middle of recuperating from a blistering climax when he contacted Kingdom and made plans to meet at Sage's house. There was protocol to follow when approaching another MC, and Shadow had disregarded it. Once he approached her without permission, it wasn't about her anymore. She shuddered to think what all this would mean.

A potential situation between clubs was bad enough without hearing that Scorpion was sick. Shadow's eyes turned shifty while he was relaying his message, so he was lying— Scorpion wasn't sick, he was on his deathbed. Right about now, her emotions were flailing around in her ribcage.

Loki walked through the door, nodded to her and Sage, and joined Cutter and Kingdom in the kitchen.

Sage took Greta's hands into her own and rubbed warmth into them. "Oh, sweetheart, we'll work this out."

Coming from Sage, it almost sounded true. After Shadow left, she received a text with the location of the hospital. More proof that Scorpion was bad off. It was also Shadow's lovely way of making clear that he had her number, because she sure as hell hadn't given it to him.

Slim arms wrapped around her hunched shoulders as Greta dropped her head into her hands.

"There's a solution and we'll find it. Nothing is going to happen to you. Not ever," Sage assured her.

Walking into the living room, Cutter declared, "There's no guarantee, Sage. It's a clusterfuck. Best not to hand out false hopes."

Callous bastard. Her chest throbbed, and she willed herself to breathe. Her other option was to lunge and claw him to death. Anything to release the frustration and rage coursing through her.

"Don't even think about it," Cutter warned sternly. His glower promised retribution if she did a tenth of what she fantasized doing to him. Sweet, fucking hell. How did he read her so well?

"Hey, at least she's trying to make me feel better," Greta retorted.

He flexed his body in her direction, but Sage flung herself across Greta.

An instant later, Kingdom shoved Cutter against the wall. "Can you keep your shit together for one fucking moment? *Stay*. That's a fucking order."

Panic rushed up her throat. Kingdom was blaming Cutter,

but it was her fuckup. Kingdom backed off, but Cutter remained against the wall, spearing her with a withering stare.

"Sorry, Cutter," she called out from her seat on the couch.

He let out a growl in response.

Worried that if she stayed any longer, she'd continue provoking him or smack him hard, Greta jackknifed off the couch and strode toward the door. "I'm outta here."

By the time she reached for the door handle, familiar fingers wrapped around her nape and turned her into his chest. Her head hung down, and he draped himself around her, enclosing her in his arms.

"I'm sorry, I'm frustrated. That's where this is coming from. Ironic that I'm not even angry at you. This is my fault. I should've protected you so that he could've never gotten close enough to breath the same air as you. But we're gonna see this through to the end and I'll make sure they can never get to you again," he pressed.

"Scorpion's on his deathbed. He will make it happen."

His forehead crinkled. "Make what happen?"

Bile billowed up from her gut, but she fought against the band around her throat and choked out, "The marriage between Shadow and me."

Say what? He must've heard wrong because there was no fuckin' way the Horseman was going to touch, much less own, the woman he loved. End of story.

Jumping from the couch, Sage rushed toward them and cried, "What did she say? What. Did. She. Say!"

Kingdom pounced on her and hauled her against his chest, urging her, "Calm down, babe, this isn't helping the situation."

Greta burrowed into Cutter like a wounded animal.

"Look at me, Greta. This ain't your fuckin' fault."

"It is," she rasped.

"We've been blindsided. You had no idea that Scorpion would die or lose his goddamn mind."

"I should've known something like this would happen because that's what he wanted for years," she persisted. "I thought he gave up once he had Shadow by his side, but that bastard doesn't forget anything, and I grew complacent after so much time had passed."

Kingdom comforted Sage in the background. Cutter palmed Greta's throat, and her quiver of breath heated his nipple through his shirt. Watching him get aroused eventually helped her breathing subside.

Sage came toward them, and Greta moved into her outstretched arms. "I swear to you that we'll work this out. You're not alone and I'm not letting anything happen to you, Greta. You're my best friend and you know how much I care about you."

Over Sage's shoulder, Greta fastened her gaze on him. He nodded, reassuring her, and she said, "He's had plans for me with Shadow since I was a kid. Since Scorpion hadn't shown any interest in me in years, I thought he'd given up his quest."

Twisting her hands, she continued, "There were signs that he was watching, though. Little things. A guy who wouldn't stop asking me out suddenly left me alone for good. A landlord who was overly friendly suddenly stopped knocking on my door. You know what I mean..."

Yeah, he fuckin' knew exactly what she meant. Any club worth its mettle would behave the same way. They didn't approach her, but they were present, slipping in and out of the corners of her life. Worst of all, their behavior meant they thought they owned her. A tension headache battered against the cage of his skull like a jackhammer.

"Go on," he ground out.

"Shadow must not have an old lady, or not one Scorpion approves of. Otherwise, he'd continue to ignore my existence."

His nostrils flared, and an animalistic sound emanated from the pit of his soul. "Not necessarily."

The bastard was sick, and although the last thing he wanted was Greta near those fuckers, he wouldn't selfishly keep her away from her father near the end of his life. If Greta was right and Scorpion had plans for her and Shadow, the Squad was there for her now. Regardless of how she felt about it, she was Squad property. That gave her options, including visiting her father safely. Reuniting with an estranged parent on their deathbed was a powerful thing, and he'd do anything in his power to make it happen for her safely.

"Babe, Scorpion won't hurt you. You're imagining the worst, and"—Greta opened her mouth to speak, but he held up his hand to quiet her—"you may be right, but you will be my old lady when we show up in Camden. Shadow or no Shadow, you're off the market. Period."

"I don't want to go," she grumbled.

From behind them, Kingdom interjected, "Cutter's right. You've gotta see him. The Squad must also address the transgression of another club lurking around our territory and approaching you without permission. Can't let that slide."

"Scorpion is not Prez or Chopper," she countered. Kingdom's face drained of color, and Sage grasped his hand. Greta hurried to add, "There's a huge difference between these men, and he's not worth my attention."

"Truth is, brave girl, you will regret it if you don't see him," Cutter counseled.

"I don't want anything to do with him," she repeated with a

little stomp of her foot. She knew she was whining, but it was bad enough that he had diabolical plans for her. Now she had to go back to her hometown, face her old MC again, along with all the people she'd abandoned when she left with her mother, and confront her father for one more epic battle before he died. She certainly didn't have any hope of reconciling.

"You sure about that?" Cutter asked gently as he caught her by her waist and stroked up and down her arm. "Not one question you want him to answer? Not one last thing you want to say? This will be your last chance."

Greta faltered, "I-I'm not saying that there isn't a part of me that doesn't yearn to reconcile with him. It's just… I'm sure it will end in disaster."

"You know, when my moms was dying, I had resentments built up because of Tommy, but I put them aside and showed up for her. True, she didn't change, but it gave me peace to know that I did right by her. I had no regrets. Then, when Prez got sick, I learned to quit being lazy and step up. Death makes you realize things and puts life into perspective. At least, you'll get the chance to face the past."

Stroking her cheek, he continued in a low voice, "You're holding onto the pain. Facing Scorpion may free you of it, and you deserve to have that." He took her mouth in a blistering kiss.

Breaking it off, he promised, "And I'll be there with you every step of the way."

In the background, Kingdom uttered, "Loki, set up a meeting with Kite, the president of the Squad chapter in Jersey just in case, for backup. Greta's doing this with Cutter. You're gonna have a little chat with whoever's in charge and seek compensation for the slight on our rep."

40

GRETA

Greta wasn't near ready to see her father, so what did the maddening man do?

He fucked her until she was too sated to fight back. Filled her with his come to remind her of her who she belonged to and then told her they were riding to Jersey. She put as much distance as she could between them on the bike, but he swerved around bends and corners like a NASCAR driver, forcing her to clutch to him for dear life.

Once they crossed the state line, Loki split off to meet up with Kite and prep for their appointment with the Horsemen the following day.

The hot sun was waning by the time they reached Camden, the city ruled by The Dark Horsemen, and her hometown.

Everything was achingly familiar. The streets, the traffic lights, even the lampposts. Everywhere they rode, pieces and parcels of her past came unglued and memories floated unhindered in her mind. Her hands itched to throttle him from behind. Stress did that to her. Made her want to take a swing at him.

By the time they drove onto the block that housed the Dark Horsemen, she was crushed against his back. Her nerves were zapping around like dragonflies in her belly. He clasped his gloved hand over her thigh and gave her a reassuring squeeze.

The façade of the clubhouse hadn't changed much. An addition had been built, but other than that, the building was stuck in the same dirt yard, along with the same scrawny trees struggling to survive in the inhospitable soil.

Cutter rolled his bike right on the sidewalk, and a prospect jumped back.

"What the fuck?!" the prospect shouted as he peeled himself off the chain-link fence.

Cutter planted his boot on the asphalt and stabilized his bike.

"Nice show of force," she commented.

Whipping off his helmet, he looked over his shoulder at Greta and quipped, "That a compliment?"

Above the prospect hung a placard with an image of a horse rearing up on its hind legs, etched in red. Greta's vision was shrouded with the faces of past ghosts, some angels, but mostly demons. Gulping down the lump lodged in her throat, she traced the edge of her choker, her lodestone. Her spine stiffened. No, she wasn't going to cower. Not this time.

The prospect approached them, but halted when Cutter zoomed his fierce expression on him. Narrowing his eyes at the prospect, Cutter snapped, "Go tell whoever's in charge that Greta's here."

The prospect stood, glued to his spot, for an extra beat. Then, shaking his head, he beelined it to the clubhouse.

Swinging off the bike, she withdrew her helmet from her head and clenched it against her hip. It dug in at a sharp angle that would leave a bruise, but she'd deal with Cutter's complaint later.

"Greta."

Their gazes connected. Standing beside her, he laid his hand on her back and rubbed small circles. She caught the lapel of his cut and thumped her forehead against his heart.

"Breathe," he commanded.

His authority radiated through her, and the knot of breath stuck in her lungs unraveled and shuddered out. She inhaled a gulp of fresh air, and like a canister of gas released, it cleared her mind. Pushing up the sleeves of her jacket, she thrust her shoulders back, her gaze level at the entrance.

"You've got this, highness," he reminded her as they walked to the entrance.

Greta shoved against the beat-up door sticking to the frame, and it swung open. Stepping inside, her vision adjusted to the dim lighting, and her breath caught.

The bar.

The plain wood was scuffed with a glut of nicks and dents. The bar was where she spent her afternoons doing her homework while following Shadow from under her eyelashes. Listening to every word he said, watching every move he made.

Eyes sharp, she scanned the gathering of bikers until her gaze landed on a grisly biker who was rounding the bar. Greta escaped Cutter's hold and flung herself on him.

Scudder.

Poppy to her. A nickname she'd come up with to tease him when he tried to distract her from one of Scorpion's rages. Wrapping her arms around his thick neck, she felt two spots burning in the back of her head. Cutter, probably glaring at her from behind.

"You remember an old man like me, princess?" Poppy's gruff voice cracked.

She clung to him tighter. Buried in his leathery neck, she muttered, "I could never forget you. Drowning my sorrows with you and a big glass of Coke with ten ice cubes, just the way I liked it."

"Liked? Don't you like it anymore?" he joked.

"Without you making my special drink, how could I?" she teased back.

Abruptly, Cutter's hand was on her nape. Manhandling her in the presence of the entire MC. Before she could react, she was whisked off Poppy and brought to his side. His rough palm wrapped around her trachea to keep her in check. Scudder's keen eyes flicked to Cutter's hand.

Without shifting his gaze from Scudder, Cutter demanded, "Who's he?"

Vibrating like a tuning fork, she hummed lightly under her breath. His grasp flexed around her throat. Pressing forward, she tested the pressure on her throat; his hand tensed to tell her he was onto her. Yeah, yeah, he'd reprimand her for taxing him in a hostile environment. His sole focus should be on her safety, blah, blah, blah. Greta leaned back into Cutter and grabbed his solid thigh, stroking it to pacify him.

"This is Scudder. He's an old friend who helped me," she sniffed softly, "through bad days."

His fingers twitched around her neck. "He better not have put his hands on you when he *helped* you."

She elbowed him in the gut. Unfazed by the insult, Scudder inspected Cutter's Demon Squad patches. Bikers shifted and gathered around them at the bar, emitting a series of low growls. Tension crackled in the air. Her gaze bounced from man to man, some she recognized, some she didn't.

Then, the old man's features relaxed. At the softening of his expression, the pack of brothers eased off.

"Glad that Greta's with a man who knows a prize when he sees one. And protects her like one."

Whew. Her chest caved in and she caught herself from slumping over in relief. Scudder held Cutter's even gaze with one of his own. Pretending to be in a huff, she moved out from under Cutter and planted a fist on her hip.

"I'll have you know that I'm not just some biker's property. I can take care of myself. Very well, I might add," she emphasized.

"She's a work in progress," Cutter remarked drolly.

Scudder snickered, "Yep, you've got your work cut out for you. Always was a handful."

Greta glared at Scudder. "Are you kidding me right now?"

Ignoring her, Cutter said, "Don't I know it. She's feisty, but I wouldn't want her any other way."

"Warms my heart to see her spirit ain't broken."

Greta waved her hands in front of the men. "Hello, I'm right here, people."

Cutter broke into a chortle.

Scudder finally acknowledged her, "That you are. You drinkin' something stronger than Coke nowadays?"

Greta gave Cutter a sidelong, questioning glance. His left eye squinted slightly, an indication of approval. Good, because she needed a drink like she needed her next breath. "I could use rum in that Coke."

"I'll be damned. Grown up into a queen."

Before she could slap him, he turned away and walked behind the bar. Waving them over, he signaled to the other Horsemen, giving them permission to approach her. Scudder might be old, but he was the guardian of the clubhouse premises.

Led by Stacy, Scudder's old lady, the women surged forward and engulfed them. Cutter might have control over her heart and body, but he was powerless in the face of these proud women. They pried her away from Cutter and pulled her into the core of their circle. Whether reacquainting themselves with her or introducing themselves to her, they showered her with devotion. Their prodigal daughter had returned, and they worshipped her as if she was the answer to their prayers. Throwing looks at Cutter, they assessed him with an audacity the brothers wouldn't have gotten away with.

Except for Stacy, she remembered these old ladies and bitches as timid and cowed. But as they swayed her in their undulating arms, they were energized, and she joined them in their reverie. Unchecked tears flowed down her cheeks as she was liberated from the pain and remorse she'd secreted away for years. All the while, Cutter circled around them like a prowling male keeping an eye on his mate.

Among her family of origin and Cutter, hope nudged her in the chest. Perhaps seeing Scorpion would be cathartic as well. A vision came to her, of sitting by his bed as he recited the Native stories of her childhood to her, her head laying on the padding of his shoulder. Cutter had told her the story of lying by his mother's side before she died. Although she'd been asleep, the moment helped pull him through his grief afterward. Who knew what unexpected gift awaited her when she met Scorpion?

41

CUTTER

Dusk blanketed the sky by the time they reached the hospital. Against the background of low, flat clouds from an incoming summer storm, a column of windows flew up above them, pouring out florescent light that took on a muted glow in the hazy drizzle.

They drove past the bright lights of the entranceway to the back of the parking lot, and Greta's hands fisted his cut like it was a lifeline. Her gesture hurt his heart. Despite her nervousness, he'd promised to take care of her, and bringing her to see her father was part of that.

Shutting off the engine, Cutter offered her a comforting smile. His fingers intertwined with hers as he tucked her into his side. At the curb of the sidewalk across from the hospital entrance, Greta hung back.

He chucked her on the chin and said, "Head up. I know you're afraid, but look how well things went at the clubhouse."

"This is altogether different," she griped.

Beckoning her back to his side, he said, "Yeah, but one thing's the same. You've got me by your side."

She hesitated for a moment, then allowed him to tug her

hand, and they crossed the street together. The glass doors slid open into a cheery, blissfully cool, bustling lobby. At the check-in counter, a woman wearing a name tag with Marge written in block letters, welcomed them. When Greta muttered her father's name, Marge clapped her hands together in glee.

"Oh! You're here to visit Mr. Wright."

Greta stiffened against him.

No fuckin' wonder because he knew that Wright was not her surname.

"At first, the young men visiting him made me a tad nervous. But his sons and their friends are such nice boys," Marge chattered on.

Greta choked, and Cutter had to pound between her shoulders to stop her spluttering.

Unaware, the woman blushed and winked. "They do like to flirt with the women. Charming aren't they?"

Greta clenched the edge of the desk as she forced a tight smile on her lips.

Looking her over, Marge inquired, "Are you family, too?"

A sharp sound came from the back of her throat.

Cutter sent her a quelling look, and with a broad smile, explained, "Sorry, my wife has allergies."

Labeling her as his wife renewed her agitation, and he roughly hauled her squirming body against him. She let out an *oomph* but pressed into the warm bulk of his large body. That seemed to have done the trick because she quieted down.

"You alright, hon?" Marge asked, with a stitch of concern between her eyebrows.

"She'll be fine. A seat and a glass of water will help. You know women when they're expecting," he ended with a shrug.

Beneath his jacket, Greta inflicted a wicked pinch to his

side. He ground down on his molars and plastered a smile on his face as the woman prattled on.

"The same thing happened to me with my oldest. Now, when you get to Mr. Wright's room, make sure to settle yourself in a cozy chair. He's in 205, the west wing. Take a left, go down the long hall to the end, and grab one of the elevators there."

She gave Greta a commiserating smile. "The first trimester is the worst, dear. Hang in there, and remember, before you know it you'll be cuddling that bundle of joy in your arms!"

"Thanks for your advice, ma'am," Cutter replied overly politely. He gave her a little salute and towed Greta away before she wrapped her hands around Marge's neck and strangled her.

Around the nearest corner, Greta spat out, "His sons? Sons, my ass. *Nice boys?* Jesus, every one of them is a cold-blooded killer. Is she insane? It's not as if they don't look the part!"

"Easy, babe. Don't lose your shit now," he said calmly.

"And you," she huffed out with a smack that bounced off his taut stomach. "Your wife. Your *pregnant* wife. I'm just sayin', this isn't the time to poke the bear, Cutter. I'm about to go Incredible Hulk on these people and you're making jokes?"

He pulled her to his other side before she got slammed by an orderly hurtling down the hallway pushing a rolling metal container.

"I don't joke about shit like that. This isn't the time to delve into a serious discussion about pregnancy, of all things, but it is a conversation we will have," he alerted her.

Spinning her around, Cutter prodded her down the busy corridor toward the elevators. Once they got there, her limbs slackened, and she leaned into him heavily. His sweet girl was exhausted. He slid his forearm around her back, and she snuggled into his chest.

They rode up to the second floor and followed the signs to the Intensive Care Unit. Doctors, nurses, and interns either zipped around them with maniacal efficiency or were hunched over screens, tapping away with intent concentration. Greta dragged her feet as they walked down a hallway and entered the waiting area for the ICU.

Half a dozen bikers lounged on the bolted seats, either on their phones or watching a TV monitor attached to the wall. One biker had a wiggling toddler firmly grasped on his lap. Another man paced the length of the wall-to-wall carpeting, like a death-row inmate. Turning on his heel, he caught sight of them and paused midstride.

Shadow.

His dark eyes churned with an emotion Cutter knew only too well. Longing. Christ, this was a shit show. He pinned the asshole with a fuck-you glare.

The asshole jerked his head and said tersely, "He's in there. I'll take you."

Cutter waved his hand magnanimously. "Lead the way."

At the sound of his deep baritone, heads swung in their direction. Several bikers shot up off their seats, their eyes grim, mouths flat. The biker with the kid moved the boy behind him, as if to protect him from Cutter. He snorted at the irony of it considering the man had likely killed men with his bare hands.

The colors of his Demon Squad leather cut had them snarling in warning, but raising her chin like the queen she was, Greta took the lead and punched the button that opened the double doors leading to the isolated unit. At Scorpion's room, Shadow signaled to the brothers manning the outside to step aside.

Nodding, Greta acknowledged them, "Gunner. Lazer."

He almost burst out laughing when their eyeballs bulged out of their sockets. Gunner cracked a smile at Greta, but nipped it when Shadow threw him a look full of daggers.

GUNNER LOOKED THE SAME, except for a few more lines around his eyes. He drew the hospital curtain open for them to step in. The pungent odor of antiseptic hit her nostrils and her nose twitched as if she was about to sneeze. A large window filtered in the twinkling lights from the surrounding hospital buildings in the darkness.

Shadow took his position beside Scorpion. Her nerves jangled like a distorted heavy-metal guitar riff as her eyes landed on her father for the first time in a decade.

He was propped up on pillows, eyes closed, his corded, tattooed forearms crossed over his torso. His once large frame was gaunt, his abdomen cavernous in a hospital gown that dwarfed him. A white cotton blanket covered his skinny, atrophied legs. Much of his hair was missing. The long braid he'd once worn with pride was gone.

Taking in his emaciated body, Greta expected to feel something. Extreme love or extreme hate. Instead, she felt nothing. There he lay, whittled down to an old, worn-out biker who'd lived too hard, and would die too soon.

Scorpion's eyes slanted open like a copperhead snake and enlarged in increments. They glittered with the instincts of a killer. Pressing the controller, the head of his bed rose as his gaze roved over her. Then, it cut to Cutter's patches, dismissing her.

He spat on the linoleum floor. "What in the fuck is a Demon Squad asswipe doin' with my daughter?"

"Seriously? After ten years, that's the first thing you have to say to me. You're unbelievable. You don't have the decency to take care of your own blood, but you have the nerve to question my choice in a partner?"

Poised to jump on Scorpion's bed and cut off the remainder of his short life, Cutter snatched her by the arm just in the nick of time and held her back. She struggled against his hold, so he hooked her by the waist, sat down and towed her over his lap. Nimbly, she scrambled upright. The dead hole inside her was rapidly filling with hate.

The urge to throw her independence in his face was riding her hard. "He's with me and there's nothing you can do about it," she snarled at her father.

Scorpion's face turned a mottled purple. His was a man's world, and a strange male from another clan was a direct insult to him and everything he stood for. His razor-sharp eyes paused on Greta's hand, rubbing Cutter's chest.

Eyes bulging, he strained forward as he roared, "Get him the fuck out of here!"

But Scorpion's body was broken and his bellow ended in a ragged cough.

Cutter casually flicked a piece of lint off his denim jeans, leaned in and nuzzled the side of her throat. Shadow's glower deepened, his dark eyes burning bright with hate.

Tension vibrated through Greta's muscles. Gathering her determination around her like a cloak, she declared, "He stays. If you wish to talk me, then talk now. Otherwise we're leaving."

Scorpion wiped spittle from his mouth with the back of his hand. "Who the fuck is he to you?"

Greta began to respond, but Cutter interjected, "Cutter's my name. I claimed your daughter."

Greta's hand stilled as she dragged in a protracted breath.

The troublemaker in her wanted to fight him on it, but she held back. As much as she hated to play these biker games, this was his way of protecting her.

Scorpion razor-sharp eyes registered her reaction. A slow, demonic grin spread over his face. "You're shit out of luck, boy, 'cause I decide who claims her."

Greta exploded out of Cutter's lap and lunged over the bed until she was nose to nose with her father. "You're not my father in any way that counts. You were nothing but a sperm donor and have no power over me."

Cutter rose behind her and caught her by the nape. At this point, her dreams of reuniting with this bastard were dashed, and second-degree murder was looking like a pretty good second option.

CUTTER WANTED to rip his shirt off, beat his chest, and crow his victory to the world because he'd publicly declared Greta as his. Pride filled his lungs as his little kitten's back arched, fur raised, ears flat. She was spitting mad and fucking cute.

"I lived with you for what? Sixteen years? You had years to behave like a real father, but instead, you spent your time destroying Marianne. You lost the right to decide what I do with my life a long time ago, old man," she sneered.

Her words hadn't wiped off Scorpion's smirk. Without an ounce of contrition, he jabbed a finger toward Cutter and snarled, "He's a worthless dog! Quit whinin' that I didn't go after you after you ran off with your momma and that good-for-nothin' piece of shit traitor, Trucker. While I'm still breathing, I'm making up for it and getting you the fuck away from him." He thrust a crooked finger at Cutter.

Escaping Cutter's hold, she clawed up Scorpion's bed before he had the chance to stop her. He plucked her off just as her arms came in swinging, fighting him to reach Scorpion. The Horsemen began to move toward them, but he held them off with a scowl.

In her ear, he warned, "He's goading you, baby girl. Don't give him the satisfaction."

Her hand flung back and cracked against the side of his temple. Fuck, that stung.

Gasping, she caressed the reddening skin. "Oh my God, I'm so sorry!"

Veering back toward Scorpion again, Greta argued, "You know nothing about him."

"You think I don't know about the man-whore my daughter shacked up with or his *reputation*," he spat out the last word with disgust. "The twisted motherfucker made a name for himself for tyin' bitches up and you're complainin' about what I did to your mother? You'll regret him as much as your mother regretted me."

Cutter almost doubled over in laughter, but held it in. The old son-of-a-bitch had no clue who his daughter was. Greta buckled against him and he caught her before she fell to the floor.

Fuck this. There was no reconciliation in sight. The suffering in her eyes made him want to tear the old man to shreds, but his priority was his woman. *Time to shut it down.*

"We're done here, old man," he declared as he ushered her toward the exit. They were almost across the threshold when Shadow stepped in front of them.

"The hell you are," the pussy biker threatened.

"That's right, son, take what you should've taken years ago," Scorpion called out from behind them. Touching Greta's sleeve, Shadow gave her an imploring look. His expression bled something poignant. Love. Had to be, because how could a biker not love her?

"Babe, I love you," he confessed in a hushed tone. "Always have. Everyone loves you. Greta, you belong here, with your family. They need you to lead them now that your father's going to leave us."

"Are you fucking serious, Shadow? Why didn't you come to me years ago?"

"I tried. God knows, I tried," he pleaded. "I was going to leave the Horsemen for you. I went to your college. Found you studying in a coffee shop. I was about to come up to you when another student stopped by your table and started talking to you. You were happy, laughing like I'd never seen before and I knew that I couldn't take you away from that. You'd built a hard-won life, and I had nothing to offer you except a future in another club. I knew that if I'd shown myself, you'd have left with me, so I left without giving you the chance."

Cutter rolled his eyes. Please, motherfucker. No one would buy that bullshit story, least of all Greta. Shadow took a step closer to her, and Cutter tightened his hold on her, but Greta detached herself from him.

Shadow took her hand and Cutter gritted his teeth from snatching her hand out of his. He'd let this play out for the sole purpose of putting Shadow and Scorpion behind Greta. This was for her so that she could get rid of these ghosts once and for all, and move on with her life with him and the Demon Squad.

"Greta, you belong with the Horsemen," Shadow said, in a cajoling voice. "You can right past wrongs and make the club what it was meant to be. A club your mom would be proud of."

She dropped her head into Shadow's chest. It was a gesture he'd only ever seen her do with him and it gutted him that she was doing it with this man, that she was letting him touch her, that she was seeking shelter in another man's arms.

Over Greta's bent head, Shadow locked eyes with Cutter and bared his teeth. He gritted out, "You can't offer the same."

Cutter's heart crashed against his ribcage. The fucker was right. He'd seen how easy it was for Greta when they'd been at the clubhouse. She belonged with them. He told her he owned her, but staring down at her head cushioned against Shadow's heart, the choice was ultimately hers. Yes, she'd returned to Cutter, but that could have easily been motivated by jealousy when she saw him with Angie. Had she submitted to him fully? Was she his completely, in the depths of her heart and soul? He drew in a rattled breath. Honestly, he wasn't completely sure. After all, her running out on him hadn't been exclusively about the arrest.

Fuck him, the son of a bitch was right. He had something she'd wanted since she was a kid, long before she'd met Cutter. The Horsemen were her kin. Greta was a princess to her core, and he couldn't rip the offer out of her hands and selfishly bind her to him.

Around the lump in his throat, he called, "Greta."

She turned around in Shadow's arms, streaks of mascara and tears tracked down her cheeks. "You've got a choice to make."

Her brows slashed down over her eyes. "What are you talking about?"

"There's shit you gotta work out with the Horsemen." His gaze lifted briefly to Shadow. "I'm trusting you'll be safe here while you do it. Loki will be comin' with Kite and his posse to deal with the trespassing issue. It will give you time to work out what you want to do, where you want to be."

Greta shoved Shadow's limbs away from her. Charging up

to him, she exclaimed, "What the hell are you talking about, Cutter? You leaving me?"

His hand reached out to caress her softly. "Never, brave girl. I'm giving you time. Time to figure out what you really want. Remember when I said that I didn't want to look over my shoulder each time some shit went down. I'm making sure you do you. You gotta figure out if there's anything here you want bad enough to stay. I love you too damn much to bully you into staying with me again. We got back together, but I'm giving us the chance to do this right."

His tone dropped to an intimate octave, "Because, believe me woman, if you choose to submit to me, there will be no going back."

Her gaze skittered away from his. His heart cracked, pieces crashing down and scattering on the hospital linoleum floor beneath his feet.

"See, you're hesitating. I want our relationship to be complete and for that to happen, there can't be an ounce of uncertainty. Our kind of life requires *complete* submission, feel me? I don't know if you can give that, and I can't live with anything less. It's your choice and I'm giving you the space you need to come to the right answer without my influence to sway you because, swear to God, if you come back to me, there will be no hesitation. You take my collar, my name, my jacket on your back. You take everything. You ready for that, Greta?"

Greta stood still, eyes blinking, but he had to step away fast before he lost his determination.

"I think not," he concluded. Nodding once to Shadow, he spun on his heel and shouldered his way through the guards. Down the hallway, he paused for a moment, waiting to see if she'd run out.

"Fucking hell," he cursed. He tore past the waiting room and slammed open the door to the stairway. Taking three steps at a time, he jumped to the landing of the next floor and then flew down to the lobby. Without a word, he passed the chatty receptionist and went out into the muggy, dense night. He jogged to his bike before he lost his nerve, revved it up, and skidded out of the parking lot.

42

———

GRETA

Greta lifted her face from her hands. Shadow's arms were wrapped around her and crushed her against him until she could barely breathe. "Babe, you're safe here. Stay with me."

A disbelieving laugh escaped her. Squinting up at him, she said, "You can't imagine how many times I've waited to hear those words from you. Too many to count. Even today, sitting by the bar at the clubhouse, I thought I wanted to hear that." She shook her head in wonder. "Even if they're true, it doesn't matter anymore. My place is with someone else."

Grasping her shoulders roughly, Shadow growled, "You can't mean that. I've waited years for this moment. The bastard is finally dying. My hard work and patience are paying off. You were always part of my bigger plan."

Greta sniffed with derision. "You can't expect me to believe that. It's been over ten years! I know you, and"—she smacked his cut—"if you had wanted me bad enough, nothing would've prevented you from coming for me. Nothing! Right now, it behooves you to have me by your side. This is all for show." Straining against him, she hissed, "I saw you the day Scorpion went up to Vermont and spoke to Marianne."

Holding her firmly in place, Shadow drew back, eyes narrowed. "You knew I was there?"

"As if I would've left Marianne alone with that abusing asshole. Of course, I was there. I was hiding and I heard what she said to you. You didn't make a move. And you knew me better than anyone. If you had shown yourself, I would've left everything for you. I would've done anything for you. Anything! Can you say the same for me?"

"It wasn't the right time," he said, avoiding answering her question directly. "Your father didn't trust me, and I had to prove to him that I hadn't helped you and your mother get out."

"If you had loved me, *you* would've helped us, not Trucker. Knowing you, you have something up your sleeve. One of the brothers must have called you when Cutter and I were at the clubhouse. Told you how I was received by the brothers and bitches. They trust me, not you, and you need that trust to make sure you become president." Eyeing him carefully, she nodded. "That's it, isn't it? Someone else is vying for the spot and you need reinforcements."

"You're wrong, " he said, harshly.

"I'm not," she retorted. Anger bled into his expression. Adjusting his grip on her, Shadow began to shake her. Thrashing against his iron clasp, she went for his eyes, but he backhanded her. Scorpion raised himself halfway up, and hollered, "Take her down! Teach her how to respect bikers."

Gunner and Lazer tackled Shadow to the ground. He lunged up again and again, but they held him down. A hand to her throbbing red cheek, she stared up at her father and spat out, "To think that I came here with the hope that you'd changed. That there was something salvageable in you."

Stumbling off the bed, Scorpion made a grab for her, but he was too weak, and she threw him off her.

"Cutter," she whimpered.

Shadow, lying on his belly, wrists twisted behind him and a knee in his back, snarled, "He left you, you cunt. If he cared for you, he would've stayed and fought for you like a man. But, he's a fucking little bitch."

Greta gave him a swift kick in the ribs and ran out of the room. She shuffled down the hall, and after scanning the waiting room, she rushed past the bikers and didn't stop until she was out of the hospital. She screeched to a halt at the curb, in time to see a small blur, a retreating biker jetting out from the far end of the parking lot. Hands shaking, she pulled out her cell and dialed. "Poppy, I need help."

43

CUTTER

Cutter had to believe she'd make the right decision. Otherwise, the ache pulsing in his chest would become a permanent companion. On his way home, he made a pit stop for two bottles of whiskey and then locked himself inside his house to wait.

Swinging the bottle to his lips, he guzzled it down until the burn mixed with the acid already churning in his gut. Spine plastered against the shut door, he promptly slid down to the ground and hung his head between his knees. The only time he lifted it was to fit the bottle to his lips. The ringtone for Kingdom went off, cutting off his swallow. He wiped his mouth with the back of his hand and reached for his cell. "What do you want?"

"Where the fuck are you?"

"Home. What's up?"

"Sage is blowing up my phone. You left Greta in Camden?"

"Yeah, Loki's there and she needed some time."

"Time for fuckin' what? That's your old lady."

"Butt out, Kingdom."

"You left her alone with those fuckers. Without tellin' me. What the fuck were you thinkin', you dumb fuck?"

"I'm doing right by her," he asserted.

"Fucking hell, you're not making up for being a slacker by throwing her away. I'm retracting my offer for VP. I can't be having an idiot like you as my second-in-command."

"Stay in your fucking lane. I'm not throwing her away. I'm giving her a *choice*. Big difference."

"You sure about that? Christ, stop whoring yourself out as a martyr. It doesn't suit you. I hope you don't end up ruining your life for your fucking pride," he remarked, before disconnecting.

Cutter scrubbed his eyelids, but he couldn't block out the image of Greta. Her bright eyes and luscious curves. They had been his. Hopefully, they would be again. Maybe Kingdom was right and he was going to regret his actions, but he had to follow his gut, and his gut had never let him down.

Hours later, he blinked, and found himself slumped on the floor. Lightning-fast pain struck and felt like his skull was cleaved in two. Rubbing the crease the floorboard left on his cheek, he groaned and rolled onto his back. He stared bleakly at the ceiling, lifted his fingers out of a pool of spilled alcohol, and shook them. Droplets of liquor sprayed him in the eye. Shaking his head, he managed to dispel his disorientation.

He'd do right by her. It might fucking kill him, but so be it. With a palm planted on the floor, he stumbled to his feet, hauled himself onto his couch and collapsed, winded from the exertion.

Boom, boom, boom.

The pounding on the door hammered inside his skull.

"Cutter, open up it's me."

Greta. He heaved himself up and stumbled to the door. It sprang open and his eyes gobbled up the sight of her standing in front of him. The urge to grab her was intense, but instead, he stepped back to let her in. For the first time in his life, he prayed that he hadn't fucked up by giving her options.

"I choose you, not him. Never him."

Dragging her into his arms, he exhaled, "Thank fuck."

She wrapped her arms around his waist and confessed, "There's only been you since the day we met. I love you. My happiness is in your hands."

The starkness in her voice wrapped around his heart. Burned through his veins and stirred his cock to life. Staring at his open palms, he focused on the sharp, horizontal line cutting across the other lines. Greta was that line. Discovering her had cut him off from the wreckage of his past and healed him. Made him a better man. He trailed his fingers down her wet cheek. "I left because I was trying to do the right thing."

"I know," she whispered, "but what's right for me is you. Only you. The best thing that's ever happened to me was us. I'd go insane if I lost you."

Fierce possessiveness rushed through him. He slammed his mouth down on hers, pushing through her lips, and devoured her. Leaving her lips bruised, with traces of blood from their teeth, he scattered open-mouthed kisses along her jaw and her arched throat. Sweeping her into his arms, he marched into his bedroom as she licked and nipped the side of his throat.

CUTTER DRAPED her over the bed and covered her with his body. Her nipples beaded against the hard ridges of his defined chest. His intoxicating musk enveloped her, and the knots in her belly unraveled, leaving her boneless. Tugging her shirt up with one hand, his other slid up her short skirt, aiming straight for her pussy. He cocked his head to the side, and she got a side-long glimpse of his smug grin, eyes alight with triumph. Cutter's thumb pushed through her slippery folds before flattening her clit.

Holding her gaze, he intoned, "You're mine, babe." Oh, the word *mine* wound her up, flaying her from the inside out. His fingers speared her, and she urgently ground herself against the heel of his palm, straining to suck his stiff, thick digits into her clenching sex. He gruffly blew out a breath against her temple, a sultry gush of tropical air.

"Repeat after me."

Dependent on the tension building inside her, she pumped her hips to get more of the right amount of pressure.

"Greta," he cautioned.

She grunted in frustration. Dammit, he was going to be difficult. Suddenly, he had his key chain in his hand and whipped it around his fist a few times. She blinked furiously. "What are you doing?"

"Repeat what I said."

Her mind flickered out. For the life of her, she couldn't remember what he'd said. "Umm..."

Chortling darkly, he yanked off her shirt and her bra. Her torso bare, he tweaked each of her nipples and then dragged the chain roughly over one, crushing the peak between the links of the silver chain. The sharp sting of metal sparked a shiver. Gasping, she arched her back.

"Concentrate," he chided, "because even if I've got my cock moving inside you, it's bad form to do anything without my permission. Say it, Greta."

"Nothing without your permission," she repeated vaguely, "Now finish me off, dammit!" His fingers surged inside her sex and twisted, hitting the right spot. Her hips twitched, and an arrogant smile crept over his lips.

"Got an ache, baby girl?" He thrust in boldly, hard and fast, but quickly removed them, and ordered, "Turn over."

She flipped onto her belly, and he pressed a palm between her shoulder blades, telling her to stay still. Behind her came the sound of his boots scuffing the carpet. Then, he massaged the chain against the puckered hole between her butt cheeks until she was a writhing mass of flesh, arching her back and spreading her buttocks for more. His fingers tangled her hair as he gathered her tresses and meticulously secured them around his fist.

She let out a strangled scream as he guided her to her knees until she was facing him on the carpet. Yearning for his touch, Greta thrust her breasts out, proudly displaying her nipples, one of them red from his earlier ministrations. Smirk fading, he took a big swallow. Good, she thought grimly.

"Extend your knees until your cunt is spread on the ground."

Gaze trained on the patch of carpet between her legs, Greta alternated her weight from side to side. Her knee ground down on something sharp, and she stifled a grimace. Her hamstrings were stretched so wide, they burned. Discreetly, she circled her hips to scrape her puffed-up clit. A spasm popped off a mini explosion at the back of her skull, and she jerked. A vein pulsed along his temple.

"I didn't give you permission to grind down on your pussy for relief." His hand landed heavily on her shoulder, and she almost buckled beneath the weight. "Get back up, brat."

As she struggled to her feet, he abruptly swung her up and landed her on his lap, knees flanking his thighs. Embarrassed by her overenthusiasm, Greta buried her face in his chest. Nuzzling her, he combed his fingers through her hair above while experimenting below with the lips of her sex. Blood rushed to the place where he played with her, engorging her clit into a hard pebble. A seductive chuckle rumbled near the hollow of her ear.

His mouth engulfed hers. Slanting his tongue over hers, he rode it full throttle. Moaning, she met him with equal force, and their tongues wrangled like wrestlers. He broke off and murmured over her skin, "I feel that wet, fuckable cunt. Your sweet cream is drenching my fingers."

He breached her pussy with four fingers in one solid thrust. A slurping sound dominated her ears as he set a fast pace. "I was gonna lap up your sweetness."

Nodding desperately, she broke off sucking on his neck, imploring, "Yes. Please."

A teasing smile lifted a corner of his lips. "If you listened and hadn't rubbed your cunt on the carpet, takin' your pleasure without permission, you'd already have my cock in that fuckable mouth of yours. Only thing I'd be deciding was whether to take your pussy or ass next. Instead, you had to make shit difficult for yourself. When you earn it," his words wound around her like a spell, "I promise it's gonna be like nothing you've experienced before. Obscene. *Nasty.*"

Greta palmed the hard ridge of his cock behind his jeans. She dove for his fly, but he withdrew his fingers from her cunt, seized her hand, and popped a smack on her flank.

"Time on your knees hasn't taught you enough. The way you're going, you'll finish up with a sore pussy but no orgasm."

The words *no orgasm* halted her in her tracks, and she wilted. Humming with approval, Cutter dragged his zipper down and spread his jeans open. His massive cock smacked against his navel. He always went commando. Simply knowing that he was ready for action, anyplace and anytime, had her salivating.

"Not convinced you deserve my cock, but I'll show you mercy. You'll pay me back, wearin' your love collar." He cupped her throat and tilted her up until their eyes were aligned. "On your chain. In public."

Wearing a choker was manageable, but with a chain? In public? Panic gurgled in her throat. "No!"

Greta went for gouging his eyes, but he had her on her back in an instant, wrists cuffed above her head. Ramming her body up, she strove to crack her head against his nose, but he straddled her waist. She continued to strain against his powerful grip, striking him with her elbows wherever she could. He leaned her sideways and looped her arms resolutely behind her. Pinning her down, he landed slap after slap on her buttocks, her flesh rising and falling in response to his precise, controlled smacks.

"Disobedient. Little girl, I go soft on you for a second and you throw my leniency in my face."

Click-click.

Manacles locked around her wrists. Sliding down her thrashing body, he wrenched her thighs open and caught a slip of skin between his teeth. Mercilessly, he suckled until his face was coated with wetness.

"I saw the Horsemen watching you, begging you with their eyes. But, they're not gettin' their little queen, are they? Oh no, they're not, because she's mine."

"Get off," she shouted between pants. Bracing his arms on either side of her, he caught the curve of her chin and shook it.

"Cut it out."

The hardness of his tone gave her pause. Smoothing the length of her inner thigh, he mused, "Look at that ripe pussy." He skimmed a finger between her nether lips. "But, it doesn't deserve a touch yet," he tutted. "Naughty kitten, I'm gonna clip those nails and build a cage for my little wildcat."

He brought her to her knees and rose above her. The tip of his cock rubbed between her parched lips and her tongue instinctively darted out. A shudder went through him. His cock was exquisite. Despite his reprimands, this was a treat because Cutter rarely allowed her to suck him off. His musky flavor hit her taste buds, and she moaned around his cockhead. Pre-come oozed out, coating her palate, and she lapped up whatever she could.

"Fuck, girl. You're earning your way back to me."

Her thumb and forefinger circled the base of his cock and followed the glide of her mouth. Looking up, she batted her eyelashes and inquired sweetly, "You want it slow and sloppy? Or fast and hard?"

He rocked his hips. "You'll find out soon enough."

Her head leaned against his thigh, causing his cock to push into the inside of her cheek. She repositioned herself quickly to work her tongue over the ridge on the underside of his penis and took her time. When she tipped her head back to swallow the head against the back of her throat, he took her hair like reins. Fucking her mouth, his shaft drove the air out of her lungs as he bottomed out, his balls bouncing against her chin. Gripping his quads, she relished the iron power of his muscles as they flexed under her fingers. Although it barely gave her enough friction, she rubbed her clit against the comforter.

"I didn't give you permission to—"

Cutter ended in a grunt when she sucked his cock in deeply. Cupping his balls, she massaged them, and his head dropped back as her name ripped out of his throat. She snaked her fingers down her torso and onto her clit in time for his semen to spurt out and spill from the sides of her mouth. Cutter plunged his fingers inside to spur her on further. Oh, did she ride those thick, flat fingers of his to her peak. Exploding violently, she shot off into the skyline and shattered like a clay target at a hunting range.

His fingers strummed her until she collapsed, and his cock slipped from her mouth. He settled in behind her and wrapped her into the shelter of his heaving chest. Talking into her halo of raven tresses, he said, "Shadow cares, ya know. I saw it in his eyes. He cares. How could he not, when there's no woman as picture-perfect as you?"

"Perhaps, but Shadow cares about his position with the Horsemen the most. You love me, he doesn't. He wanted me by his side to reinforce his takeover. I know him inside and out, and I know you inside and out. A perfect example was the fact that you walked away to give me the chance to make up my own mind. Not once has Shadow done what was right for *me*. It's true that, as a kid, he was the first person to see me, really see the hurt little girl inside me. And at the hospital, she got the attention she craved from him, but acknowledging my hunger and knowing where my heart lies are two different things. You're my heart."

Cutter eased her off him, swung his legs over the bed and planted his elbows on his knees. Facing away, he said, "Princess, you're meant to be at the top of the pecking order. I can't offer you that with the Squad. Kingdom offered me the position of vice president, but it won't be the same."

"Cutter, I already have a career that I love, and I have no intention of dropping it for any club. I'm already advising Sage as she takes her place alongside Kingdom in the Squad. Being the old lady to the vice president would simply make what I already do official, but I'd do it anyway. Another reason I rejected the Horsemen is because the Squad is my club. My loyalty is here, with you and them."

He expelled a ragged breath and, pivoting toward her, said, "Say that again, babe. You don't know how long I've yearned to hear it."

EPILOGUE

GRETA

Cutter had moved her into his place permanently before the week ended.

Among half-opened boxes and piles of books, Greta lounged against him on the couch, a book propped up on her chest. A game was droning on in the background. It was becoming one of her favorite reading positions.

A silver hoop dangling from Cutter's index finger dropped in front of the page before her. Squinting, she read "Property of Cutter" inscribed on the burnished silver. Snatching it with greedy fingers, she flung the book down and turned around to face him. The collar was crushed between them; Greta pressed her lips against his.

"It's a day collar. You can wear it backward and hide it underneath your hair when it's down if you're at work or running errands. No one would be the wiser."

Her heart pinched. In the midst of proclaiming his love for her, he was respecting her limitations.

"It'll make it hotter when I take you home and mount you from behind. Pull up that thick hair of yours and see my name etched in silver while slamming into you. *Grrr.* We should try out my theory right now."

A needy moan slipped out of her as Greta clasped his head and smashed his lips down on hers. Once she released him, he spoke in a husky rasp, "Try it on."

She scooped her hair to the side and arched her neck. Cutter clasped it around her throat, and the weight settled comfortably above her collarbone. Although she couldn't tell what it looked like, it felt glorious.

Sprawled on his chest, she laid her head on top of her linked hands. Eyes heavy-lidded, his tawny lashes threw long shadows over the broken line of his nose. He slid a palm over her collarbone, tracing the edge of the cuff. Following the dip of her waist and the rise of her hip, his palm rested on her outer thigh. He stilled. His head shot up and his gaze zeroed in on her Horsemen tattoo.

He caught her hand and flicked his tongue on the inside of her wrist. Trailing an invisible path up her forearm, he suckled on the sensitive skin of her inner elbow. She gave him a wobbly smile, and mouthed, "I love you."

Crushing her beneath him, his lips sealed over hers for a searing kiss. His mouth pulled away and he professed, "Fuck, highness, you take my breath away."

Cutter shimmied down the sofa and his tongue laved the healing tattoo of The Dark Horsemen morphing into the emblem of the Demon Squad. She'd asked Hoodie to design it, and he'd found a way to honor her past while embracing her future.

"Glad you approve."

Cutter gave her a sharp glance.

"You got inked up without me. A man touched you without my permission."

Greta shifted nervously, wetness gathering at the apex of

her thighs.

"Sage was there with me the whole time."

"Like I give a fuck. That's gonna earn you a punishment."

"Oh yeah?"

Cutter flipped her onto her stomach, pulled her hips up, and kneeled behind her.

"You're looking too excited. Set this up on purpose, did you? Brace yourself 'cause it's gonna be a long wait."

A slap rained down on her flank and she sucked in a ragged breath. Massaging the raised flesh, he murmured, "Love you, babe."

"Back at you. Now, show me," she pleaded.

And, true to his word, he did.

THANK you for reading Cutter's Claim! I hope you loved meeting Cutter and Greta. The next book in the Demon Squad MC series is Loki's Luck.

A DAMAGED BIKER.

A younger woman.
An exchange of sex for secrets.

TO PUNISH **himself for his baby brother's death, Loki is determined to live a life of abstinence—no partying, no women, no nothing. He stays focused by throwing himself into managing the MC's new gym. But when he's roped into teaching a self-defense class, the supervisor threatens his self-control. The annoying little pixie loves butting into his business, but Loki's gaze keeps returning to her luscious curves. Again and again.**

MORE BY MONIQUE

Steamy Biker Romance Series

Kingdom's Reign (Book 1)
Cutter's Claim (Book 2)
Loki's Luck (Book 3)
Stanton's Sins (Book 4)
Puck's Property (Book 5)
Whistle's War (Book 6)
Her Hidden Valentine, A Squad Novella (Book 7)

Lupu Family Mafia Romance Series

The lives of these powerful men revolves around three core elements: duty, sacrifice, and family. There's little time for women, and no time for love.
Each one of them will be cut off at the knees, humbled by a woman. Oh, how far these mighty men will fall before they learn the age-old lesson that the only way out is through...

The Chosen Heir (Alex's story)

The Recluse Heir (Luca's story)
The Savage Heir (Nicu's story)
The Perfect Heir (Tatum's story)
The Secret Heir (Prequel to Sebastian's story)
The Bastard Heir (Sebastian's story)
The Princess Heir (Emma's story)

Empire Academy Series
A High School Bully Mafia Romance Series

UNFORGIVABLE (Starlene's story)
UNREGRETTABLE (Crina's story)
UNFORGETTABLE (Gabriela's story)
UNDENIABLE (Zoe's story)

ABOUT THE AUTHOR

Growing up in New York City, I used to walk the hot pavements in the melting heat of the long summers, and dream. Uptown to downtown, eastside to the westside, and underground to catch a subway racing out into the boroughs. During my wanderings, my magic pencil spun out fantasies full of romance, with first meetings, heartbreaks, and reunions. Sometimes my boy crush (unrequited, of course) starred as the hero.

I grew up, and after a stint in art school, became a lawyer 'cuz a woman's got to make a living. I came from parents who fled to France as refugees, and as an attorney, I dedicated my work to helping survivors of trauma and persecution.

I believe in them. In their grit, in their determination to hold on, to pull through and, somehow, someway, to keep themselves intact, body and soul.

Perhaps that is why I am drawn to writing stories of men and women who live through heart-rending pain, desperate yearnings and, ultimately, reach a place of redemption.

For a long time, I fought the urge to veer off the expected, safe path until I couldn't go on unless I took a chance and made a change. I began to write, stopped, and began again. Finally, I gave in and here I am.

Come join me on my journey…

Check out more Dark and Spicy Bonus Material about Cutter and Greta here!
https://BookHip.com/ZCZTTV

Join Monique's Newsletter: https://www.subscribepage.com/moniquemoreau
Join my reader's group, she'd love to hear from you: Possessive Alpha Reads

Learn all about Monique's books: MoniqueMoreau.com